THE
KEY
TO
THE
HALF
WORLDS

THE
KEY
TO
THE
HALF
WORLDS

A world of choices,
but which world to choose?

ANDREW CHAPLIN

The Book Guild Ltd

First published in Great Britain in 2016 by
The Book Guild Ltd
9 Priory Business Park
Wistow Road, Kibworth
Leicestershire, LE8 0RX
Freephone: 0800 999 2982
www.bookguild.co.uk
Email: info@bookguild.co.uk
Twitter: @bookguild

'Dracofarne Map' Illustrated by Paul Futcher, Lorraine Inglis Design

Typeset in Aldine401 BT

Printed and bound in the UK by TJ International, Padstow, Cornwall

ISBN 978 1911320 043

British Library Cataloguing in Publication Data.
A catalogue record for this book is available from the British Library.

With heartfelt thanks to my wife, Dawn,
for her ideas and for making sure this story reached the printed page.

Also, I am grateful for the encouragement from my sons Alex and
Simon, for whom this was their bedtime story of choice
when they were growing up.

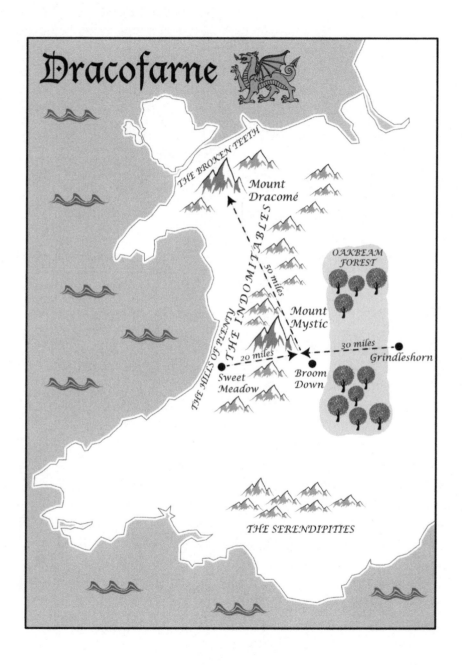

one

Like any other school morning, Richard got on the school bus at the bus stop, only this time it would prove to be more of a bus *start*, the start of a journey which would scare the living daylights out of him. It would thrill him. It would damn near kill him. And it would change him. In fact, it would change everything, everywhere – inside out, upside down.

But Richard was blissfully unaware of any of this, as the bus wended its way out of his village, Grindleshorn, ultimately heading for the town of Pemberton, five miles distant, where his school lay in wait. Moreover, he would have laughed himself silly if you had told him that he would soon be dealing with killer fog and deadly and devious dragons at one end of the spectrum, while meeting the girl of his dreams at the other.

As the bus continued to climb and grind its way out of Grindleshorn, he caught a glimpse of a group of trees in the vale below. He knew these particular trees very well, as they were in his back garden. He and his brother James had nicknamed the trees the 'Wild Wood', but right now Richard's mouth had gone dry and his eyes were out on stalks. The Wild Wood had become a Frenzied Forest. The trees were shaking about violently, as if there was an earthquake going on. It wasn't anything to do with the old bus as it wrenched its occupants about, because everything surrounding the Wild Wood looked

1

as serenely non-moving as you would expect. Then the trees snapped back into their reassuringly immobile state. Richard, now sweating, quickly looked around the bus to see if anyone else had seen any of this, but nobody was looking in anywhere near the right direction, which – thankfully – helped him resist his impulse to ask if anyone had seen his Wild Wood dancing the salsa. That was definitely a good thing, because 'Banghead' Brunning was on the bus, and he would have loved to have ammunition such as this to make Richard's school life a good deal less comfortable than it already was. Banghead enjoyed calling him 'Nature Nutter' on account of Richard's love for nature and wildlife, and he would have so relished the excuse to add something like 'Weirdo' to the description.

Richard knew he had not imagined the moving trees. He was both disturbed and elated; he had always felt something magical and edgy whenever he walked among them. It almost felt as though he had some kind of ancient relationship with the trees. Imagine what Banghead would do with *that* if he got to hear of it!

Eventually he calmed down, and with the prospect of a long journey ahead, began to drift into his favourite activity – daydreaming. Right now he was in the Pemberton Boys Senior School cricket team, saving the match against the visiting (and dreaded) team from the school in nearby Granthorn. So far, he had scored an impressive ninety-seven runs, and was starting to entertain the possibility that he might score a century. Calmly, he prepared himself while the boy at the far end of the pitch stood poised, menacingly rubbing the leather ball against his cricket flannels, ready to demolish Richard's stumps. Suddenly the boy started his run, and swung the ball rapidly towards Richard. Richard lifted his bat and struck the ball with a resounding 'Crack!' and it flew effortlessly, higher and higher, into the perfect cloudless blue sky. Richard paused to smile at the scene he had just created, but his moment of happiness quickly evaporated as he started to reflect on how he never really seemed to excel at anything. While he was on the school playing field supposedly practising cricket, Mr Marsden the sports teacher spent most of his time supervising the 'first eleven' team, leaving the remaining boys to supervise their own match. This consisted of the biggest boys informing everyone that they alone would be batting, and that everyone else should either be a bowler or a fielder. Richard liked the game and wanted to learn to play it well, but inevitably he ended up fielding, dreaming of a fairer world.

He didn't dislike school, it was just that he seemed to be average at most subjects, except for English and Art, which he was good at. Yesterday Mr Randall, the English teacher, had asked his class to write a short story on any subject they liked, so long as it was fictional – it had to be a story from the imagination. Richard had plenty of imagination and he wrote what he felt was a pretty good detective story. The hero, Detective Chief Inspector Jack Mullen, was perplexed. He was wondering why his best officer, Detective Inspector Will Mathias, had so far completely failed to solve a spate of bank robberies, and was more than a little surprised to learn that Will had recently changed his battered old VW for a shiny new Ferrari…

Suddenly, the bus hit a particularly rough section of the road, causing all on board to be thrown around like sacks of potatoes. Richard's forehead thumped on the window he had been staring out of, bringing him rudely and painfully back to the present as lush vales and hills crept by, heralding the foothills of nearby Wales, only a matter of miles to the west.

He was a slightly-built thirteen-year old boy, with a prominent shock of ash blond hair and captivating blue eyes set in a rather round face, which his mother said was 'lovely'. He hated this. He certainly didn't want any of his friends to think he looked 'lovely'.

Grindleshorn was a quaint old village, full of houses that had been there forever, many with walls leaning at crazy angles. One of them, The Manor, had been owned by Richard's family for generations. It was an average size, as far as manor houses go, set towards the edge of the village. It was reached from the village road by a crescent gravel drive. The handsome red brick of the house was perfectly matched by the surrounding tall red brick walls, which, as his mother often said rather stuffily, made the house 'secluded'.

The garden at the back was a wonderland, and Richard still felt this, even at the age of thirteen. It was very big, mainly laid to lawn, with a fish pond and of course the Wild Wood at the end of it. Richard loved being in the garden. Sometimes he would play badminton, cricket or football with James or with friends. Sometimes he would let his pet rabbit Rocket out of his hutch to stretch his legs. Getting Rocket out of his mother's vegetable plot and back into his hutch was the hard part. At other times, Richard would walk past the fish pond and onward to the trees, and he would imagine he was walking through a great forest on some fantastic quest.

Now the bus had stopped outside the school's gates.

'Everyone off!' called out the driver.

Richard trooped into school with the other boys. Just before he got to his classroom, he heard a familiar voice.

'Richard!'

It was his best friend Tom.

'Mum says I can stay at your house over the weekend!'

This was good news. Tom had a new tent, and they were going to give it a trial run by pitching it in the garden and sleeping in it for one night.

The morning stretched on. Eventually it was lunchtime. Having eaten, Richard and Tom wandered around the school playground area with twenty minutes to go before their next lesson.

'Fancy a game of football?' asked Tom.

Richard looked at him. Tom was a happy-go-lucky sort of boy, slightly on the plump side, always quick to smile. He looked rather scruffy, his dark hair sticking out randomly in a state of permanent surprise, his clothes seeming to sit on him in a slightly untidy dejected pile. His brown eyes locked onto Richard.

'Well?' demanded Tom.

'It's too hot to do anything like that,' replied Richard. Then he thought for a moment. 'Tom, you know in English this morning when Hargreaves was telling us about anagrams?'

'Yes,' replied Tom, and he then launched into an impression of the impossibly pompous Mr Hargreaves. 'An anagram, as you doubtless know, isn't a telegram to a girl called Anna... er...well anyway, it's a word or phrase formed by the letters of another in a different order. For example, there used to be a magician on television called Paul Daniels, and an anagram of his name is, er, almost Dull Spaniel. Well I certainly thought he was rather dull, in fact I became rather dog-tired of his show...er...I think you get my drift.'

Richard smiled. It was a very good impression.

'Tom, let's work out anagrams of our names,' said Richard.

Tom nodded. 'I've not got anything better to do.'

They walked to a nearby low wall and sat on it.

Richard found some paper and a pen. First, he wrote down Tom's name: Thomas Bradley. After several attempts, their best effort was: Sly Mad Breath.

'Hold on,' said Tom. 'We're missing an 'o''.

'Okay,' responded Richard. 'How about that well-known Irish crook: Sly Mad O'Breath?'

Tom grimaced and said, 'Let's try your name.'

Richard wrote down: RICHARD CRANFIELD. The best they could come up with sounded like a newspaper headline: CLAN RID FRIED CHAR. 'Char' was Richard's idea, and having explained to a disbelieving Tom that one of its various meanings denoted a type of fish, something very strange started to happen as they stared down at the paper. Some of the letters in 'THOMAS BRADLEY' and 'RICHARD CRANFIELD' were moving: T, O, M, S, R, D, E, R, I, R. They continued moving until they had arranged themselves into: STORM RIDER.

The colour drained from both boys' faces.

Slowly, Richard turned to Tom and said, 'Did you see what I think I just saw?'

Tom stammered, 'I c-could swear I saw some letters move from your name to spell 'STORM RIDER'.'

They looked down at the paper again, and the phrase 'STORM RIDER' was no longer there. Stunned, the boys continued to stare at the paper, but their names stubbornly remained with their full complement of letters. It was then that Richard decided to tell Tom about the shaking trees he had seen from the school bus. Tom just nodded; anything seemed believable from now on.

'Pee-eep!' The end-of-break whistle had blown.

'Tom, don't say anything about this to anyone,' whispered Richard as they filed into the classroom, 'it's hard enough surviving at this school, without being known as a couple of complete nutters.'

That evening, Richard was at home in the dining room having dinner with his mother, father and James. His favourite meal was his mother's steak and kidney pie. She made it with amazing pastry which melted in the mouth, and had just served a perfect example of her pie, with steamed dumplings, carrots, parsnips and roast potatoes. Normally Richard would have wolfed it down, but now he was deep in thought, eating his food slowly and mechanically.

His thoughts were interrupted by James, who was saying, 'Let me guess, dear brother. You are, yet again, no longer with us. You are either orbiting the planet Zog wondering if the inhabitants are friendly, or you are at the bottom of our garden with the fairies discussing how we can stop our wildlife becoming extinct.'

James was two years older and very different from Richard. James didn't have much time for dreams or imagination; he was always accusing Richard of being 'wishy-washy' and saying that he should 'get out more'.

Richard gave James a withering look, then moved his gaze around the table and took a deep breath. 'This will sound rather silly,' (at this point James was vigorously nodding his head in agreement, a huge smile on his face), 'but Tom and I were messing about with anagrams at school today, and when we wrote down our names, some of the letters started moving around on their own, spelling 'STORM RIDER', then moved back to spell our names again!' He looked around the table to see how his revelation was being received. 'Okay, so I'm weird,' he finished crossly.

After a long embarrassing silence, his mother assured him he wasn't weird, and asked if he would like some more pie. His father, as usual, didn't want to get involved in anything he considered trivial or irrelevant, and suggested Richard should do his homework straight after dinner. James, still smiling, slowly shook his head.

After dinner, Richard dutifully went up to his bedroom to do his homework, hating the fact that his family seemed incapable of anything remotely resembling emotional contact. *I'm not weird*, he thought bitterly. He was glad he hadn't mentioned the shaking Wild Wood – he would probably have been marched straight to the lunatic asylum. The fact is, it happened, and one day he would damn well show them.

He sat down at his writing desk. Tonight it was maths. Maths wasn't his favourite subject, and for some time he stared blankly at the swathe of figures and equations in front of him. Try as he might, he kept seeing those letters, inexorably moving together to form 'STORM RIDER'. This has got to be a message meant for me and Tom, he thought, but what does it mean, and who sent it? What was that old song that Mum likes? Oh yes! It goes: 'Riders on the storm'. Maybe Tom and I are going to form a band?

Finally, with great mental effort, he managed to pull his mind back to the task in hand, and somehow he completed the exercises. Then he looked at his watch and saw it was only half-past seven.

'Good,' he thought, 'I've got time to read a bit more of my book.'

He got up, walked over to his bed, launched himself onto it, and took the book that was lying on the bedside table. He made himself comfortable and opened it where the bookmark was.

The title was: 'The Otherworld Agent'. There were two versions of the planet Megalon, each existing in a different dimension. In one dimension, the Megalonians had developed a death ray machine which they intended to use to take over other worlds, whereas in the other dimension...they hadn't. The trouble was that the Megalon world without the machine had got to hear about the one with the machine, and they were working at finding a way to get into the other world to steal it. Now, a certain Max Manfred worked for an agency that had been set up to keep the Universe stable by preventing different dimensions from interfering with each other, and unfortunately for him, this particular Megalonian inter-dimensional mess had just glooped its way into his in-tray...

Suddenly Richard put the book down. He wanted to ask his father something. He rushed downstairs, and found him in the living room sitting in his armchair writing on a pad of paper.

'Dad,' called Richard, slightly out of breath.

His father, frowning, looked up. 'Have you done your homework?' he asked.

'Yes,' replied Richard, feeling that his enthusiasm had just had cold water dumped on it. However, he persevered. 'Dad, do you think there are other worlds in the Universe with life, and do you think there are other dimensions, other worlds that you can't see, but they're there anyway?'

Richard's father was a professor at Pemberton University, and his subject was Astronomy. Richard loved to talk about the stars and planets on the rare occasions he could get his father's attention. Unfortunately, his father always seemed to be caught up in his work at the university, and on the few occasions when he came home early, he never had much time to talk to Richard (or James for that matter). But tonight, Richard was in luck.

His father turned away from his paperwork, his eyes searing into Richard's like a laser. 'Other worlds with life? Well, the Universe is essentially without end as far as we know, so you might think there have to be worlds out there with life somewhere, but I'm not sure. I think life on Earth is pretty special and that the chance of it happening elsewhere is rather unlikely, except for simple forms such as bacterial life, which we now believe may be present on Mars. I certainly think it's very unlikely there is any other intelligent life. I mean, we've been monitoring the Universe for a long time, listening for radio signals for instance, but so far nobody has picked up anything resembling a signal from intelligent beings. We've only received naturally occurring signals from things such as dying stars. As for other dimensions, that's probably just science fiction. Mind you, really strange things happen around black holes – a black hole is formed when a star of a certain size dies and collapses in on itself creating an incredibly dense region, sucking in everything that's near it, a bit like water going down a plughole.'

Then he seemed to lose interest, looking down again at his paperwork; but Richard wasn't about to give up. 'Dad, what strange things happen around black holes?'

His father slowly looked up at Richard. 'Well,' he replied, this second interruption causing irritation to creep into his voice, 'there's a theory that time and distance become completely distorted. If you think of the normal Universe as a continuous carpet, then at a black hole, the carpet is sucked in and the fabric of space is turned in on itself. That's where the stories of wormholes in space come from. You know, where you can move from one place to another in no time at all, or move to a completely different dimension or Universe. Anyway, it's time you went to bed.'

Richard dutifully did as he was told. He would have loved to ask his father many more questions, but at least he now had plenty to think about. It seemed to Richard that nothing was really as it seemed, and that anything was possible. He drifted into sleep, dreaming of other worlds – but not for long. A strange 'whooshing' sound had invaded his room through the partially opened window. He sat bolt upright in his bed, feeling goose bumps of fear as he stared at the curtains covering the window, beads of moonlight filtering through the stitching of the material. It was a deep, slow, repeated sort of whooshing. It was coming from outside and seemed to be very close. His heart pounding, he got out of bed and began walking towards the window. Before he got to it, the light leaching through the curtains blinked out for a second or two, then returned. Suddenly he became aware that the whooshing had stopped.

He quietly moved to the window, and slowly parted the curtains, just enough to allow him a view of the garden below. The moonlight lit everything in sharp relief. All seemed normal – nothing was out there that shouldn't be. Richard continued to gaze out of the window for some time, his pounding heart gradually settling down to its normal rhythm.

Suddenly, he caught a glimpse of a huge dark shadow moving near one of the garden's walls, just before it passed out of sight. What the hell could produce a shadow like that? A giant bear? An elephant? His heart was racing again and he felt the cold sweat of fear. The shadow had moved too quickly for him to make out any detail, but then he became aware of another shadow playing on the wall. A massive writhing snake? No. As it twitched this way and that before moving out of view, Richard realised he had been looking at a shadow cast by an enormous tail. There had been something monstrous there, an enormous something with a long tail, something that whooshed and could blot out the moon. Something that was probably still lurking very close by. Surely it was far too big to get into the house…surely?

He stood transfixed by the window, mouth agape, his whole body quaking with terror, waiting for the shadows, or worse still whatever was making them, to return. Eventually, he shut the window as quietly as he could, drew the curtains, and got back into bed, knowing that he could not tell his family any of this because they simply would not believe him. He also knew he would be very wide awake for the rest of the night, assuming of course that whatever-it-was allowed him to get through it.

TWO

Richard glanced at his alarm clock for the umpteenth time. Now it was half-past six, and the morning light was starting to illuminate the curtains. He felt a sense of relief; surely the daylight would banish the terrors of the night. But then came a creak from the landing. Oh no, it had got into the house after all. He dared not breathe or move. There was a long, long pause – it was trying to figure out where Richard was. Another creak – it was nearer. Richard gripped his duvet as though it might provide him protection from the thing when it burst through his bedroom door. Then it cleared its throat before going downstairs. It was his mother.

Eventually, he got up and went downstairs for breakfast. James had already had his, and had cycled off to spend the day at a friend's house in a nearby village.

Richard's father was in the living room writing on his pad of paper. Had Dad gone to sleep at all? His mother assured Richard that his father had indeed gone to bed and slept last night.

Together, Richard and his mother set into a sumptuous meal of bacon and eggs with a little fried apple and some fried bread.

'Did you sleep all right?' she asked. 'You've got dark rings around your eyes.'

'I had a nightmare, that's all.'

Afterwards, he helped with the washing up, then went out into the back garden to let Rocket the rabbit out for a run. In the daylight, everything seemed normal and friendly. Maybe the daylight really had vanquished any monster that had been at large in the night.

Richard walked over to Rocket's hutch, which was positioned next to an outbuilding that used to be horse stables, but his father now used as a workshop. Richard had helped his father build the hutch. It had been designed to be fox-proof, and was made of wood with a sloping roof and a wire mesh front.

He stopped in front of the hutch, or rather what used to be the hutch. It was in pieces – broken wood and mangled wire mesh were all that remained. He stood there, his mouth dry as a desert, his stomach tightening into a vice-like knot. A fox couldn't have done this. And where was Rocket?

He glanced around. There didn't seem to be anything else out of place. Then something caught his eye, in a nearby tussock of grass. On closer inspection, he saw it was a shred of fur, coloured like Rocket's fur, tinged with blood. Richard felt sick. Repulsed, he took a step backwards, and felt strangely off-balance. He looked down and saw that he was standing on the edge of a slightly lower area of lawn. That was odd, as this part of the lawn was pretty flat: in fact, it was where they played cricket. He then noticed that the area appeared to have been flattened. The grass and daisies were all squashed, and Richard was surer than ever that he was dreaming. The depression he was standing in was created by a monstrous foot. There were three toes (or claws?) that pointed in one direction. He measured the print using his own feet and found that it was almost four shoe-lengths. His head was spinning. He looked around and now could see other footprints, some fainter than others, but all the same basic shape and size. He counted eleven of them, all around where the hutch used to be.

Suddenly it all became too much. He ran to the house shouting, 'Mum, Dad! Something terrible has happened!'

His mother came out of the house, closely followed by his father. 'What on Earth is it?' his mother asked.

'I think Rocket is dead! Look – over there!'

Richard led them to the scene of destruction. His mother and father gawped when they saw the remains of the hutch, and their eyes almost popped out onto the grass when they saw the footprints.

Presently, his parents began to recover the power of speech.

'Who could have done this?' spluttered his father.

'Yes, who?' repeated his mother, slowly shaking her head.

'For heaven's sake, why can't either of you consider *what* did it?' pleaded Richard, his upset turning into frustration.

'What are you saying?' asked his mother helplessly.

'I mean, they look like dinosaur's footprints, like a tyrannosaurus or something!' Richard had maintained a keen interest in dinosaurs for many years.

'Look, Richard,' started his father with presumably what he hoped was the voice of benevolent wisdom. 'There's an explanation for this that doesn't involve creatures that don't exist anymore.' He took a long breath and continued, 'I reckon that someone got into the garden last night and played a nasty sick practical joke, making it look as though some monster had broken into the hutch and eaten Rocket. Whoever it was must have had a model of a monster's foot and used it to create the footprints. This person was probably disturbed at some point and ran off before more footprints could be made. This explains why there are only prints near the hutch. It's got to be something along these lines, Richard.'

Richard wasn't at all sure about this explanation. Could the shadow on the wall he'd seen last night have been cast by a person? It was such a large shadow that surely it would have to have been made by a group of people. Actually, a crowd of people. 'Okay, Dad,' he sighed. 'I want to go inside now.'

Later, Richard's father called the police, and a policeman duly arrived. He looked over the scene and said there had been some instances of vandalism in the village over recent weeks, and they had today arrested a boy of age sixteen in connection with the offences. The policeman was sure that the demise of Rocket and the creation of the footprints was this boy's work.

Richard's father then set about clearing away what remained of Rocket's home. He offered to replace the rabbit, but Richard wasn't sure he would ever want another one. Besides, Richard was of an age where the time invested in looking after Rocket had started to seriously conflict with his growing 'number one' interest, which was: girls. The trouble was, it was a frustratingly difficult subject to follow up if you attended an all-boys school.

Richard's cousin, Nathan, attended a mixed-sex school in Gloucester, and was forever giving Richard a running update on who his latest girlfriend was. The last he'd heard, it was some girl in Nathan's class called Natasha, who had previously dumped one of Nathan's mates. Richard had commented that they could call themselves 'Nat and Nat', but Nathan had failed to see the funny side.

Richard's only opportunity to socialise with girls was outside school, and that primarily meant girls living in Grindleshorn, and that meant being brave enough to walk up to a girl whom he may not know, or only know by sight, and engage her in conversation without going red and stammering. How much easier it would be to get to know girls if they were actually in his classroom, he mused. Then he smiled. He already had a girlfriend, or at the very least, he thought, a good friend he really liked who happened to be female. She was Nicci Bannon, the daughter of Dr David Bannon who was a colleague of his father's at the university. She was full of life, and was able to see eye-to-eye with Richard over the difficulties of living with a father totally immersed in his work.

Richard was really upset when Nicci started to attend a boarding school. For a while, he got to see her every now and then during the school holidays, but the lack of contact during the school terms eventually took its toll and the friendship tailed off. But right now, the business with Rocket had temporarily demoted the subject of girls into second position.

Richard remained on edge for several days. His parents left the landing light on throughout the night, and kept their bedroom door open in an effort to reassure him. James had told Richard that he certainly wasn't going to lose any sleep over the Rocket incident. In which case, thought Richard, why had James taken to leaving his bedroom door ajar? He wasn't fooling anyone.

A week rolled by, and there were no more nasty surprises. Maybe the police had caught the culprit after all. Maybe the huge shadow on the wall that night was some kind of weird optical illusion and was actually made by one person. Or maybe it was nothing to do with Rocket's demise, in which case what was it to do with?

This was the weekend Tom was due to stay over with his tent, and Richard now felt much more back to his normal self. He felt confident enough to camp in the garden with his best friend.

It was a fine sunny Saturday morning. Richard had finished his breakfast and had gone to his bedroom to continue reading his book, 'The Otherworld Agent'. Max Manfred entered the dimension in which the death ray machine existed, and was then promptly captured by a group of Megalonians who were waiting for him. Unfortunately Richard would have to wait before discovering how Max fared, because he had just heard the sound of a car's tyres on gravel. It had to be Tom.

Richard quickly put the book down, jumped off the bed,

and rushed downstairs. He almost collided with the front door, he was in such haste, then opened it and took in the welcome sight of Tom, pulling out a suitcase and, Richard happily noted, Tom's Alpine Adventurer two-man tent, from the rear tailgate door of an old Volvo estate car.

Tom's mother had just got out from the driver's side, and she was standing there with her eyes closed.

'Hello, Mrs Bradley,' Richard ventured.

Mrs Bradley's eyes opened. 'Oh hello, Richard,' she said with a smile, as though surprised that anyone should appear from a house when a car turns up noisily in the drive. This was 'situation normal' for Mrs Bradley. Somehow, although she was with you physically, part of her was definitely elsewhere. Richard liked her a lot. Her eyes seemed to draw you in to far-off lands. A loose-fitting flowing dress covered her slim frame and she wore simple open sandals. The great thing about Mrs Bradley, Richard thought, was that she didn't seem to be affected by the world's rules and restrictions. She just did what she wanted to do, and got on with it. In a word, she was unpredictable, and in another word, fun.

Mrs Bradley was so much more interesting than his own mother, thought Richard. Mrs Bradley encouraged flights of imagination, ran a gift shop and had potholing as a hobby, whereas Mum pretty much limited herself to housework and gardening. Tom got into potholing first, then Mrs Bradley thought she'd give it a go, liked it, then realised she could sell in her shop any interesting stones or crystals she found when potholing. Smart or what?

Then Mrs Bradley broke Richard's reverie. Frowning, she asked abruptly, 'Have you ever felt that this world is missing something?' Without waiting for a response, she continued, 'There's something happening here, something amazing.'

Richard was rather taken aback by this. 'Er, well, Tom and I are camping tonight…that should be quite exciting,' he hazarded, although he wasn't sure that camping in the garden could be classed as 'amazing'.

'No,' she said, 'something very important…something to do with roots…no, I've lost it…but definitely roots,' she finally finished (rather inadequately as far as Richard was concerned).

Tom, who by now was standing next to Richard with his tent held in one hand and suitcase in the other, was becoming impatient. 'Mum, you can check out 'roots' on Gardener's Question Time, but right now, we'd like to put this tent up before nightfall,' said Tom.

Mrs Bradley smiled at her son. 'Of course, cheeky,' she chuckled. 'Hello Rachel!' she added as Richard's mother appeared at the front door. 'I'll collect Tom tomorrow at six o' clock. Have fun, boys. That goes for you too, Rachel!' With that, Mrs Bradley smiled beamingly at everyone, then jumped into the car and drove off. Rachel smiled uncertainly, waving goodbye mechanically as the car receded, before turning to the boys. 'Richard, help Tom in with his things. It'll soon be time for lunch,' she said.

After lunch, Richard and Tom rushed out into the back garden, sharing the weight of the awkward bag that contained Tom's tent. Suddenly Richard stopped, and Tom who at that moment was moving forward rapidly, lost his grip on the bag and fell over.

Richard grinned. 'Clumsy or what? Since you're obviously not capable of putting one foot in front of the other, I'm happy to make allowances just for you and pitch the tent here.'

'No way, you git!' laughed Tom, getting back onto his feet.

Richard knew that Tom loved visiting his house. They all called the land at the back of the house a garden, but in truth it was better described as a park. Richard had told him it was four acres in area. What Tom would have given to live somewhere like this.

They had got as far as the fish pond, which nestled

alongside the garden wall to their left. It was a beautiful natural-looking stretch of water, bulrushes and white flowered waterlilies moving to and fro in the slight breeze.

But Richard wasn't smiling any more. 'Tom, I'd rather we pitched the tent not too far from the house.'

Tom smiled kindly at his friend and said, 'That's all right. Look, the police caught that boy who…who killed Rocket.'

'But that boy swears he never came anywhere near our house,' replied Richard, frowning.

'You bet he does! Don't forget he still won't admit the damage he's caused to other people's property, even though seven people have independently identified him. Also, he's got one of those 'monitoring order' thingies on him at the moment, so I think we're safe.'

'I suppose you're right,' responded Richard, brightening a little.

'What are those brown marks on the lawn over there?' asked Tom. 'Oh, sorry mate. Me and my big mouth.'

Richard put the tent bag down and walked towards the marks, Tom following close behind. 'Dad has filled the footprints with soil and put grass seed down…look, you can see the young grass coming through.'

Tom was impressed by the size of the marks. 'Wow, it would have to be something huge like a dinosaur to make tracks like these,' he blurted, hastily adding, 'but it's a good job that dinosaurs died out sixty five million years ago and that the boy who made these marks is no longer around. Don't you think?'

'I know, Tom, but it's just that weird things have been happening over the last few weeks. First, I see the Wild Wood dancing about, then we see our names on a piece of paper change into 'storm rider'. I'm sure we weren't dreaming – we both saw it. Is 'storm rider' a message from aliens or something? Then I wake up in the night, at least I think I wake up, hear a whooshing sound and for a moment it goes black outside. By the time I get to my window, I see a huge shadow moving quickly out of view.'

Tom thought for a moment. 'The whooshing,' he suggested, 'could have been the sound of the boy running away – you know, when you run with jeans on how the cloth can rub and make a, well, a whooshing sound. In the quiet of the night I bet you would hear it.'

'But the whooshing sound was deep and repeated quite slowly,' countered Richard.

'Right,' replied Tom glumly.

'And how do you explain the light going out?' asked Richard.

Tom brightened at this. 'Well, at the moment you looked at your window, a bat flew past blotting out the light,' he said with an air of satisfaction.

'It would have to be a damn big bat,' suggested Richard.

'Okay,' said Tom thoughtfully. 'How about this. The noise the boy made disturbed a heron standing on your roof – you know as well as I do there are often herons up there keeping an eye on the fish pond. The heron flew right past your window blocking out the light. They have huge wings don't they?' Tom was warming to the theme now. 'And you also heard the slow whooshing caused by the heron's wings,' he said triumphantly. 'Could you make out any detail at all from the shadow you saw?'

'Not really, I only got a glimpse before it was gone.'

Richard didn't tell Tom that he thought the shape had a tail, as he didn't want to set him off on an analysis of how the tail was in fact the heron's long legs, sticking out backwards as the bird flew. Actually, thought Richard, that might just be a possibility, but his gut feeling was that it wasn't. He decided to change the subject. 'What about 'storm rider'?'

'That's a tough one,' said Tom, frowning. 'Mum thinks

that you and I are sort of 'in tune', and that was why we both saw the words form a message, which she believes was a message from the Universe – as she puts it. She also said that we'll soon find out what it means. I did ask Mum if she knew what it meant, but she said she didn't know. She believes the message is meant for you and me, and only you and I can find out what it means.'

Richard looked at Tom. 'Your mum believes in the power of thought, doesn't she?'

'Yes. Why do you ask?'

'Hmm,' pondered Richard, 'she said she felt that something amazing was going to happen.'

'Oh, that's just Mum's way,' replied Tom, shrugging his shoulders.

'I see,' said Richard.

Eventually, Richard and Tom reached a wide neatly-cut yew hedge that divided the long lawn into two halves. Richard wanted to pitch the tent there, but Tom convinced him that it would be fine to be even further away from the house – it would be more like proper camping.

So they walked down the grand stone steps flanked by stone balustrades that bisected the hedge. Now they were on the lower half of the lawn, the lawn that led to the Wild Wood. Richard wanted to pitch the tent near the foot of the steps, but Tom persuaded him to move on, towards what could only be described as a most remarkable sight.

In the middle of the expanse that was the lower lawn, was an outcrop of grey-blue rock that looked for all the world as if some passing giant had one day decided to plonk it there, perhaps because he just couldn't be bothered to find somewhere else more appropriate.

It was about three metres high by four metres wide. The boys gazed in awe, watching its surface literally sparkling in the sun. It seemed alive, as though it was radiating some kind

21

of beautiful energy. It was made of granite, and it was the embedded fragments of quartz that caught the light. Countless years of weathering had smoothed its edges, making it look like some kind of abstract sculpture. Richard and his family knew it rather unimaginatively as 'The Rock'.

Suddenly, Tom dropped the tent and ran to the sparkling beacon. He leapt on to it, climbed nimbly to the top, and shouted at the top of his voice, 'Look at me! I'm on top of the world!' Grinning, he scrambled down and rejoined Richard.

'Did you feel anything while you were up there?' asked Richard.

Tom wasn't expecting this particular question, and his grin slowly receded as he thought about it. 'Now you mention it,' he pondered, 'I felt really good. Still do, in fact. Isn't that strange?'

'It is,' replied Richard quietly. 'I feel the same way whenever I'm near it, or best of all, touching it. If I'm feeling a bit low, I often walk to The Rock, touch its surface, and my worries seem to disappear. The world seems a happier place. Trouble is, the effect doesn't last.'

The boys stood in silence for a few minutes, lost in thought as they took in the strange beauty of The Rock. Finally, Tom picked up the tent and began to move towards the beckoning Wild Wood. 'Come on, Richard,' he urged. 'Let's get this tent set up.'

Richard followed reluctantly. In the end, they pitched the tent at the far end of the lawn, near the Wild Wood, where the manicured grass mingled with the scrub leading to the trees. Soon they were surveying their handiwork. It was, according to Tom, a two-man tent, designed to cope with being pitched halfway up a mountain in the Himalayas. Richard, however, was content to leave it pitched on the lawn. It was certainly a very nice tent. Tom's mother had recently bought it for him for his thirteenth birthday, and this would be the first time it had been slept in overnight.

Night came all too soon for Richard. It was now dark, although the starlight would stop the night getting too dark. Richard's parents were standing by the tent's entrance looking in on the boys lying inside their sleeping bags, the scene lit by an electric torch that Richard was holding.

'Okay, if you need anything, the house isn't far away. Sleep well,' said Richard's father.

'Goodnight boys,' said Richard's mother.

With that, they left the Alpine Adventurer and its occupants to get on with it. Anyone watching the tent from the outside would have seen the light go off, hear someone say, 'Was that you rustling?' then someone reply, 'Not me, mate,' the light turn on again, 'Think it was a hedgehog,' the light go off again…until finally they were both asleep.

Richard slept badly that night, dreaming that the Wild Wood had started moving about again and was engulfing their tent.

Three

It was Tom who woke first. The morning sun lit the tent up inside sufficiently for Tom to see that Richard was still asleep. Tom sat up, his joints aching a little after lying on the hard ground all night. He got out of his sleeping bag and unzipped the tent door. Still wearing his pyjamas, he slipped outside.

Richard became aware of someone shouting. 'Richard! It's gone! I don't believe it!' As he started to wake up, he realised the voice was Tom's.

'What's gone?' grunted Richard, rubbing his eyes.

'For God's sake come out here *quickly*!'

It was obvious that Tom wasn't messing about. Richard sprang out of his sleeping bag and joined Tom outside the tent, and there both of them stood transfixed. The thing that had gone was…the house.

They stood in stunned silence for several seconds.

Finally Richard croaked, 'We have to be dreaming.' Slowly, he turned around and saw that not only had the house gone, but the Wild Wood had grown from a large group of ancient oak trees into a large ancient forest, the green canopy seeming to stretch forever into the distance. The trees he knew and loved were there, but where had the rest come from?

Turning back to where the house used to be, he recognised the rolling hills, and saw that The Rock was where it should be (albeit partially obscured by bushes that had magically appeared), but the entire village of Grindleshorn had been replaced by grass, bushes and small groups of trees. Then he noticed a wisp of smoke drifting upwards from one of the hills in the distance. Now he could see the smoke was coming from the chimney of what looked to be a rather quaint little thatched cottage. Threading its way past the cottage was the road to Pemberton – how the school bus struggled up that hill – but the road looked different, in fact it looked like a dirt track rather than a tarmac highway.

Then Richard became aware of something else. The birds seemed very loud, or did they seem loud because there were no traffic sounds, no dogs barking? 'Tom, this is just crazy. I'm going to phone Mum and Dad.'

Richard fetched his mobile phone from the tent and started to make the call, before stopping and staring at the screen.

'What's the problem?' asked Tom.

'It says 'No network available', and the signal indicator isn't showing anything. But that's not right – the signal is really strong around here.'

'Yes, but where *is* here? You know what? Mum was right. Something amazing *has* happened.'

'Yes, she was right,' a voice said behind them. 'And by the way, ditch the phone. It won't work here.'

They spun around, and saw a young man of average height standing there, smiling. He had a kind face with steel-blue eyes that twinkled, and was wearing what could be best described as a smock which stopped just below his knees. The smock was a dark blue colour, and it was tied with a black leather belt around the waist. He wore brown leather sandals, and held in his right hand a gnarled metre-long wooden stick. He was clean-shaven and had long dark brown hair pulled back into a pony tail, but most strikingly, he had pointed ears.

Eventually Tom managed, 'Who are you?'

'My name is Toby Nonsuch, and in case you're wondering, I'm a wizard.'

Tom's fear gave way to angry frustration. 'You don't particularly look like a wizard, and anyway, I don't believe wizards exist. Perhaps we should call you Harry Potter or… Gandalf? At least Harry Potter has a wand and Gandalf has a pointy hat so that you're never in doubt that *they* are wizards!'

Toby's brow furrowed. 'So, you don't believe in wizards, yet you know a Harry Porter and a Gandalf, who *are* wizards?'

Tom's frustration had become exasperation. 'Not Porter! Potter! Where have you been?'

It seemed that Toby had no wish to further inflame Tom's obvious annoyance. 'Er, you mentioned tall hats and wands,' he volunteered, clearly hoping to move the discussion to a calmer place. 'Wizards used to wear tall hats all the time, even inside, which really is impractical as the ceilings in our houses are definitely on the low side. As for wands, they're as much use as sunglasses in a snowstorm. You know, once a young wizard broke into my house. He was reading one of my spells when I disturbed him – I think it was my Tax Return spell, which causes taxation officials to turn up at your front door, desperate to return all the tax they've taken over the years. Anyway, back to the story. Without hesitation, the young wizard thrust his little wand at me saying, 'Don't come any nearer or I'll let you have it.' I replied, rather coolly I think, 'That's not a weapon of sorcery.' Then levelling my staff at him, I said, '*That's* a weapon of sorcery.' It worked a treat – he dropped his wand and ran off.'

Tom muttered, '*That's* out of 'Crocodile Dundee'.'

Toby thought for a moment. 'No. Definitely no crocodiles involved.'

'Never mind.'

'You see, you can't squeeze sufficient sorcery into a small stick to so much as light a candle – that's why we have big sticks or should I say staffs, like this one,' he said pointing to what Richard and Tom had first thought was his walking stick.

Toby seemed to be warming to his theme. 'You may be confused by my lack of a beard,' he continued, in spite of Tom who was vigorously shaking his head in disagreement. 'Well, until quite recently, wizards favoured beards because it made them look older and more venerable and wise, but now people are looking for more approachable, younger, trendier wizards – so the beards had to go. Besides, female elves really go for clean-shaven wizards, I can tell you.'

'All I want to know is what the hell is going on here!' growled Tom.

But Richard's interest had been aroused. 'Elves?' he blurted. He had always felt an affinity with the concept of elves. Elves were supposedly high-minded, decent folk. He wished his school could be elf-only, and that he had been given special dispensation to attend it.

'Yes, I'm an elf,' Toby replied warmly, apparently sensing that Richard was at this moment definitely the friendlier of the boys.

'That I suppose explains the – '

' – pointed ears. Yes, that's right,' nodded Toby.

Richard remembered the house. 'Where is my home, and why is everything similar but different? This has to be a dream – none of this is real, is it? *You're* not real, are you?'

'Please sit down both of you,' said Toby. 'We need to talk.' So saying, he gestured towards the ground and sat down cross-legged, and in spite of their disbelief of pretty much everything at the moment, they followed his example.

Toby eyed the boys intently. 'Many centuries ago in the ancient world,' he began, 'there were several races of people. The most significant of these in terms of numbers were humans, elves, goblins and dwarves. Initially all the people got on reasonably well with each other, but the humans gradually started to upset things. Humans have always been more aggressive than other peoples, and not having the ability to practise sorcery made them very resentful towards anyone who could practise it. Unfortunately for them, humans had to rely solely on technology and ingenuity to solve problems.

'For example, a long time ago a human called John Whirlpool spent years of his life designing and building a machine out of wood and string and goodness knows what else, that washed clothes pretty much by itself. One day John decided to show off his machine to the public, hoping to make some money out of his invention. He had a pile of dirty clothes which he showed to his audience, then placed them into a great wooden vat filled with water. Finally he released a stone weight that proceeded to power an amazingly complex contraption, which ultimately caused wooden paddles to thrash the clothes about in the vat of water.

'After what he called 'the cycle' had finished, he took out the clothes, which although clean, had unfortunately been torn into shreds. Seeing his audience start to turn away, he pleaded with them to let him try again. An elf in the audience shouted, 'You'll need those clothes back as they were then, won't you?' John thought the elf was joking, and smiled and said, 'That would be nice.' Before he knew it, the elf had used sorcery to put the clothes back together, only now they were completely clean. 'I'm sorry, mate,' said the elf, 'I meant to make the clothes as they were in the beginning. I'll soon make them dirty again.' But before the elf could invoke the spell, someone in the audience asked a telling question: 'What's the point in making the clothes dirty again? This elf has cleaned them with a wave of his hand!' Then someone else said, 'Yeah, why do we need this contraption? If I want my clothes ripped up, I give them to my dog!' John, quickly realising that his demonstration was doomed, decided at this point to abandon his invention…and he strangled the elf instead.

'The point is, my friends, that humans really didn't get on well with anyone else other than humans. It got to the stage that humans hated sorcery and people that used it so much that they tried to obliterate its existence. They refused to use the word 'sorcery', and instead used the horrible word 'magic', saying that sorcery was no more than a magic trick, an illusion – not real. They went further than this. Eventually they said that since sorcery didn't exist, neither did the people who practised it, and any person or creature remotely connected with sorcery didn't exist either. All sorcery-connected people and creatures were labelled as myths.

'In fact, humans started to believe these lies so much that eventually the resulting build-up of mental energy split the world into two versions, your version with humans, and the version that you are now in, without humans – with the notable exception of you two, of course. You see, never underestimate the power of thought! If enough people see the world in a particular way, that's the way the world becomes, rather like a dog comes to look like its owner, or is it the other way around? Anyway, why humans ever got so upset about their inability to practise sorcery, I'll never know. Actually, even in my world, most people and creatures can't do sorcery – it's jolly difficult, you know.'

Toby had finished speaking, but Richard and Tom just stared at him in total amazement as indeed they had throughout the whole time he was talking.

Eventually Richard stammered, 'Y-you mean there are two versions of the world, or two dimensions, even parallel universes?'

'Yes, that's it,' responded Toby.

Richard was starting to think that at any moment he might meet Max Manfred, the Otherworld Agent, in his new quest to put the two versions of the planet Earth back together again.

But it was clear that Tom was not thinking along the same

lines at all. 'Richard, surely you're not going along with all this rubbish?'

'Okay, then. Explain where my house has gone!' retorted Richard.

'Er…good point.'

Richard turned back to Toby. 'So in your version of the world, my house was never built, and most of the forest wasn't felled?'

Toby smiled and nodded. 'You are very perceptive, young human. The world divided into the two versions, well before – in your version – the forest was felled and your house was built.'

'And how can I get back to my world, to my family?' asked Richard.

'I'd like an answer to that too,' chipped in Tom, clearly feeling increasingly excluded from the conversation.

Toby's smile had vanished, and he looked at them with sadness in his eyes. 'I don't yet have all the answers, but I will tell you what I know. In order to move between the two worlds, the place and time needs to be right. The place needs to be somewhere where the two worlds overlap – the remaining trees from the ancient forest at the bottom of your garden fall into this category – and that's where you pitched your tent. However, the time part isn't so simple. Time is rarely synchronised between the two worlds. In other words, sometimes your time is ahead of ours, and sometimes it's behind, and every now and then, it's the same. When it's the same, and you're in the right place, a portal is created and you can pass from one world into the other. You see, I've been monitoring the timing of our two worlds for years, and recently saw the timelines were starting to converge, so I've waited here several days – waited for the time to become the same, waited for you two to arrive.'

'Waiting for *us* to arrive?' cried out Richard and Tom in unison.

'Well, my friends,' said Toby, 'I have been – how can I explain this? – I've been calling you into this world, using the power of thought, in the hope of saving both our worlds from destruction. That 'storm rider' message you got in the school playground was a kind of wake-up message from me. I'll do my very best to get you back into your world as soon as possible so that you can be reunited with your families and friends. I'm so sorry to do this to you, but please trust me – you two are needed right now to stop really bad things happening to our Universe.'

So they weren't going mad when they saw the letters on the sheet of paper move around, finally spelling 'storm rider'.

Richard looked into the elf's eyes, and could see fear and pain there. Then Richard looked at Tom. 'Tom, do you trust Toby?'

Tom hesitated. 'It kind of makes sense, I guess…you know, your vanishing house and the storm rider stuff.'

Richard nodded and turned back to Toby. 'Tell us more,' he said.

At that moment, they heard a low roaring sound in the distance.

'What the hell was that?' spluttered Tom.

Toby gulped visibly and his eyes went wide as dinner plates. 'We need to get into the forest, *now*,' he urged.

'Into the forest?' blurted Richard. 'I think that sound came from the forest!'

'No it didn't,' said Toby grimly, starting to run in the direction of the forest. 'Follow me – quickly!'

'What about my tent? It's brand new! Mum'll kill me!' wailed Tom.

'Leave the tent and everything in it!' bellowed Toby. 'We need to get into the trees before something really kills us!'

The boys ran like they had never run before. Hearts hammering, they careered through rasping bushes and nettles, which was not good as they were both wearing shorts and hadn't got around to putting on shoes. But the pain they would normally have felt from their torn legs and feet was, for now, lessened by the abject fear of something deadly getting ever louder and closer.

After what seemed like a lifetime, they were inside the forest, doing their best to avoid tree trunks and saplings that threatened to bundle them to the ground and leave them at the mercy of whatever was after them.

Suddenly, Toby steered them to a great oak tree. 'Stop here and listen,' he gasped.

They stopped by the great tree and listened for some time, hearing only bird-song and the buzzing of insects, together with their painful breathing and the pounding of their hearts. Eventually Toby whispered, 'We're safe for the moment, I think. We can talk now, quietly, that is.'

'What *was* that sound, Toby?' asked Tom shakily.

'I'll explain later. We need to move on quickly,' replied Toby, as he pushed bushes at the base of the tree apart to reveal a large hole in which was placed a leather bag. He pulled out the bag and emptied its contents onto the ground. Richard and Tom gazed down at a pile of clothes and shoes. Toby gestured towards the pile. 'These are for you, my friends,' he announced.

'But we already have clothes,' said Richard, 'although our shoes are inside the tent,' he finished ruefully, looking down at his bloodied feet.

'My friends,' said Toby patiently, 'in order for you to pass off as elves, you need to wear elvish clothes.'

'Pass off as *elves*?' gasped Richard.

'If you look like humans, you'll attract unwelcome attention,' explained Toby. 'People will think you have come from, or are going to, a fancy dress party. Remember, as far as this world is concerned, humans are myths, only to be found in fairy tales. You'll probably get people trying to pull off what they think are your false human ears. No, I'd go for the elf option, if I were you. Oh, and you'll need to lose those watches on your wrists.'

'No way!' said Tom. 'Mum'll...'

'Kill you?' suggested Toby. 'No, if you wear them, you'll stand out like sore thumbs. We don't have wristwatches in this world – only fob watches, I'm afraid. And like I said before, you can't keep your phone, Richard – we certainly don't have anything here like that. Your watches and the phone will have to be left in this hole. They should be safe there.'

Toby looked meaningfully at Tom, and stretched out his hand.

'What?' said Tom, frowning and shrugging his shoulders.

'Your phone too, Tom.'

Tom slowly dug into a pocket and very reluctantly handed his phone over. 'How did you know I had a phone?' he asked.

'I'm a wizard. I know stuff.'

'You're kidding!' moaned Tom. 'It's the latest model – and it's got all my text messages and photos on it. And what's more, I've only had it a few days. Mum'll...kill me,' he ended quietly.

Watches and phones now stashed in the hole, the boys started handling the clothes and shoes. 'Actually, these are cool clothes,' said Tom, smiling. 'I don't mind being an elf.'

'Well, I'd feel pretty daft wearing this stuff back home,' said Richard. Then something occurred to him. 'Toby, will it all fit? More to the point, will the clothes fit Tom? Nothing ever quite fits my scruffy friend, does it Tom?'

Before Tom could find a suitable retort, Toby said patiently, 'It will all fit perfectly, right down to the elvish underpants.'

'Sorcery, right?' prompted Richard.

Toby smiled, and gestured to the clothes pile. 'These clothes and shoes are Richard's, and these are Tom's,' he said as he divided them into two separate piles.

Soon the boys were wearing their new clothes and shoes. Amazingly, they fitted perfectly, even in the case of Tom. They were wearing smocks with black leather belts around the waist, similar to Toby, except Richard's smock was grey, and Tom's was brown. Also like Toby, they wore brown leather sandals; but unlike Toby, they wore hats. The hats were jaunty hats, rather like the sort of hat Robin Hood was supposed to have worn.

Toby smiled. 'You both look good,' he said, satisfied. 'Now you are elves. But you must remember to keep your hats on when there is anyone around – those funny rounded ears of yours need to stay covered up until your hair grows sufficiently to conceal them. Now we need to move on.' So saying, he pushed the leather bag containing the watches into the hole, then arranged the bushes so that the hole and its contents were completely hidden from view.

'If anyone asks,' said Toby, 'you are both my apprentices. You're learning the wizardry trade. All right?'

The boys nodded nervously.

'Right. Follow me. We've a long walk ahead of us. The 'Green Goblin' inn is on the far side of this forest.' And with that, Toby marched off purposefully, ever deeper into the forest, the boys following in single file.

'Toby, what was that thing that was after us?' asked Richard.

'All will be revealed soon. Right now, I'm afraid I need to concentrate on where we're going.'

'Oh…okay then.'

Chatting proved to be a great way to ease the tension. 'Do you *really* think I'm scruffy, Richard?' asked Tom, as they picked their way through a sea of waist-high green ferns.

'I sure do, me old mate!'

'Well, in that case, girls must like scruffy boys, me old loser!'

'What do you mean?' asked Richard, beginning to feel uncomfortable. 'Are you saying you've actually got a girlfriend?'

'I might be!' smiled Tom.

Richard was cross now. 'Look, have you or haven't you?' he demanded.

'Actually, I have,' replied Tom, rather smugly.

'Well, go on then!'

'Okay. I was helping Mum out in the shop, you know, serving, when this girl came in.'

'Yes?'

'Well, she walked straight over to me and said she was looking for a crystal necklace. So I showed her our jewellery shelf, and there were a number of necklaces with various stones or crystals attached to them. Mum had disappeared into the back room, I think to check the stock or something – now that's a thought.'

'What is? For God's sake, get on with it!'

'I'm wondering if Mum deliberately disappeared, so that she wouldn't cramp my style – it's the sort of thing she'd think of. Anyway, the girl started handling the necklaces, and seemed to be having trouble making her mind up. Then I remembered something Mum asks people when they're having trouble deciding what to buy, so, I asked the girl who the necklace was for – and that's when I hit the jackpot!'

'What do you mean?'

'She looked at me full in the face and said, 'It's for me.''

'What? She said it was for you?' laughed Richard.

'Very funny. I was quoting her. It was for herself. So that's when I said that any of the necklaces would look good on her, but in particular, the one with a gold chain and violet amethyst crystals.'

'What's amethyst?'

'That's exactly what she asked. So I explained that amethyst is a kind of quartz, and wow – it did look great on her when she tried the necklace on. Then she looked in the viewing mirror and asked me what I thought, and in no time I'd clinched the sale.'

35

'So that was it?'

'Not quite.'

'Go on.'

'Well, I then mentioned that some of our stock was obtained from potholing expeditions, and amazingly it turns out that she does a bit of potholing too, and that she's recently moved into the area, in fact, she's now living in Pemberton! So I asked if she'd like to join me on one of my potholing club's outings – and she said 'Yes'. And since then, we've been seeing each other pretty often.'

'What's she like?'

'Really pretty. A bit shorter than me. Brown eyes. Brown skin. Black hair in long ringlets.'

'She's black then?'

'Yes, as it happens.'

'You jammy, jammy…friend,' said Richard, who was glad for Tom, but at the same time was upset, because Tom's success served to highlight his lack of success with girls.

'Her name?'

'Dawn.'

'Nice name.'

'Yes, I like it too.'

'I don't think I'll ever have a girlfriend,' said Richard sadly. 'I wish our family had some business like your Mum's, where you get to meet lots of people.'

'Richard,' said Toby, who had been smiling as he listened to the boys' fervent conversation, 'I think you'll be meeting plenty of people in my world, and I'm sure, soon enough in your own world. Just take one day at a time, my friend, and you'll be all right.'

Strangely, Toby's words made Richard feel a lot better.

All this time, Toby had continued to maintain a relentlessly fast walking pace, and now the boys were starting to struggle to keep up. They were thinking more and more of something to eat – perhaps there was a fast food restaurant lurking in a forest clearing nearby?

Richard decided he didn't want to dwell on uncomfortable subjects such as food (or girls for that matter). Thankfully, he found himself remembering how he would walk in the Wild Wood at the end of the garden and imagine himself on some grand mystical quest. Now that dream had come true! Richard had always thought that imagination and dreams were infinitely more powerful than anything else in the world. Why then, wasn't this 'roaming of the mind' encouraged at school? Surely school shouldn't all be about: 'This is how you do it'. Wouldn't it be great to be asked: 'How would *you* do it?', and then be rewarded for giving the wackiest, most off-the-wall suggestion!

Richard plodded on through the forest, which, rather than being dark and forbidding, seemed quite welcoming, the ancient trees generously spaced with frequent sun-filled glades. His thoughts ranged between family and the power of dreams, not to mention numerous unanswered questions concerning the new world he was in. He reckoned Tom was probably hoping to check out his new outfit with a mirror should he ever find one – no longer Tom the Slightly Dishevelled, but now Tom the Coolest of Elves, with girlfriend – although unfortunately for Tom, she just happened to be in a different dimension.

The boys' thoughts came abruptly to an end when Richard walked into Toby, closely followed by Tom walking into Richard. Toby had stopped, and was motioning the boys to be quiet. He was pointing at something. There was a clearing in the near distance, with a group of animals occupying it.

Tom whispered, 'They look like white deer – I can see their antlers, although they look more like horns than antlers – yes, I think they're straight without any prongy bits.'

Toby smiled. 'You are looking at a herd of unicorns,' he said quietly.

37

'But these have two horns, not one!' exclaimed Richard in a kind of hushed shout. 'Unicorn means 'single horn', doesn't it? Besides, unicorns don't exist!'

'First,' explained Toby patiently, 'you forget that my world is full of creatures that you humans have stopped believing in. Second, when unicorns were first discovered deep in forests such as this, it was thought they had single horns. As you can see, the horns are very close together. From a distance the two horns look like one. By the time it was realised that unicorns had two horns, it was too late. Books had been written and the name 'unicorn' had travelled throughout the world. Anyway, what would you call it? Maybe a bicorn? Doesn't have quite the same ring to it, I think you'll agree.'

Richard reminded himself to always expect the unexpected. It wouldn't be the last time he would have to do this. Suddenly he realised that the unicorns had vanished.

'They spotted us,' whispered Toby. 'They don't like it when the forest gets too busy. Either that, or something else scared them off.' He seemed to visibly shiver for a moment, then continued, 'Anyway we need to keep moving.' Richard decided he didn't want to ask what that something else might be, at least not yet.

Toby led them cautiously into the clearing that the unicorns had vacated. They hadn't got very far into it before the ground under foot suddenly started to feel rather springy. Suddenly Toby stopped and turned around, pushing the boys back the way they had come. 'Get back!' he implored, 'It's a traaa – ', the ground beneath their feet now having given way. They had been standing on planks of wood covered with loose vegetation. One end of each plank was tied to a length of cord, and right now, all the cords were being pulled on with great vigour. Toby and the boys howled as they fell into the hole that had opened up. It was about three metres deep, and they landed heavily at the bottom, lost balance and fell over. They stood up as quickly as they could, every bone aching.

'Anything broken?' asked Toby.

The boys shook their heads.

'Good,' said Toby. 'What I was trying to say just before we fell, was that we've walked into a trap – which, of course, now seems pretty obvious. I'm really sorry about all this. I should have seen it coming – forest clearing and spooked unicorns.' He sighed. 'They'll be here in a moment.'

'Who'll be here in a moment?' asked Richard.

'Those guys,' said Toby looking up. 'Trolls.'

Richard and Tom looked up to see six faces peering down at them around the perimeter of the hole. They looked pretty much like giant stocky humans. They were about three metres tall. Apart from their size, one feature that definitely separated them from the human form was their noses, which were large and bulbous.

Keeping his gaze set on the trolls, Toby half-turned his head to the boys and started talking in a hushed tone, much in the manner of a TV naturalist describing creatures in front of him to his viewers which he doesn't want to spook (the creatures, that is). 'These are male trolls,' he whispered. 'Actually, it's quite difficult to distinguish male trolls from female ones at a distance, as they're all basically huge and hairy. Both male and female trolls wear their hair to their shoulders, but this is the point, male trolls have beards, whereas…ahh…' Toby's commentary had petered out, his brow now furrowed in thought. The boys looked at him expectantly. 'Yes?' said Richard with eyebrows raised, inviting Toby to continue. Toby obliged. 'Er, now I think of it, some female trolls have beards, so it's not quite as simple to tell them apart as I've led you to believe. The trouble is, clothing doesn't work either…some female trolls wear skirts, but then so do some male trolls. Hmm.'

Richard feared that Toby was going to continue his thesis on the intricacies of troll identification, but mercifully the trolls had other ideas. 'Strewth!' exclaimed one of them, his voice deep and gruff. 'We've caught a wizard if I'm not mistaken, and a couple of young…er – '

'Elves,' said Toby helpfully.

'Right,' said the troll. 'Now all you have to do is hand over any money or valuables you're carrying, and we'll let you out, free to go where you will. So how about it?'

'I think not,' replied Toby, a thin smile playing on his lips. 'Pull us out of here, and then we'll see what we can do to meet your request.'

The trolls all looked at each other. 'Well, it was worth a try,' said one.

'Let's help 'em up, then we'll talk things through,' said another rather darkly.

'Right then. Let's get you out,' said the troll who had first spoken after they'd fallen into the hole. He seemed to be the leader.

'I'll go first!' called out Toby. He looked down at the terrified faces and whispered, 'I'll think of something.' All Richard was thinking of was the very real possibility they were about to become lunch.

'Yeah, all right. The wizard first,' said the troll leader, his tone now a little less confident.

A large hand at the end of a large hairy arm was extended into the hole. Toby caught hold with his left hand, his right hand grasping his staff. With astonishing ease, the troll pulled Toby out of the hole.

Toby found himself quickly surrounded by the six trolls, but seemed quite unperturbed. They wore loose-fitting gowns made of a coarse fabric, tied around the waist with cord. Richard noticed that none of them wore shoes – it seemed that trolls must have very tough thick-skinned feet.

'Before we talk about anything, I'd like you to help my friends out of your hole,' requested Toby pleasantly.

But the trolls had other ideas. 'Give me your staff, and we won't harm you,' demanded the lead troll, using his most frightening gruff voice.

Toby spun around so that he faced the troll, his staff held out towards him. The troll started to slowly back away. 'I'll certainly give you my staff, all right!' cried Toby.

So saying, the end of Toby's staff glowed bright blue, and a blue line of crackling dancing light exploded from the end, connecting with the troll. It seemed to Richard that loyalty was not high on a troll's agenda, because the troll's associates immediately ran off, stopping at what they presumably felt was a safe distance.

Toby slowly raised his staff into the air, and the surprised troll at the end of the writhing beam of energy also started to rise. It was as though the energy beam was a pole, with the unfortunate troll stuck on the end of it. Up and up rose the troll, until he was hovering just below the tops of the trees. 'Put me down!' he shrieked.

'Like you put us down into your nasty hole?' asked Toby. 'Okay, I'll drop you like you dropped us.'

'No!' screamed the terrified troll. 'Let me down gently and we'll let you go! We won't take nothin' from you! Y-You can have anything you like from us – we've got money, jewellery an' stuff. I, *we*, promise not to do anything against you!'

Toby rubbed his chin with his spare hand, as though deep in thought. After prolonging the troll's agony for a little while, he said, 'I don't want anything from you, and I *will* let you down gently, although I warn you and your pals that if any of you do anything to make me unhappy, I'll gladly roast you all alive.'

Toby looked at the trolls now cowering at the edge of the clearing, and they gave him a barrage of fearful nods. He returned his gaze to the sky-bound troll, and slowly lowered his staff, the troll descending on the beam of blue energy. When the troll was a couple of metres from the ground, Toby cut the beam, and the troll crashed to the forest floor with a howl. He slowly got to his feet, feeling his body for any broken bones.

'You said you'd let me down gently,' groaned the troll.

'I did let you down gently,' grinned Toby. 'I was sorely tempted to drop you from the top of the trees.'

'Fair enough,' said the troll quickly, now seemingly very keen to please.

'Now get my friends out of that hole,' demanded Toby. 'And then I want to talk about potential changes to your lifestyle.'

The lead troll gestured in the direction of the nearby huddle of trolls. 'Quick! Get 'em out!' he bellowed.

The trolls rushed to the edge of the hole, and in no time Richard and Tom were standing next to Toby.

'Are you two okay?' asked Toby.

'We are, if you can do more stuff like that!' said Richard.

'Yes,' agreed Tom. 'That was incredible. Your staff really works! Real sorcery! You're one cool wizard!'

'Thanks, Tom,' said Toby, looking a little embarrassed, and, ensuring that only the boys could hear, he whispered, 'The fact that trolls aren't very bright definitely helps.' Then he thumped the ground with his staff, causing the nearby group of trolls to flinch. He glared at them while they nervously fidgeted, clearly wondering what the wizard had in store for them. 'Sit down, all of you,' commanded Toby, addressing the trolls. They obediently sat on the ground. 'Can't you lot find something more constructive to do than mugging people and taking their valuables?' he asked.

After a long silence and much head-scratching, the lead troll replied, 'No. Can't think of anything at the moment.'

Then he started to look aggrieved. 'We were forced into this way of living by you elves,' he said.

'Oh? How's that?' asked Toby.

'Well, we used to, in a manner of speakin', look after bridges,' mused the troll. 'Those were the days. We each had our own bridge. I had a home-from-home under my bridge. I had a comfy chair, magazines to read, and of course my collecting tin for the bridge toll. It was a shame, but some bridge users got real shirty when I popped up onto the bridge asking for the toll. I'd tell them that someone had to keep an eye on the bridge, you know, protect it from vandalism and the like. It seemed pretty reasonable to me that the person providing the protection couldn't be expected to live on air – hence the need for a small charge per person using the bridge.'

'Another view is that trolls all over the country were 'protecting' bridges that had no need of protection,' said Toby wearily, 'and so I think one can reasonably conclude that you and your kind were simply embezzling money out of the public.'

'Yeah well, you're an elf, and that's your view,' replied the troll. 'It was you elves that ganged up on us, and destroyed our livelihood. Elves took it on themselves to form the Highway Department, and one of the first things they did was to stop us living under our bridges. I tell you, they sank vertical metal bars into the ground under my bridge, forming a kind of cage, which stopped me from going underneath. Now, my bridge crossed a river, so the only way for me to get under it was to wade into the river! I even tried mooring a boat under the bridge, but by the time I got out of it, the bridge user had already crossed. In the end, I was forced to camp by the side of the bridge, which wasn't fun when it was raining or snowing, I can tell you. The trouble then was that folk using the bridge would see me well before they got to it, and some would simply find another way across the river. Even worse, really

43

nasty folk would inform the Highway Department, and they'd send out an enforcement dragon to move me on. So I gave up, and joined up with these guys you see here, who've been forced from their bridges like me, and now we make our living by relieving unwary travellers of their money and valuables.'

'One possibility you haven't mentioned is getting a job,' suggested Toby. 'I don't know…such as farm work or something.'

In spite of their obvious fear of the wizard, the trolls burst out laughing. 'We're *trolls* for goodness' sake,' the lead troll chuckled. 'We don't do proper hard work!'

'Well, I'm going to do something for you that might change your minds about that,' said Toby. He waved his staff in a wide arc, and the trolls, in abject panic, tried to scramble away, perhaps expecting to be roasted as Toby had threatened earlier. But no sparks flew off the end of Toby's staff, nor did it so much as glow. The trolls stopped their backwards shuffle, wondering if Toby's staff had gone wrong. 'I'm going to leave you with those money boxes,' said Toby.

'What money boxes?' asked the lead troll.

'The money boxes behind you,' replied Toby. The trolls turned around, and saw a group of six small wooden chests with hinged lids. They looked like pirate's treasure chests, albeit very small ones. 'Now, before you get too excited,' continued Toby, 'there isn't any money inside the boxes. But for every week of honest work you do, you'll find a gold coin – an eldrum, in fact – appears in the box. If at any point during the week you steal something, for example, then the timer resets and the week starts anew. So if you want lots of eldrums, stay on the straight and narrow!'

'Thank you,' chimed the now-grinning trolls. Then the lead troll's eyes narrowed, apparently smelling a potential rat. 'Do you promise the box won't do anything nasty, like explode or something?' he asked.

'No, I promise that all it will do is produce coins,' smiled Toby, 'but only if you behave. If you don't behave, it'll simply remain an empty box.'

The trolls got up off the ground and ran to the boxes, and in no time a bit of a tussle developed. Then the source of the problem became plain. The lead troll had taken all six boxes for himself.

'It's one box per troll!' growled Toby. 'If any person has more than one box, then none of the boxes will ever produce coins. Okay?'

'Yes of course,' said the lead troll. 'I only got hold of all the boxes so that I could hand them out to my friends in an orderly manner.' It was obvious that his companions weren't convinced.

'Okay. We're going on our way, and I don't want to find you lot lurking in this forest ever again,' said Toby. 'Is that understood?' Judging by the trolls' fervent nodding heads, it was.

At last, Toby and the boys passed through the clearing. As they walked on, they could hear at least one gruff voice in the distance behind them saying, 'Who's got my box?'

There was a period of silence as the trio pondered their experience with the trolls. It was Richard who eventually broke it. 'So all the fairy tale stories in my world about trolls under bridges were taken from reality, the reality that existed before the world divided into two dimensions?' he asked.

'That's it,' said Toby.

'But,' continued Richard, 'those stories were usually about trolls wanting to eat anyone crossing their bridges. The trolls *we* met only wanted to rob us.'

'I'm afraid, replied Toby, 'that the eating part of the story is another example of your world embroidering the truth, my friend.'

'That was brilliant sorcery back there with the boxes,

Toby,' chipped in Tom. 'What a great way to get those trolls to live decent lives!'

'Well, I hope it works, Tom,' smiled Toby. 'I certainly don't expect to find them in this forest again!'

For the next half hour or so, nobody said much. Everyone had plenty to think about, as they picked their way through the never-ending forest. It was Tom who eventually broke the silence. 'That's odd,' said Tom, his voice sounding rather distant. Richard and Toby stopped walking and turned around to see what Tom thought was 'odd'. In hindsight, 'odd' was a woeful understatement.

FOUP

Tom was standing several metres down the forest path, gazing at a whitish bank of dense fog, which was oozing and swirling its way around and past the trees. The fog bank reached right up to the forest canopy, but otherwise was strangely localised – it was only fifty metres or so wide, resembling a large clump of cotton wool out for a stroll in the forest.

Richard was mesmerised by this peculiar sight. He wondered what the fog was doing here on a hot summer's day? Its presence jarred against the backdrop of the sunlit-dappled glade it was gliding into, as it started to cast its steadily growing shadow over Tom. It was almost as though it was heading for him, as though it was being guided, or even had intelligence. Richard suddenly became aware that the leading edge of the fog seemed to be made up of a mass of swirling tendrils; and now he thought of it, they reminded him of spindly beckoning hands. All of a sudden, it seemed to be getting cold, *so* cold that Richard started to shiver – and what was that? No doubt about it. He could hear strange, unearthly, intoning voices saying, 'Come and join us. Join our great cause. Sleep now and awake in glory! Join us and sleep, sleep…'

'Tom!' cried Toby. 'Get away from that fog! Tom! Tom!'

Toby's shout of warning woke Richard as though from a dream. 'Wh-what?' muttered Richard, as Toby rushed past him.

The fog had reached Tom, its tendrils (or hands?) swirling around him. Then Tom slumped and fell to the ground without making a sound. Unfortunately Tom would have to wait for Toby's attention, because Toby was fully preoccupied with the fog, his staff outstretched towards the looming cloud. Without warning, a mass of whitish, writhing, foggy hands burst out towards Toby, grabbed his staff, and started to pull it in. 'Join us and sleep…' the voices continued to intone.

'No you don't!' growled Toby, as he was steadily dragged towards the swirling mass. By now, half of his staff was inside the heaving whiteness, and it wouldn't be long before *he* was as well, if he didn't let go. 'Disperse, foul demons!' commanded Toby. 'Feel the warmth of life in your cold, dark souls!' As he said this, the writhing fog around his staff, which had now almost reached Toby's hand, started to glow yellow, quickly deepening to orange.

The voices stopped intoning, and screamed. 'You hurt us!' screeched the voices. 'You hurt us! We burn! Burn! Make it stop!' The orange glow around Toby's staff grew to encompass a large area, causing the screaming voices to reach fever-pitch. 'Ayeee!' shrieked the voices. 'Let go of it! Let go! Let go!' Suddenly, the fog parted from Toby's staff, leaving a large tunnel within, inside which, the end of the staff burned brightly. Then an 'arm' broke out of one side of the main fog mass, and, twisting and turning, accompanied by the sound of a howling wind, this 'arm' snaked away into the trees behind, acting as a kind of vacuum cleaner hose, into which the remainder of the fog was sucked. In a few seconds, the fog had disappeared into the forest, allowing the sun back in.

Richard rushed to Tom, who still lay in a crumpled heap on the forest floor. He quickly knelt down and rolled Tom over. His face was ashen-white. To Richard's relief, Tom opened his eyes, and smiled weakly, colour rapidly returning. 'Are you all right?' asked Richard.

'I think so,' said Tom haltingly. 'I remember this weird fog, then I got really cold; but somehow felt all right because, well, these sort-of voices were calling. Then you were here. You know, I still feel cold.'

'Don't worry,' said Toby who was kneeling close by, staff in hand. 'You'll soon warm up. It's good that you don't remember anything from when you were inside the fog. That's a blessing. All-in-all, you've had a lucky escape.'

'Escape from what?' asked Richard.

'I believe it was a group of demons, it seems with a common purpose in mind,' replied Toby grimly. 'Demons are essentially the souls of evil people, and normally they go around on their own, you know, generally lurking around old buildings with unpleasant histories – bad ghosts, you might call them. But this lot – and there were an awful lot of them – were acting together. And the only way they would act together, is if something greater than themselves was in control. I think I know what that something, or rather, who that someone, is. Someone who has no qualms when it comes to unleashing dark sorcery, and just happens to be responsible for the danger that our worlds are in. Drusilla.'

Richard's eyebrows raised. 'A woman?' he asked.

'Yes, well, at least a female elf.'

'Elf? I thought elves were good people!'

'In your world, there are good people and bad. Elves are no different. Drusilla is probably the most powerful wielder of sorcery in my world, but there again, *I'm* quite powerful in a different way, hopefully a good way. So all is not lost!'

'Anyway,' smiled Richard, 'you saved us again. You sent those demons packing. What was Drusilla using them for?'

'I think they were a kind of task force, patrolling the area for any folk who haven't yet submitted to her will. The demons sensed that Tom wasn't 'on board', so they made him unconscious in order to carry him back to their mistress for questioning and probably worse. They would have moved on to Richard and myself if I hadn't given them something to think about!'

'Will they be back?' shuddered Tom.

'I don't think so,' said Toby. 'They'll be looking for easier pickings, now. I hope those trolls back there don't run into them – they're a rough bunch, I know, but even *they* deserve better than to end up at Drusilla's mercy.'

Toby and Richard helped Tom to his feet. 'How do you feel, Tom?' asked Toby.

'A little unsteady, but I'm all right,' he replied with a thin smile.

'Good,' said Toby. 'We're not far from the inn. Let's push on.' So they resumed their walking, looking this way and that in fear of anything else that might want to attack them.

Soon, the trio reached the edge of the forest. Below them swept a green vale with a small group of thatched houses in the middle of it, next to a meandering river. The evening sun suffused the calm scene with a warm rosy glow. 'That village is called Broom Down, where 'The Green Goblin' inn is, and that's where we shall spend the night,' said Toby. Then a smile crept over his face. 'Would you like to know how the village got its name?' he asked. The boys nodded expectantly.

'Well, the story goes that there was an elf-sorceress who was fed up with crows nesting on top of her house's chimney, blocking it and causing the house to fill with smoke. So, clutching a broom, she got out her ladder and climbed up onto the roof at one end of the house, finally reaching the rather tall chimney – '

'Why didn't she use magic, sorry, sorcery, to unblock it?' interrupted Tom.

'Well, Tom,' replied Toby, 'as I've said before, sorcery is not easy to do. Every time you do it, it depletes your 'enchantment' charge, and you have to work hard to build it back up. It drains your energy. That's why folk who practice sorcery only use it sparingly.'

'Okay,' said Tom, apparently satisfied.

'Right,' resumed Toby. 'So, using the full length of the broom she started dislodging the nests. Unfortunately she was at full stretch, lost her footing and fell off the end of the roof, still clutching her broom. Passers-by saw her plummeting to the ground with the broomstick, now jammed between her legs, and they decided that she was flying on the broom, if a little on the steep downward side. Sorceresses later became nicknamed 'witches', because the broom was made of witch-hazel, and the village became known as Broom Down, because the *broom* was literally, well, *down*. Sadly the unfortunate sorceress died on hitting the ground, and hence was denied the opportunity to set the record straight. Since then, the myth of witches on broomsticks has been ruthlessly exploited by the tourist industry in Broom Down. You can't move without bumping into so-called genuine witches' brooms for sale.'

Toby looked to see how the boys had received his tale. Richard was smiling, but Tom was frowning. 'Why didn't she use sorcery to save herself when she fell?' asked Tom.

'Well,' smiled Toby, 'nobody knows for sure, but I'm certain she tried to invoke a spell the moment she lost her footing. The trouble is, she only had a couple of seconds before she hit the ground, and I can tell you, it's hard to invoke any spell in that time. When you consider she was also in a bit of a panic, I don't think she would have had time to say anything other than *Aghhh!*' He again looked at the boys, who were now both grinning. 'Right,' he said cheerily. 'Let's find The Green Goblin.'

Whereupon they walked as fast as they could down the hill towards the village, with food, drink and a comfortable bed on their minds. Before long, they were traversing the humpback bridge that took them across the river to Broom Down, just as day was dissolving into night. Lights were appearing in the windows of houses, and all was quiet except for a distant babble of voices and occasional laughter. They walked down the deserted main street and eventually came to the source of the noise – The Green Goblin.

It seemed a welcoming place. A yellow glow of light issued from the windows, and the movement of people inside could be seen. Richard looked up at the inn's sign which showed what he thought might be a goblin. It was certainly very green, and sported a huge toothy smile. As the sign moved to and fro in the slight breeze, Richard could almost believe the goblin was real, and at any moment might drop down from the sign and say, 'Evenin'.'

'Evenin',' said a nearby voice. Richard spun around to see a green one metre high slightly rotund creature, looking very much like the picture on the sign. It was wearing a string vest and a brown suit that was badly in need of ironing. Its green hairy chest seemed to shine through the holes in the vest, and its large green hairy bare feet slapped on the path. It winked at them, smiling hugely (and toothily) as it walked past, finally disappearing into the inn.

'I think I've seen it all now,' Tom managed, his jaw hanging in disbelief, his eyes wide.

'I can assure you that you haven't,' said Toby quietly. 'Now, my friends, when we go in there, I want you to stay close and let me do the talking. As long as they think you're elves, they won't pay any attention to you.'

Richard and Tom nodded. They were going to stick like glue to Toby. They walked up to the great gnarled oak door, and Toby swung it open. A cacophony of voices and the smell of beer hit them as they walked in. It looked pretty much like any country pub you would find back home, Richard thought. But the clientele were certainly different. There were quite a few green goblins milling about, which presumably was how the inn got its name. There were also several groups of elves.

'It's good to see yer, Wizard Nonsuch!' a rough voice called out. Richard turned and saw the barman was waving at them from behind the bar. He had a jolly face with rosy cheeks, brown curly hair and a rather large brown beard. But the strange thing was that he was bare-chested. He wasn't wearing a shirt or anything else on top. Richard thought that perhaps the barman felt hot and so had taken his shirt off. How off-putting to have to stare at a sweaty hairy chest as your drink is being poured out.

Toby led the boys up to the bar. 'Ben,' he said warmly. 'Please meet my two apprentices, Richard and Tom. We need three rooms for the night.'

Ben, beaming a huge smile, leant over the bar and shook the boy's hands very firmly. 'I've got three rooms together for yer,' said Ben. 'Now, how long have yer been learning the art of sorcery with Toby, then?'

Before the boys could think of an answer, Toby quickly said, 'They're from the other side of Oakbeam Forest, and they've joined me to commence their training. I believe they've a natural flair for sorcery, but don't yet realise it.'

Ben roared with laughter. 'Well I hope they stay with yer longer than that lad yer were teaching last year,' he chuckled. 'He certainly mastered that disappearing spell!'

Toby's face and ears reddened. Gritting his teeth, he turned to the boys. 'Ben is talking about an apprentice who attempted a disappearing spell,' he said ruefully. 'He disappeared, but didn't reappear as he should have done. So I followed what we wizards call the 'spell trail', and eventually found that he had by chance reappeared on a lovely desert island populated solely by a group of beautiful young elvish women who had been ship-wrecked there. He told me that, since arriving on the island, it hadn't taken him long to decide he wasn't cut out to be a wizard, and if it was all right with me, neither he nor his new-found friends actually required rescuing. Seeing the island and the women, I quickly realised it was unlikely I would ever see him again, and indeed I haven't.'

Toby decided it was time to stop Ben causing any more trouble at his expense. 'Anyway, I'll have a pint of Old Hen's Foot, and the boys will have Apple Smash,' he said, forcing a smile. 'A giant selection of chicken, ham and cheese sandwiches for the three of us, please.' The boys hoped that Apple Smash didn't taste as bad as it sounded. The sandwiches were probably the safest choice, when compared with some of the hot meal selections chalked up on the nearby blackboard menu – Forest Grunt, Weasel Shock Pie and others sounding even less appealing.

'All right then, wizard folk! I'll bring the drinks and sandwiches out to yer in a jiffy,' roared Ben above the general din.

Toby smiled at Ben, then led the boys to a nearby table where they sat down. He carefully placed his wizard's staff against a nearby wall. Richard and Tom looked around the room. It was quite busy. A group of green goblins were sat at a nearby table, laughing their heads off every time one of them belched or farted. At another table, a group of elves cast occasional disdainful glances at the uncouth goblins. Richard noticed that the barman had placed their drinks and a huge plate piled high with sandwiches on a tray. He swung open the hinged bar top and door, and walked into the room carrying the tray. The barman clipped and clopped on the flagstones as he walked towards them. His horse's body had been hidden behind the bar. Now the mystery of the bare-chested barman was clear to all. He was a centaur, front end – man, back end – horse. He arrived at their table, deposited the tray, and with a broad smile and flick of his tail, headed back to the bar. The boys gawped like fish out of water.

Tom was the first to recover from the shock. 'Toby, now can I say we've seen everything?'

'No.'

'I knew you were going to say that.'

Some time later, the boys recovered sufficiently to try their drinks. The Apple Smash was a reddish-brown colour with a little froth on top. They gingerly sipped the liquid, then decided it was actually all right. Soon Richard was halfway through his drink, feeling much better. 'Toby, why is this stuff called Apple Smash?' he asked.

'Oh, it refers to the way it's made,' said Toby.

'How is it made?' asked Richard tentatively.

'Well, the apples are put into a huge vat, then giants walk on them – '

'Giants?'

'Yes, giants – big guys, about six metres high when full-grown. You know, 'Fee-fi-fo-fum' in your world's fairy tales. So as I said, they walk on the apples. Now when you weigh over a ton, I can assure you that apples are converted into juice pretty easily. The added benefit is that it keeps giants off the streets.'

The boys slowly nodded, looking completely dazed. Malevolent fog, trolls, goblins, centaurs...and now giants!

Toby continued, 'They're so clumsy, you know. They tend to bump into houses and step on people by mistake, that sort of thing. Mind you, they're generally polite and quick to apologise. In fact, you know if one's about – you'll hear lots of crashing sounds and frequent use of words and phrases such as: 'Sorry', 'Whoops', 'Oh bother' and 'Did I do that?''

The boys were silent for a while, not daring to say anything, fearful Toby might tell them something else concerning this world which would unsettle them even more than they were already. Meanwhile Toby had started eating a sandwich, reminding the boys how hungry they were. Finally having eaten, Richard could no longer hold back the question he was itching to ask. 'By any chance, are there any of these, er, giants, around here?'

'Probably not, Richard,' said Toby, attempting a smile of reassurance. 'The last time I believe a giant was seen in Broom Down was close on ten years ago. The giant wandered into the village asking for directions to the nearest apple orchard. He was looking for work, you see. A passing elf suggested that the village's Employment Office could help him out, although the service might be a bit slow. The giant asked why there might be a problem with the service. In response, the elf pointed to the giant's right foot. He had inadvertently stepped on the Employment Office building, which was now completely flattened. The elves that worked there, having narrowly escaped, unsurprisingly gave him directions to the furthest-away apple orchard on their list.

'But fear not, my friends. The vast majority of giants live in mountain caves, many miles from here. They normally only come down to the lowlands to work in apple orchards, which, as you might expect, are generally located well away from villages. Now, it's getting late – '

'Pardon me, wizards!' It was Ben, who had arrived with a bundle of leaflets, which he placed on their table. 'I thought,' continued Ben, 'that the lads might be interested in some of the attractions I run in Broom Down, in case you have some time to spare. There's a tour of the famous Broom Down witch's house. The story goes that a long time ago this lady elf got up onto the roof of her house – '

Toby interrupted, 'I've told them that one, Ben.'

'Oh, right,' said Ben, looking a bit deflated. 'Well, it's damn good value. And you get the chance to try out a genuine witch's broom! Don't be upset if you can't get it to fly – most folk don't have the knack.'

'The only use for those brooms is sweeping,' muttered Toby under his breath.

'Now here's another good one,' said Ben, beaming. 'Go to an apple orchard and watch giants at work. Very exciting, because you get to see lots of giants, close up. I do a good rate for personal insurance, not that it's dangerous of course! But it's better to be safe than sorry. Oh, and you can all drink as much Apple Smash as you like for no extra charge.'

'Ben, thanks,' said Toby, smiling up at the centaur, 'but we need to move on in the morning. Perhaps we can try some of your tours another time.'

'Right you are then, Toby,' replied Ben, moving back to the bar, clearly disappointed.

When Ben was out of earshot, Toby motioned the boys to move closer to him. 'Before we go to bed,' whispered Toby, 'I must tell you what is going wrong with my world, how it will affect your world, and the vital role you boys have to play.'

However, it was all too plain from the fearful looks on the boys' faces that they didn't like the sound of this unwanted responsibility that seemed to have been thrust on them.

Nonetheless, it appeared Toby was not about to be put off. 'I didn't want to drag you into all of this,' he said, 'but I think you'll start to understand when I reveal something about you both that neither of you are aware of. Let's go to the 'snug' around the corner where it should be quieter. I'll get hot chocolate drinks for everyone.'

Soon they were sipping their hot drinks around a table in the little snug room, with a fire crackling in the nearby grate, warding off the creeping chill of the evening. Toby seemed pleased that there was no-one else with them. He leant forward and spoke in a quiet, measured way. 'When your world and my world separated long ago, each world became only a half-world. Much of the wonder and boundless creativity of the original world was lost, and dark forces have since been at work in both our weakened worlds trying to take them over. Your world has had many wars and conflicts, and so has mine.

My world has had conflicts such as those between giants and dwarves in the mountains, and between elves and wood-pixies in the forests. These conflicts were all about people with different cultures wanting to live in the same places, but not with each other. Fortunately, nowadays most feuding has ceased, and the vast majority of people and creatures have learned to live in harmony with each other. But, these days, your world has a general terrorist threat that is threatening its very existence, and – '. Toby paused, looking around, then moved his head close to the boys and whispered, 'My world also has an evil force that is threatening its existence, and that force is, as you already know, Drusilla. Over many years, she has built up an evil empire, and she intends to enslave both worlds, and ultimately recombine them under her power. I, for one, want the worlds to recombine and be the better and stronger for it, but as a free world, not enslaved by anyone, least of all by someone as ruthless as Drusilla. Her real name is Betty Golightly, but she changed it to a more fitting name for a person committed to the cause of mass enslavement and misery.'

'But where do *we* come into all this?' asked Tom.

Toby hesitated before saying, 'There's a well-known ancient prophecy in my world that foretells that a time will come when the elvish and human half-worlds will unite briefly in time and place, and that two young human boys with elvish lineage will enter the elvish world at a time of great need on a quest to prevent a dark force there from enslaving both worlds. It goes on to say that the boys will need to find a book created by good sorcerers a long time ago called 'The Key to the Half Worlds', and then to use its power wisely, or all will be lost. One thing for certain, my friends, is that the dark force is very present in my world, and growing ever stronger.'

Richard was frowning in disbelief. 'Toby, are you telling us that Tom and I are the two boys?' he asked.

'Yes. That's it.'

'We have elvish lineage?'

'Yes. Before the worlds parted company, human and elf folk married quite a bit, and I have ancient records that show that the ancestors of your families, Cranfield and Bradley, were not solely human. Generations ago, at about the same time, your ancient grandfathers married elvish women. I thought you'd like to know that the records describe both elves as 'very beautiful'. I think that explains your good looks!'

Richard was yet again a fish gasping in too little water – mouth wide open, eyes bulging alarmingly. 'That's crazy!' he spluttered at last.

'No it isn't,' said Toby firmly. 'Haven't you and Tom felt different from other people? Haven't you both dreamt of something better? It's the elvish part of you, your zest for life!'

'So why us?' asked Tom. 'Why not other members of our families who have the elvish ancestry?'

'You two are the ones who have woken to the calling of the elf part of you – without realising it. In a way, you selected yourselves. You were both in the right place at the right time.'

'Maybe that should be the wrong place and time,' muttered Tom grimly.

'And before either of you ask about your ears,' continued Toby, 'you won't be surprised that the reason you don't have elf-ears is because you have only a tiny bit of elf-blood in you. It's tiny, but I believe you'll find in time that it's surprisingly useful to you. Now let me tell you what I think Drusilla knows. She knows that the prophecy is being fulfilled – she will have felt you two entering this world from your own, and I have to say she's looking for you. I know she's looking for you, because – ', and at this point, he hesitated and looked furtively around, ' – because, let's say, I've seen evidence of it.'

Richard looked sharply at Toby and blurted, 'The thing

that made that roaring sound when we were on the other side of the forest was looking for us, wasn't it?'

Toby returned Richard's gaze. 'You are very perceptive, my friend,' said Toby. 'It was looking for you boys, on her behalf.'

'Was it wanting to capture us, or kill us?' asked Richard.

'I believe that Drusilla wants you both captured,' answered Toby. 'She wants to find out how you got here, and she'll try to use you both to help her gain access to your world. Yes, I'm very confident that she wants you both alive, at least for as long as you are useful to her. We need to defeat Drusilla and return you two to your own world, to your families. Now this is very important. What Drusilla does not know is the detail of how our two worlds interact in terms of time and place. She has been trying to get her hands on the book mentioned in the prophecy for many years. It has been handed down by generations of good, well-intentioned wizards, and it describes how the worlds interact, how you can monitor the interaction, and how you can pass from one world to the other. If she gets hold of this book before you two do, she will use it to enslave your world in much the same way she is already enslaving mine. She has the power to do this. She just needs to know how to use the power to achieve her ambition.'

'Toby, let me guess,' sighed Richard. 'You've got the book?'

'Yes, but Drusilla doesn't know that,' said Toby. 'The only way she would guess that I have the book is if she realises that I'm looking after you two. What would I be doing other than taking you both to the book? The first place she would look would be my house – and I have to say she'd be right to look there. That's why it's vital that nobody guesses who you two are until we have completed our business with the book. You see, many folk now work for her, and it only takes one of them to work out who you are, and then to report back to her that you have been seen with me.'

'What do we have to do with the book?' asked Tom.

'Well, the book contains a number of spells,' explained Toby. 'The 'padlock' spell is a kind of safety spell, designed to prevent evil sorcerers from using the book. It locks or unlocks all other spells in the book, and I quote, 'can only be invoked by two people with mixed elf and human lineage' – that's you, boys. The ancient sorcerers who created the book didn't think to invoke this spell, because there simply weren't any evil sorcerers around at the time. This means that at the moment, all spells in the book are available for use. Both you boys need to place your hands on the book with mine, while I read out the locking spell; then the other spells will be locked out.'

'That seems simple enough,' said Tom thoughtfully, stroking his chin.

Toby nodded approvingly before continuing. 'The spells Drusilla would like to get her hands on are the ones that allow the timelines between the worlds to be manipulated, enabling her to open and close portals pretty much where and when she chooses. No doubt she would send her forces through the portals to cause mayhem in your world. She certainly won't wait for natural portal openings – they only happen once in a blue moon!'

Toby paused to sip his drink. 'The ancient sorcerers intended the portal spells to be used to encourage elves and humans to move between the two worlds, the ultimate aim being to reunite the elvish and human worlds into one world. This aim in mind, the book includes a recombining spell. The idea is that when elves and humans have got used to mingling with each other and have decided they'd like to make the arrangement permanent, the spell can be invoked to recombine the worlds so that, as before, one world is created with a rich blend of elvish spirit and human ingenuity – this time, hopefully, a harmonious world. I hope that one day the time will be right to invoke the recombining spell. Mind you, it can't be invoked just like that – it needs two people with mixed elf and human lineage, and seven sorcerers to make it happen! Anyway, to cut a long story short, I need to get you boys to the book so that you can invoke the padlock spell. Then, if Drusilla gets hold of the book afterwards, it will be of no use to her. At least that should save your world from her unwelcome attention. Then I will carry out my plan to destroy her power-base – in other words, to destroy her hosts of dragons, and free my world of her grip.'

'Toby,' said Richard, 'yet again you've mentioned dragons, but what really bothers me is your use of the phrase 'hosts of' in connection with these particular dragons,' whispered Richard fervently, looking very directly at the wizard.

Toby avoided Richard's penetrating gaze and suddenly pulled out his fob watch. 'Oh, look how late it is!' he announced, jumping to his feet. 'We need to get to sleep – we've got an early start to make tomorrow. We shall stay in one room for safety – I'm afraid you two will have to share the bed between you. I will sleep on the floor. My staff will wake me if danger approaches. I'll make it look as though the other two bedrooms have been slept in. Now follow me, boys.'

Staff in hand, Toby led them to the bar where he paid Ben for the evening and the rooms. 'We'll be away early in the morning, Ben,' said Toby. 'I'm sure I'll be visiting Broom Down again soon. I'll see you then.'

'Right. Are yer travellin' far?' asked Ben.

'We'll go where the mood takes us. It's part of their training,' said Toby, nodding at the boys. 'I take them to all sorts of places where they can try out their sorcery skills.'

They all bid Ben farewell, and made for the door that led upstairs to the bedrooms. As they climbed the creaking stairs, they could still hear the continuing belching and farting sounds from the green goblins below, accompanied by the inevitable guffaws of laughter.

FIVE

Toby and the boys stepped out from the front door of The Green Goblin, and quietly closed it behind them. It was early in the morning and there was no-one else about. They squinted at the sun that had just risen above the distant hills, promising a hot summer's day.

It had been an uneventful night. Richard and Tom had been so tired that they had almost forgotten how terrified they were, and had gone straight to sleep. Now, in the hard light of day, they all had the look (and smell) of people who had not washed recently and had slept in their clothes.

'The first thing I need to do,' said Toby, 'is visit a friend here in Broom Down. He's one of those rare elves who likes technology and invents things. Follow me.'

Toby led them to a cottage on the outskirts of Broom Down. Whoever lived in the cottage didn't spend much time looking after either it or the garden. They passed an open rickety wooden front gate which looked about ready to part company from its hinges, then walked along the path leading to the cottage, the path disappearing in several places under encroaching vegetation. The garden itself was a chaotic wilderness of long grass and brambles. They reached the cottage, which at one time would have been described as 'charming', but no longer. The thatch was covered in green mould with birds nesting in it. A window had been partly boarded with wood where a pane of glass had presumably fallen out long ago, and the front door – which was obviously once shiny and red – was now bare grey wood beneath a rash of faded red paint peelings, the rusty door knocker hanging limply at an angle from one remaining screw fixing. Toby rapped on the door with his staff, causing a momentary blizzard of paint flakes. After a short wait, the door opened and a small elf peered around it. When he saw Toby, he smiled and opened the door wide. 'Come in, Toby! It's good to see you!' he said briskly. He spoke in short quick bursts, rather like a machine-gun. All the words were there, but they were so fleeting, it was all too easy for a word to get away without the listener even being aware it had arrived.

The elf looked middle-aged. His hair was a dark unruly mop, and he wore a white lab-coat covered in grubby marks and stains. His movements were quick, and bird-like.

'Shamus, can I bring my trusted apprentices in with me?' asked Toby cheerfully. 'Maybe they could look at some of your inventions in the front room, while you and I take a look at our project?'

'If it's fine with you, it's fine by me. Welcome, all of you,' Shamus rattled off in reply while ushering them inside and shutting the door.

Toby pointed to the front room and asked the boys to wait in there. 'Shamus and I won't be long,' he said. 'I'm seeing how he's getting on with something he's making that we hope to use against Drusilla. The fewer people that know what Shamus is up to, the better. If Drusilla found out, Shamus and I would be in great danger. So I'll see you shortly, boys.'

Toby and Shamus disappeared into the back of the cottage, while Richard and Tom went into the front room as directed. The room was sorely in need of decoration and had no furniture in it. Most of the floor space was covered by weird gadgets. The boys couldn't work out what many of the gadgets were meant to do – they were too strange for words. But some were more recognisable: a wind-up vacuum cleaner, a wind-up food mixer, and a wind-up drill.

'Do you think Shamus is going to take on Drusilla's dark forces with a wind-up pop-up toaster?' said Tom, failing to stifle his laughter. Richard slowly shook his head, a broad smile on his face.

Soon, Toby and Shamus returned. They were looking pleased with themselves. 'Shamus has done an excellent job,' said Toby. 'Drusilla had better watch out. Now we must take our leave – we've a long walk ahead.'

But Richard didn't want to leave it there. He looked at Shamus. 'So you're creating some kind of weapon to fight Drusilla?' he asked.

'Well,' replied Shamus, who clearly wasn't expecting such a direct question, 'I normally make gadgets for use in and around the home by elves who want life made easier by means other than sorcery. Actually, I'm doing rather well; household gadgets are becoming very fashionable with elves these days. But as for Drusilla, we can't fight her with sorcery alone – so yes, I'm working on a physical weapon.'

'Which, as I said earlier,' added Toby, 'we don't want you to have any details of at the moment, just in case either of you ever finds yourself, God forbid, being questioned by her or her minions. Now, boys, we really must go.' This was the cue for Shamus to show them to the front door, and bid them farewell. Whereupon the trio walked back along the path, taking care to step over the gate which had now given up all hope, having completely fallen off its hinges.

'Right, boys. My home is a day's walk, beyond those hills,' said Toby, pointing at some distant hills with his staff, 'and we should get there tonight if all goes well. A meal and a bath beckon. Talking of food, have a Wizard Nonsuch travel biscuit.' Toby pulled out from a pocket some large round biscuits that looked as though they were made of oatmeal. He passed them around as they walked down the road out of the village.

'Ugh! These biscuits taste awful!' groaned Richard.

'Yes, that's right!' smiled Toby. 'One biscuit will put you off food for quite some time, which I think you'll agree is a great way to stave off hunger.' The boys' mutterings of discontent didn't seem to affect the wizard in the least.

After an hour or so walking through open moorland along the rough dirt road, Toby led them onto the moor itself. 'This is the shortest route to where I live. It also takes us away from the road and away from folk travelling on it – we don't want to advertise our presence to more people than is necessary.'

Soon, they reached a small copse of trees at the foot of the hills, where they stopped for a rest. The sun was now high in the sky, and they were all very hot and weary. They sat under the cool shade of the trees, and Toby passed around a flask of water. They were about to get going again when all went dark and a violent swirling wind sprang up. There was a deep whooshing sound from above.

'My God! What's that? Tom, Toby, run for it!' shouted Richard in panic, leaping to his feet. Something huge was landing near the trees, but he couldn't see its shape clearly through the airborne dust. He could feel the shock through the ground as whatever-it-was finally landed. Richard ran blindly into Tom who was doing exactly the same thing. Together they then ran off in what they hoped was the right direction. There was so much dust in the air that all they could see were dim outlines of uncertain shapes. Then they ran headlong into a tree trunk, tripped over its roots and fell over. As they started to pick themselves up from the ground, the boys noticed the tree's red roots which ended in what looked like yellowish ivory. As the dust cleared a little more, it became obvious they were looking at the foot of an animal, an animal with massive claws. Almost in a dream, their eyes travelled up what was surely the leg, up and up, until they saw a huge head looking down at them. It was a red scaly head with large nostrils, rows of sharp teeth and penetrating yellow eyes with dark reptilian pupils. It spoke in a deep, posh and fruity voice. 'Hello,' it said.

Things didn't look good. One, they had been standing on the foot of what they could now see was a massive red dragon. Two, the dragon had spoken to them. Three, it was presumably only a matter of time before it ate them. Stunned by the finality of this logic, they slowly became aware that Toby was standing next to them, and was talking crossly to the dragon. 'What do you think you're doing?' he shouted. 'Are you trying to show the whole world where we are? These boys have got enough to deal with without a great red dragon dropping in on them. The agreement was you would keep watch on my house while I was away, but that doesn't include making social calls, my friend.'

The dragon was looking very uncomfortable. 'I'm sorry, Toby,' its cultured voice very much at odds with how Richard expected a dragon might speak. 'I flew to McDragons for a quick meal. On the way back I saw you three, and thought I'd drop by to apologise to Richard.'

Richard was now immune to further surprises, feeling totally numb. He found himself saying to the dragon, 'How do you know my name?'

The dragon looked at Toby. 'Can I tell Richard about my, er, involvement?' it asked rather sheepishly.

'Yes, why not,' sighed Toby.

'The dragon turned its head back to Richard. 'I'm a friend of Toby's,' it explained. 'One night, Toby realised that this world would soon connect to your world for a short time. Toby wanted to visit you and Tom to make sure that everything felt right – to make sure that you were the chosen ones. So in order to get to the right place in time, I flew him there under cover of darkness. We flew over Tom's house, close enough for Toby to 'sense' him, and know he was definitely 'chosen'. Then we flew over your house, and got close enough for Toby to know that you were also definitely chosen. Then I did something I shouldn't have. I saw a rabbit down below, and I don't know what came over me. I was hungry, and without thinking I swooped into your garden – such a big garden, plenty of landing space – and, er, I removed the rabbit from its cage. It was only after I'd eaten it that I became aware of an angry Toby telling me that the plan was not to land and wake up the entire neighbourhood, and that I'd just eaten your beloved pet. I'm so sorry. Please forgive me.'

The dragon was now looking miserably at Richard, and a tear ran down its face. Richard's brain was starting to work again. 'So it was you that made the whooshing sound, you that blotted out the moon, you that made the footprints on the lawn, and you that smashed Rocket's hutch – then ate him.'

'Sorry.'

'Well…thank you for your apology,' said Richard, probably with more kindness than the dragon deserved.

By now, Tom had decided that the dragon was friendly and quite possibly a bit of a softie. 'Are there other dragons like you?' he asked.

'Lots,' said the dragon. 'Most of us live in the mountains, where Toby lives.'

Tom hesitated. 'So let's get this straight,' he said carefully. 'We're walking into a land full of dragons?'

Toby seemed keen to play down Tom's point. 'Red dragons have lived in harmony with other folk for hundreds of years,' he said earnestly. 'They generally don't eat people – these days they get food from shops and markets like everyone else. Besides, dragons are not great socialisers, and tend to keep themselves to themselves. Don't worry boys, you'll soon get used to them.'

Richard was frowning. 'I notice you're talking about red dragons, he said. 'Are there other types of dragon?'

Toby nodded. 'Indeed there are other dragons, and I'm sorry to say they're not friendly. They are black dragons, created by Drusilla from stolen young red dragons.'

The dragon looked grimly into the distance. 'We red dragons have unfinished business with her,' it said with sudden venom. 'Now I really must return to Toby's home.'

The great red beast backed away and slowly and gracefully unfurled its huge leathery wings. It truly was a magnificent sight. It had a serrated crest running from the top of its head, down its long neck, over its arched back, the crests getting ever smaller as they snaked their way atop the long sinuous tail, ending at a large backward-pointing arrowhead at the tip.

Somehow the dragon looked familiar to Richard. Why was that? Suddenly it came to him. 'Toby, this dragon's exactly like the dragon on the Welsh national flag!' he gasped.

'That's not surprising, Tom,' chuckled Toby. 'The ancient Welsh didn't dream up the dragon you now see on the flag. They drew it from life!'

The dragon was looking a little peeved. 'Please don't call me 'this dragon'. I have a name you know.'

'I'm sorry,' said Richard hastily. 'Please tell me your name.'

'It's Dave,' the dragon replied proudly.

'Dave the dragon?' blurted Richard, trying hard not to burst out laughing.

'Dragons like short, simple names,' said Toby quietly, shooting a meaningful glance at Richard.

'Right,' said Richard, getting the point and not smiling anymore.

Fortunately Dave had another matter on his mind. 'Toby, all the time I've been on my viewing ledge on Mount Venerable, I haven't seen anything at all suspicious happening around your home. It's been very quiet.'

'Thank you, Dave,' said Toby. 'I promise I'll return the favour. Nobody would want to go anywhere near my home with you around!'

'It's a pleasure, Toby,' smiled Dave. 'It's been very nice having the time to myself. Now I'd better be getting back. See you all later.' So saying, Dave took to the air and headed over the hills, of course leaving a small dust storm behind.

When the dust had died down and they'd all finished coughing, Toby clapped his hands together. 'Right,' he said crisply. 'We need to get moving if we're to reach my place by nightfall.'

So the trio walked on, the terrain quickly becoming mountainous, ever more having to climb steep rocky outcrops and cross deep gullies.

Richard and Tom were having an animated conversation, and not surprisingly, the hot topic was dragons. 'Dragons that speak and are friendly and that at least don't generally eat people – as Toby told us – it's incredible!' spluttered Richard.

'I wonder what it's like to be *generally* eaten by a dragon?' mused Tom, looking across at Toby mischievously. '*Specific* eating might be just your toes?'

Toby ignored Tom. 'Dave is very friendly. Actually, he's one of my best friends.'

Tom continued his line of questioning. 'Toby, I remember Dave saying he flew you to our world. So you rode on him?'

'Yes,' nodded Toby. 'You sit on his back between crests near the base of his neck, holding on to the crest in front. Dave always flies very carefully when I'm riding on him – no aerobatics, just straight and level.'

'So why didn't *we* ride him?' asked Tom. 'It would have saved us having to walk the rest of the way.'

Richard could contain himself no longer. 'What's wrong with you, Tom Bradley?' he snorted angrily. 'We didn't ride the dragon, because it's dangerous! There's a good chance that you'd slip and fall off. There is absolutely no way I'm flying on anything. I don't like heights.'

'Keep your hair on, matey!' retorted Tom, his face reddening. 'I'd really like to fly by dragon. Not something you normally get to do.'

'You're mad,' muttered Richard.

What was about to escalate into a full-blown argument was nipped in the bud by Toby's timely intervention. 'My friends,' he said, 'you're both forgetting that the reason we're not flying, is because we need to keep a low profile. Believe me, three people riding on a red dragon would get noticed, particularly because very few people in the world are sufficiently friendly with a dragon for it to even think of giving them a ride. Where I live, the only dragon ever known to take passengers, is Dave… oh, and another dragon I know. Anyway, I'm not sure Dave would manage with three of us – he'd have trouble getting off the ground.'

But now Richard looked even more worried than before. 'Toby, back in my world, why did you move the letters to spell 'storm rider' when Tom and I were playing with anagrams? Please tell me it wasn't anything to do with riding on dragons.'

Toby stopped walking, and turned to face the boys. 'I chose 'storm rider' because the prophecy tells that two human boys with elf-blood will fly on dragons and will battle with the evil power; so for 'storm' think 'battle', and for 'rider' think 'dragon rider'.' Then he shrugged his shoulders and said, 'But, hey, it's only a prophecy and it might be wrong.'

Richard suddenly stopped walking, standing crossly with his hands on his hips and looking very directly at the wizard. 'You don't think the prophecy's wrong, do you Toby?'

'No, I'm afraid it's likely to be correct,' he replied. 'Sorry.'

'Oh that's just great. I'll be terrified, but at least Tom will be happy – he'll actually enjoy the flying.'

But it seemed that Tom was not completely comfortable

either. 'Actually, I don't like the sound of the 'battling with the evil power' bit,' he said, his voice quavering.

'My friends, it's best we take each day as it comes,' said Toby, smiling warmly. 'Let's be content with where we are now, and let tomorrow take care of itself.'

They walked on, the boys anxiously looking around every now and then, as well as looking up. Eventually Toby pointed to a large hill in front of them. 'Over that rise you'll see where I live. Let's get a move on. The sun's getting low.'

So, the trio set off again, now with an added urgency in their stride. For a while, nobody said anything, all lost in their own thoughts. Tom finally broke the silence. 'Toby, don't you have to worry about dragon fire?'

'No, Tom.'

'Why not?'

'Because dragon fire is a myth,' explained Toby. 'It was a story made up by knights who fancied the idea of hunting dragons. Dragons don't by choice hunt humans because, as far as dragons are concerned, humans taste really horrible. On the other hand, a nice fat deer makes a fine meal.

'So these knights needed to find an excuse to hunt dragons. One of the knights was called George. He made up a story that dragons breathed fire and were using their fire to burn down villages just for the hell of it. George then set fire to a few villages and blamed the fires on the dragons flying overhead.

'So, now having public support to slaughter dragons, he set forth. He found numerous dragon caves, but each time he approached, the dragon in question would simply fly off, not wanting to get involved, then return after George had given up waiting for it.

'One day, George came across a cave with a dragon inside that had recently died of old age. He realised his name would be mud if he didn't bring back a dead dragon, so he inflicted a few sword wounds on the carcass and dragged it to the nearest village, saying he had fought the dragon for two hours, and was finally victorious. George's fame quickly spread throughout the realm, and it wasn't long before he was made a Saint, St. George, in fact.'

In spite of himself, Richard couldn't help smiling at this. 'When I get back to my world,' he said brightly, 'I'm going to have to campaign to have the St. George Cross flag banned. Read all about it: St. George was a fraud!'

Before they knew it, the trio had reached the top of the hill. In front of them was a beautiful vista of rocky hills and mountains, stretching as far as the eye could see.

Toby pointed to his house. It was halfway up the nearest mountain, a stone building built into the rock. It was certainly remote; no other dwellings could be seen. Toby's mountain was on one side of a deep long valley, both sides flanked by a series of equally magnificent mountains. Threading its way along the green, verdant valley floor was a river, looking for all the world like an enormous silvery snake. Dotted along the valley were the unmistakable shapes of cattle and sheep, grazing the abundant grass. The comforting cacophony of their voices wafted on the breeze.

Large birds were circling over the mountains, soaring effortlessly, their eerie cries echoing off the rock. The boys didn't need to be told that these birds were eagles. Richard wished that he could fly away with the eagles, and leave all his troubles behind.

For some time they stood, gazing at the entrancing scene laid out before them. There was certainly no indication here of evil at work. Everything appeared idyllic. It was hard to believe that Drusilla was plotting to subject all of this to her rule.

Toby finally broke the moment. 'We need to get moving,' he said.

Within an hour they were on the mountain path leading to Toby's home. Richard spotted a red dragon lying on a rocky ledge on a next-door mountain. The dragon launched itself over the edge and flew away, finally disappearing behind a distant mountain. It must be Dave, thought Richard – his long vigil had at last ended.

'Toby, has Dave been on watch throughout the night as well as the day?' asked Richard.

'Yes, he has,' replied Toby. 'Dragons can see well at night.'

'Surely he must have slept sometimes?'

'Well, dragons have a special trick in the sleep department. Dave will have been snoozing throughout both the day and night, but one eye will always be slightly open, watching. It's incredible – he can be asleep, but will always be alert. Only a dragon can get away with kipping on the job!'

After much foot-slogging, they finally reached the house, just in time to see a fiery red sun sinking behind the mountains. The combination of altitude and disappearing sun lent a chilly feel to the air. The shivering, weary and hungry trio were desperate to get inside.

In the failing light, the house seemed almost indistinguishable from the mountain. This was not surprising, as according to Toby the house was built from stone taken from the mountain, only one wall of the house showing externally. The rest of the house, in fact virtually all of it, was inside the mountain.

Positioned centrally in the external wall, there was a heavy gnarled wooden door, flanked by two small windows on either side. The door was fitted with an imposing black metal door-knocker fashioned in the shape of a dragon's head, and the windows were protected by vertical black metal bars – it seemed that Toby was keen on security.

The slope of the mountain above the wall formed a natural stone roof, through which a stone chimney rose in the middle.

The trio walked up to the door. There was no keyhole. Toby moved a little closer to the door, and it quietly opened of its own accord. 'The door only opens for me,' he explained, as he crossed the threshold into the darkness within. 'I'm just lighting a lamp. Good, now please come in.'

The boys walked into what was clearly an entrance hall, now lit by a cheerful warm glow. The door closed silently behind them, of its own accord.

'Make yourselves at home, boys,' said Toby. 'Put your hats on the hat-stand; I imagine you'll be glad not to wear those for a while.'

The boys gratefully did so. Their ears had been liberated from a whiffy itchy sauna.

The flickering light illuminated a long hall, punctuated with a number of closed wooden doors. The walls were made of grey blocks of stone, without any adornment, not even a picture. The plainness of the hall was relieved to some extent by the wooden beams supporting the ceiling, and by the presence of the hat-stand and a very attractive old grandfather clock. The clock spoke with a slow comforting tick-tock.

The ceiling was actually the mountain itself, the raw rock hewn surprisingly flat. Indeed, the floor was also fashioned from the mountain, without any attempt to cover it with so much as a rug.

Toby had opened the first door on the left, and had lit the lamps within. 'Come on in and make yourselves at home while I get the fire going,' he said invitingly.

The boys entered the room, and were taken aback by the contrast with the hall. It was a large living room, again with stone block walls and a natural rock ceiling supported by wooden beams, but it was comfortable and cosy. It sported a thick-pile purple carpet, with gold-coloured curtains covering a single window. A large rustic fireplace was the main feature in the room, and the newly lit friendly warmth of the crackling flames rising from the logs in the grate drew the boys to it like a magnet.

There were a number of sumptuous-looking leather armchairs surrounding a low wooden table on which was a spent coffee mug, a couple of books, a number of magazines, and Toby's recently abandoned staff. The magazines were all back-copies of the Institute Of Sorcery journal. One of the books particularly caught the eye – it was entitled: *Sorcery Versus Science: Can Science Ever Be Taken Seriously?*

The walls of the room were largely covered by wooden bookshelves stacked untidily with books and literature. A solitary oil painting hung above the fireplace: it was a painting of a male elf with more than a passing facial resemblance to Toby, but older, wearing what looked like wizard's attire.

'Who's that, Toby?' asked Richard, pointing at the painting.

'Oh, that's my father. He's a wizard – a good one, too. He's retired now. A few years ago, he decided he'd had enough of wizardry and offered me this house. I couldn't believe my luck! I had completed my training and qualified as a wizard some time before, so I immediately moved in as resident wizard; and here I still am, keeping the family business going, doing what I love doing.

'Dad moved with my mother and my younger sister to a cottage in the lowlands a few miles from here. Mum and Dad have always wanted a garden – something that's not really practical here! Nowadays, they seem to spend all their waking hours gardening. Their garden looks fantastic, and Dad tells everyone it's all down to green fingers, but I suspect that sorcery fingers may also be involved.'

'So has your house been handed down by generations of wizards?' asked Tom.

'It's been handed down by several generations of Nonsuch wizards,' replied Toby. 'You see, my great-great grandfather, Archie Nonsuch, built this house. He chose this remote location in the mountains so that he could concentrate on sorcery without interference from any busy-bodies. Many people seem unhealthily desperate to find out what's going on in wizard's sorcerariums – I think they expect to find horrible creations lurking, like bug-eyed monsters and such.'

Tom's eyes were almost popping out of their sockets. 'Sorcerarium? Is that a kind of sorcery workshop?'

Toby nodded.

'Are there any, er, weird creations, in your sorcerarium?'

Toby smiled. 'No, Tom,' he replied. 'As I've said before, sorcery is hard work, and we good wizards prefer to focus our energy on helping the world, which generally doesn't require us to conjure up bug-eyed monsters – if that's what you meant.'

'Oh, right,' said Tom, trying not to show his disappointment, 'and where *is* your sorcerarium?' He had tried to make it sound as though he really wasn't that interested in finding out.

'It's right here,' said Toby, pointing vaguely at one of the walls. 'It's a room right inside the mountain.'

Richard suddenly remembered the reason they'd journeyed to Toby's house. 'Toby, shouldn't we do the business with the book right now?'

'I'm afraid we'll have to wait until tomorrow morning. The ancient wizards that created the padlock spell were a little romantic in their approach to sorcery. They couldn't resist restricting the use of the spell somewhat. I can even remember the precise words: 'Let it be known that this spell can only be invoked after the first cockerel crows and thereafter until the first eagle soars.''

'That's rubbish!' snorted Richard, trying to stifle his laughter. 'How do you know when the first cockerel has crowed? It might be miles away and you wouldn't hear it. If there was a nearer cockerel, it may not be the first to crow in the morning. As for the first eagle, how do you know when it's soared? I suppose a good pair of binoculars would come in handy.'

'All good points,' smiled Toby. 'Fortunately, we wizards

have a common understanding that the first cockerel crows at six o' clock in the morning and the first eagle soars at ten o' clock in the morning.'

'Between six and ten in the morning would have been clearer.'

'It would have,' agreed Toby. 'You see, we wizards are like lawyers – we don't want the public to start to understand what we do and then find ourselves out of a job. Now, sit down wherever you like, and I'll rustle up some hot drinks while we wait for our meal to arrive. I've ordered a selection of elf-breads – they're rather like the garlic bread you have in your own world, but more interesting. I'm sorry, but I haven't time to cook you a meal tonight. I hope hot chocolate and the elf-breads will suffice.'

The boys nodded vigorously. They were ravenous.

Then Richard asked the obvious question. 'You get deliveries out here?'

'Oh yes,' responded Toby, but before he could elaborate, there was a loud knocking sound. 'Ah, that'll be the elf-breads. I could do with some help to carry in the food boxes, boys.'

The boys happily got up and followed Toby out of the living room into the cold hall, then to the front door.

'No need to put your hats back on, boys,' said Toby as the door opened of its own accord.

'That's odd, Toby,' said Richard, squinting into the darkness now revealed. 'There's no-one there.' Then he became aware there was a strange sound coming from outside, like the wind – but it couldn't be the wind. It was a low rasping sound, slowly repeating. 'My God! There's something out there – I can hear it breathing – shut the door!

Suddenly there was a heavy swishing sound and a huge head appeared in the doorway. Richard and Tom screamed and ran down the hallway as fast as their legs could carry them. They reached the end of the hall to hear the head say, 'Hello.'

It was a familiar, very well-spoken, voice. The boys turned slowly around, now realising to whom the head belonged. 'I'm sorry I gave you a fright,' said the dragon apologetically. 'I wanted to get your elf-breads to you before they got cold, so I flew pretty fast. When you opened the door, I'm afraid I was still catching my breath.'

'It's my fault, Dave,' said Toby. 'I didn't think to tell the boys who would be delivering the food.'

Toby turned to the boys and said, 'Dave often picks up food for me from Broom Down – it takes him ten minutes to fly from there to here, whereas, well…you know how long it takes to walk it. Now, are you two all right?'

Richard and Tom nodded, trying to give the impression they hadn't really been all that frightened.

Toby looked at the grandfather clock. 'You're right on time Dave,' he said. 'Nine o' clock on the button. Now you need to get back to your family…which reminds me – how is Danielle?'

'She's fine,' replied Dave. 'The potion you gave her has completely healed her wing. She says that she's not going to fly straight into the cave ever again. She's going to arrive as Diana and I do – land outside, then walk in. Mind you, I'll believe it when I see it! Youngsters – who'd have them?'

Toby smiled. 'Before you go, the elf-breads?'

'Coming up, my good wizard.'

Using a great clawed foot, Dave pushed a stack of boxes through the doorway into the house, the yeasty almond aroma of warm elf-breads wafting its way through the house.

'Thanks for this, my friend. Put it on my account,' said Toby, rubbing his hands together in anticipation of the feast in store.

This was the cue for Dave to withdraw his head. Illuminated by the light spilling out from the doorway, the boys could see his vast red body turning around, preparing for flight. His wings unfurled with a deep, leathery rustling sound, until becoming fully extended. Then the wings began to beat up and down, the whooshing sound reverberating around the mountains, the customary dust-cloud rolling into the house as Dave finally took to the air. Toby shot a meaningful glance at the door, which promptly closed, but not promptly enough to prevent everyone coughing.

Having recovered, Toby and the boys picked up the boxes and took them through to the living room, depositing them on the low table. Then they sat down and in record time devoured the elf-breads.

'You know, I definitely like elf-breads,' Richard said, feeling nicely full, lying back in his armchair with a mug of hot chocolate in his hand. Tom and Toby nodded with wide smiles.

The three friends stared into the dancing fire, lost in their thoughts. Eventually, Tom murmured, 'That was really scary, what happened at the front door.'

'Yes, it was,' Richard quickly agreed.

'It's nothing to be ashamed of, boys. Anyone who isn't scared witless when a huge dragon lurches into view needs their head examining,' said Toby. Then, with a great effort, he stood up. 'Drink up boys. Don't worry about the mess on the table – we'll clear it up in the morning. It's time for a hot bath followed by bed. We'll move two beds into my bedroom so that we're all together; I thought you might feel safer with everyone in the same room, not that there's anything to fear in the Nonsuch house. Does that sound good?'

Richard and Tom nodded, and after finishing their drinks, everyone headed off for a well-earned good night's sleep. Fortunately Toby's bedroom was spacious, comfortably accommodating the two additional beds.

Richard and Tom were very grateful that Toby was with them in the room. As if to further reassure them, Toby had brought his staff in with him, and had propped it up against his bed within grabbing distance. Still glowing from their hot baths, everyone fell asleep, the weariness from their recent journey having finally caught up with them.

But Richard's sleep soon became troubled. In his dream, he was in Toby's house, and could hear occasional faint tapping sounds. He spent the rest of the dream being very scared, moving around the house with Toby, trying to find where the sounds were coming from, and trying to determine what was making them. Suddenly Toby was no longer with him, and the sounds were getting louder...

Richard woke in a cold sweat. All was quiet, save for the steady breathing of his sleeping friends. He smiled inwardly. It was a nasty dream. Then he rolled over and slept peacefully until morning.

SIX

Richard and Tom were woken by their noses which had detected the smell of bacon and eggs cooking. Daylight from the hallway dimly lit the windowless bedroom through the open door, illuminating the outline of Toby's empty bed. The boys jumped out of their own beds, dressed quickly, and set off into the hallway following the wonderful smell. Their expedition took them past the grandfather clock which showed that it was half-past seven. Plenty of time to do the sorcery thing with the book thought Richard.

They came to a door towards the front of the house that was half-open. From within, they could hear the spitting and crackling of frying food. Richard eased the door wide open to reveal a kitchen lit by daylight from a single window. A cheery voice welcomed them inside.

'Good morning! Sit down at the table wherever you like and have something to eat.'

'Thank you,' the boys said as they walked to the table, before sitting down.

The kitchen-diner was spacious with a large oblong wooden dining table at its centre, around which six wooden chairs were arranged. The boys sat at two of the three table places that had been provided with cutlery.

The raw stone walls were liberally covered with a

smattering of wooden cupboards and shelves, populated with a topsy-turvy mixture of jars, plates, bowls and other culinary equipment. There were also some wooden drawer units, supporting a wooden work-top, and in one corner was a large old-fashioned sink fitted with a hand-pumped water outlet and a wooden draining surface.

One wall had a large fireplace set into it. A log fire was roaring in the open grate. Above the fire was a wrought-iron structure, on which a frying pan had been placed. Toby was tending the sizzling frying pan with its cargo of eggs and rashers of bacon.

Not long after, the only sound that could be heard was that of fervent eating. When the eating was over, a fly on the wall would have observed three full people sat around the table, smiling smugly at each other. In fact, there *was* a fly on the wall, but this particular fly was only focussing on the dirty crockery and cutlery that Toby was now collecting from the table.

Richard promptly jumped up, asking if he could assist with the washing up, as did Tom (rather belatedly, Richard thought).

'No need, thanks,' smiled Toby. 'It's all disposable.'

Richard frowned. 'Surely disposable kitchen stuff is made of paper, cardboard or plastic? But *these* plates are made of something like china, and the knives and forks are made of metal. So what makes them disposable?'

Suddenly the piled up crockery and cutlery exploded with flashes of yellow, green and crimson – *Bang, Bang, Crump, Kerblang!* It was absolutely deafening, the noise ricocheting off the hard stone walls. It went on for quite some time, rather like an overly vigorous indoor fireworks display, and one that any right-minded Health and Safety person in Richard's world would definitely have stipulated should have been outside. Eventually the noise subsided.

'You can come out now,' suggested Toby.

Richard and Tom slowly extricated themselves from their hiding place under the table. They looked completely dazed, rather as you might after stepping off a fast-moving roundabout.

'What happened?' slurred Richard, blinking, and holding very firmly onto the table.

'The washing up happened, that's all,' said Toby.

'Can anyone smell lemons?' asked Tom, swaying about rather alarmingly.

'Ah, yes,' said Toby. 'This particular kitchen set came with a lemon-scented wash-up. The last batch was strawberry with a hint of blackcurrant.'

The boys decided not to ask any further questions relating to washing-up. Clearly disposable kitchenware here really did mean…disposable.

The fly on the wall remained where it was. It had seen all this before, but thanks to the fact that it could only ever remember the last thing that had gone through its mind, it had forgotten that the food left on the plates always ended up dissolving into thin air before it had a chance to get to it. It would have a long wait. But maybe not quite so long, if the spider that had been stalking the fly for the last few minutes had anything to do with it.

Toby clapped his hands together. 'Okay. The *Key to the Half Worlds* book is waiting for us in the sorcerarium and the first eagle hasn't soared yet – so let's make the book safe,' he said brightly.

Still recovering from the kitchen's explosions, Richard pulled himself together, and said rather too loudly, 'Right! Let's do it!'

'Yeah,' said Tom, not wishing to be left out, 'let's do some serious sorcery!'

Toby smiled approvingly, and led the boys into the hallway,

all the way down its ever-darkening length to the door at the end. Toby gestured with his right hand, and the door silently opened, revealing a barely discernible corridor, leading to blackness. He walked into the corridor and lit an oil-lamp on the wall. The growing flickering light revealed that the long corridor led directly to yet a further door at the end of it. They walked to the door and after another movement of Toby's hand, it opened in the half-light to reveal a chamber.

As the boys entered the chamber, their eyes were drawn towards weird fantastic shadows on the rough stone walls and ceiling. The source of the shadows soon became apparent. There were several tables in the centre of the room, their surfaces covered with a riot of glass flasks, interconnecting tubing, tripods and burners. The light was projecting this scene of mayhem in the form of scary shadows.

The shadows started to disappear as Toby lit oil lamps positioned around the room. 'Welcome to my sorcerarium,' he said, with an expansive sweep of his hand. 'This is the most secure room in the house. As you can see, it's a chamber that's been carved out of the centre of the mountain. The only way in is through the door you've just passed through. That door, as you've probably guessed, is the product of sorcery and opens only at my command. Now let's move to the far end of the room where my library is.'

Toby led the boys past the tables with their sprawling spaghetti of chemistry-set apparatus.

'What do you do with all this stuff?' asked Richard, nervously eyeing a luminous green jelly-like substance in one of the flasks that appeared to be moving of its own accord.

'Is it to do with eye of toad and leg of newt?' asked Tom, grinning.

Toby stopped in mid-stride and turned to face Tom. Toby's face was a picture of mock disdain as he spoke. 'You'll be surprised to learn, young Tom, that eye of toad and such-like are not part of the sorcerer's repertoire. The use of animal body parts in sorcery is down to witch's tales – total myth. It's also not very nice as far as the animals are concerned. In fact, I hold a certificate that states that no animals, dead or alive, are used here.'

'So what do you do with all these tubes and flasks and things?' asked Tom rather sheepishly.

'Oh, that apparatus is just for show – to put nosy folk off the scent. Over there is the apparatus I use,' he said, pointing at a large old battered brown cardboard box stamped with the words: 'Handle With Care'. 'I use it to practise alchemy, which is basically about producing special metals from more common metals.'

'That?' snorted Tom, screwing his face up contemptuously.

'Open it, my friend,' invited Toby.

Tom walked to the box, gingerly opened its flaps, then fell back in complete astonishment. A column of fizzing blue-green energy burst out, hit the ceiling, and promptly spread out to cover most of it. Then weird blood-red fiery shapes appeared; dancing around, twisting, stretching and morphing into other shapes, while seemingly playing with the heaving blue-green background.

Richard watched the scene, his eyes wide with wonder. Suddenly he had an insight into what he was seeing. The red shapes were symbols. The ridiculous box was projecting some kind of chemical symbology onto the ceiling, rather like the symbols in the Periodic Table he was studying in Chemistry at school.

'Now, if I combine this element with a bit of this one…' murmured Toby as he waved his arms around, manipulating the symbols on the ceiling. 'Then we bring in this one and…'

There was a 'Thump!' as the energy column sucked itself back into the box leaving the chamber just as it was before the box had been opened.

The boys held their breath, wondering what would happen next.

Toby gestured towards the now-closed box. 'Tom, open it again, please.'

Slowly Tom moved back to the box and opened it, more cautiously than the first time. But this time, nothing happened. It just seemed to be a normal box.

'Look inside the box, Tom. It's perfectly safe.'

Tom peeked inside. 'It's full of shiny stuff!' he shouted excitedly.

'Grab a handful, Tom.'

Tom did so. He presented his shiny handful.

Richard's eyes bulged. 'Gold ingots?' he spluttered.

Toby was smiling. 'The purest of gold, my friends. This is one use of alchemy, but much more interestingly, I can use alchemy to manipulate the fabric of life.'

Tom, however, seemed to be thinking more about the financial aspect. 'Could I keep some of the gold, Toby? I don't get much pocket money...' he started breathlessly, stopping when he realised Toby and Richard were staring at him.

'Gold for the purpose of making money, Tom?' chuckled Toby. 'That's not at all why I perform alchemy, although I admit I've been known to produce a little gold for funding the wizardry business when it hasn't been doing too well. No, I use alchemy to increase my sorcery strength – all for the good, of course! A metal here, a different metal there, heated with extracts from certain plants, and if you do it right, the whole lot suddenly changes into a drinkable fluid that can enhance a wizard's power of sorcery. The trouble is, if you drink too much it can make you crazy. I reckon that Drusilla has been bingeing on wizard's rocket fuel.'

Tom, looking shamefaced, quickly stuffed the gold back into the box.

'Now, my friends, to the matter in hand while we still have time,' said Toby. 'Let's visit my library.'

The boys followed Toby past further chemical paraphernalia, which they now knew was an elaborate sham, finally reaching the end of the chamber. This part was fitted with several rows of wooden bookshelves, brimming with books, mostly on the bulky and ancient side with leather coverings decked with deep gold embossed lettering. Richard and Tom noticed a book entitled: *Humans: Fact or Fantasy?*, but their subsequent mirth was cut short by a voice screaming, 'It can't be! It's gone!'

seven

Toby was frantically rifling through the shelves, and to say he was distraught would be an understatement. 'It was on that shelf!' he wailed. 'I know I haven't put it anywhere else. Maybe I put it on another shelf. I must be going mad!'

The boys looked on helplessly until Toby at last stopped going through the books for the umpteenth time, and slowly slumped to the ground in despair. The calm and collected air that normally surrounded him seemed to have vanished. Eventually he looked up at the boys and said, 'I'm sorry about this. The worst thing possible has happened. The Book has gone. But how? This is the most secure room in the house. And where is The Book now? If it's gone to her, I've got to do something very quickly.' Then he buried his head in his hands.

The boys still didn't know what to say. Richard headed to a nearby chair positioned next to a wall, intending to collapse into it, but just before he got there – he stumbled. Looking down, he saw that he was standing on little fragments of rock. The fragments were lying on the floor in the form of a short narrow ragged ribbon, near the wall. Then he felt his eyes being drawn up the wall, and he suddenly became aware of what looked like a fault line in the raw rock of the mountain. His eyes followed the fine crack in the rock upwards. Very strange

– it was almost perfectly straight and vertical. It suddenly took a sharp left, and then he saw it. The crack formed the outline of a near perfect oblong with sides of about one-and-a-half metres in height by one metre in width, the bottom of the oblong being a few centimetres above floor level. Could it be?

Richard spun around, seeing Toby still sitting on the ground with his head in his hands. Richard pointed to the wall. 'Toby! What's all this?'

Toby looked up sharply. He pulled himself up from the floor and ran to Richard, Tom in pursuit.

'That wasn't there before,' said Toby pointing at the thin outline in the rock. 'And neither were these rock chippings on the floor.' A grim determination had set in. 'Let me get my rock hammer. I'll be back in a minute.'

Toby ran out of the chamber, quickly returning with a massive hammer, of the type used in quarrying. 'Stand back, boys!' he shouted.

He moved within striking distance of the outlined rock, swung the hammer back over his shoulder, and heaved the head of the hammer onto the target. There was a resounding 'Crack!' as it hit the wall, followed by the sound of a small avalanche as fragments of rock fell onto the floor, revealing as the dust settled – a tunnel.

The light from the room illuminated the tunnel sufficiently for all to see that it went straight and level for a few metres, then dipped downwards out of sight. A cool draught of air could be felt ushering out of the tunnel into the room.

Toby had definitely regained his composure now; the old Toby was back, but with the added resolve of someone who is on a deadly serious mission. His gaze settled on Richard. 'Richard, you've uncovered this tunnel, and in doing so, highlighted the fact that nothing is impregnable in this world. I can't think of anywhere safer to keep something than in the centre of this mountain, but it goes to show that if someone wants something badly enough, eventually they'll find a way to get it.'

Toby put his hand into the tunnel, allowing his fingers to brush over the cut rock. 'Look how perfectly this tunnel has been hewn from the rock. Only dwarves could have done this. Before they broke into the room, they even took the trouble to keep the last inch or so of rock in one piece so that they could put it back into place after leaving. You've got to admire their workmanship.'

'Dwarves?' gasped the boys in unison.

Toby sighed. 'Yes, dwarves. Short people – mind you, with the improved nutrition we have these days, many of them are as tall as your average elf. They tend to be stockier than elves, and the males are more likely to have beards than elves, but the real clincher is gold. Tell any dwarf that 'there's gold in those hills', he or she will grab a pickaxe before you know it and head off hill-ward. An elf would just continue with his or her crossword. Anyway, the main thing to know about dwarves is that they live in mountainous areas where they quarry into rock searching for precious metals and minerals, which they then sell on to the rest of us. Now, before the worlds divided, dwarves lived mainly in the areas you call Scotland and Wales. Many of the cave systems that people in your world believe to be natural formations, were actually created by dwarves. Since then, dwarves have improved their quarrying skills over the centuries, and these days they produce chambers with sides as flat as those of the tunnel behind me.'

The boys gazed at Toby as they took this information on board. As Richard finally came to terms with this new perspective on dwarves, something that had been lurking at the margins of his thoughts for some time suddenly hit centre stage. 'Toby! Last night I dreamt that I heard tapping sounds coming from somewhere in the house. I reckon I really did hear those sounds!'

'I think you might well be right, Richard,' replied Toby, his brow furrowed in thought. 'So they entered this room last night and took the book. That gives us a few days for Drusilla to get hold of the book and work out how to use it – '

'Drusilla?' interrupted Richard.

'Yes, it must be Drusilla,' continued Toby. 'The dwarves that made the tunnel were almost certainly employed by her. The vast majority of dwarves are good trustworthy folk, but there will always be some who find Drusilla's offer of pure gold too tempting.'

'How did she work out that the book was here?' asked Tom.

'A good question,' said Toby thoughtfully. 'Her spies must have seen you two boys with me and somehow worked out, or guessed – in spite of my efforts – that you were the two humans described in the prophecy that would find the book and stop it being misused by dark powers. Well, Drusilla knows where I live, and would quickly realise I was taking you to my home, and therefore that my home was where the book was likely to be. The other problem is that Drusilla and I go back a long way, and she knows that if there's any fighting of dark powers or saving of the world going on, I'm likely to be in the thick of it. So I think she put two and two together, and unfortunately for us, made four.'

'Wouldn't it have been easier for her to fight her way into the house from the front?' asked Tom. 'Since she's so powerful, she could easily fight off one red dragon. You said yourself she has hordes of black dragons.'

'No,' replied Toby. 'She'd reckon that an attack from the front would most likely turn out to be messy. The house was being watched by a red dragon, so rather than approach from the front and risk an unnecessary major conflict with my friends who include a number of red dragons, elves and one or two giants, she instead approached the house through the mountain, it seems without anyone noticing. The only way we can find out why neither I nor any of my friends were aware of this tunnel being made, is to follow it and see where it ends up. Although the creators of it have no doubt long since left the area, we might find some clues on the way that will help us when we pay Drusilla a visit.'

Richard now had some concerns to air. 'Toby, there are two things that bother me. One, are you proposing that we all get in this tiny dark tunnel and follow it until we bump into whoever made it or worse? Two, in the event we survive our journey in the tunnel, are we then to wander off to Drusilla and ask her to return our book?'

'Yes, that's it – more or less. We have to get you boys to the book as soon as possible so that you can make it safe before she gets a chance to start using it. Until you invoke the book's padlock spell, your world and mine is in great danger as long as the book remains in Drusilla's possession. Remember that I'll be with you both every step of the way.'

'I know we have to go,' said Richard, his voice trembling. 'It's just that I can't stand tiny dark airless spaces, and I'm not that keen on the prospect of visiting a powerful lady-elf wizard with loads of black dragons foaming at the mouth at the thought of seeing us.'

'I'm not keen on visiting her either,' said Toby, 'but believe me, I'm probably the best person to have around when we confront her. As for the tunnel, I'll lead the way with a light – so it won't be dark. Oh, and it won't be airless, as you can tell from the draught coming out of it.'

Tom chipped in. 'If it helps, Richard – in my humble capacity as resident expert potholer – I'm used to confined underground spaces, and am more than qualified to look after you!'

'Thanks, Tom,' said Richard, 'I really appreciate that.'

Toby clapped his hands in order to move proceedings on.

'Let's get together all we need to set off on our quest,' he said.

Soon, Toby and the boys were standing around the tunnel mouth, ready to proceed. They were all wearing heavy hooded cloaks in anticipation of the cold journey, the boys wearing their hats – in order to cover their funny rounded ears, as Toby so pointedly put it!

All the lights in the house had been extinguished. Toby and the boys were as ready as they would ever be to leave by this new, unwanted exit. First, Toby stepped into the tunnel, crouching to avoid hitting his head on the tunnel roof. Then Richard, then Tom. Slowly they shuffled on, ever deeper into the cold tunnel. Toby held his staff in front of him, the uppermost end of which glowed dimly with a yellowish hue, sufficient to show the way.

Richard whispered, 'I hope your light doesn't go out, Toby.'

'It shouldn't,' Toby whispered back. 'I put new batteries in the staff this morning.'

'Batteries!' snorted Tom with derision. 'Your staff is powered by *batteries*?'

Toby stared at Tom as though he was mad.

'Ah, a joke,' said Tom very quietly, looking down at his feet. 'I'm guessing then it's actually powered by sorcery.'

For what seemed like an eternity to Richard, they shuffled along behind Toby. By and large, the tunnel was straight with a moderate downward slope, punctuated with the occasional slight turn. The remarkable thing was how the tunnel builders had navigated so precisely through the mountain.

Eventually the air in the tunnel seemed to be getting a little fresher, then without warning, Toby halted. 'Quiet, and don't move,' he hissed. 'There's a light ahead that's not mine, and I can hear something. I'm turning my light off now.'

The comforting light ebbed away, but was replaced by a very dim glow. Could it be daylight? And now the sounds

Toby had heard were plain for all to hear. From somewhere ahead, they could hear an occasional tapping sound, like metal on rock. Then shuffling sounds, and the sound of rocks being moved.

'The dwarves must still be here!' Toby whispered. 'Follow me as quietly as you can. We're going to take a peek. They're making so much noise, I don't think they'll hear us. Okay?'

The boys nodded uncertainly, then resumed their shuffling behind Toby for several metres until he raised a hand, indicating they should stop. They had reached the end of the tunnel. Ahead, they could see the dim outline of a large cave which after several metres turned sharply to the left into a much better lit section. It was obvious that at that point the cave exited to the outside world.

Scanning the part of the cave they could see, there didn't seem to be anybody there other than themselves, although they could still hear the tapping and shuffling noises which seemed to be coming from around the corner. After a while, Toby indicated they should move out of the tunnel into the cave. In spite of the dangers lying ahead, Richard for one felt immense relief at being able to stand straight again.

'I'm just going to close off the tunnel with a plug of rock,' whispered Toby. 'I'll fill the whole tunnel in some other time. It would make too much noise if I did the whole job now.'

He pointed his staff at the opening they'd just come out of. The end of his staff glowed yellow briefly, there was a soft 'Phut!' sound, and the hole in the rock disappeared. It was a perfect repair – the grain of the rock continued seamlessly through the area where the hole had been.

Toby turned away from his handiwork and listened for a moment, then whispered, 'They're making a lot of noise, so I think we can creep forward without being heard. I wonder how those rocks came to be piled up over there? Anyway, keep well clear of them – we don't want to start a rock-slide.' He paused, brow furrowed, as he continued to stare at the vast rock pile. Then he got it. 'Of course! It's the rocks they excavated when making the tunnel. No wonder no-one noticed them tunnelling – they did it all within this cave, hidden from outside view!'

Then Toby got back to the task in hand. 'Now keep close behind me in single file, and please be as quiet as mice.'

They moved slowly forward. At one point, Tom accidentally kicked a small rock which ricocheted off another rock, coming quickly to rest. The resulting clattering seemed to reverberate all around the cave, and they all froze, expecting the worst. Hardly daring to breathe, they waited for dwarves to come rushing around the corner, brandishing pickaxes. They waited, but eventually it became clear that the dwarves were making too much of their own noise, seemingly too preoccupied to have noticed the clatter that Tom had made.

Eventually, Toby motioned them to continue moving. After some minutes, they reached the point where the chamber turned left. Toby signalled for everyone to crouch down, then guided them to a small group of rocks jutting out from the left-hand wall of the cave, situated at the point the cave changed direction. They reached the protection offered by the rocks and huddled there. The cave was brightly lit here, shafts of sunlight sweeping above their heads. Toby whispered, 'Keep your heads down. I'm going to take a look at what we're facing.'

Gingerly, Toby straightened up sufficiently to see through a crack near the top of the rocks. This was good news – he could see without being seen.

He was momentarily blinded by the glare coming from the distant mouth of the cave, but soon became aware of a figure silhouetted against the light, moving near the right-hand wall of the cave about twenty metres away. He took his time scanning every nook and cranny of the cave, searching for any other figures, but it seemed that the figure in front of him was alone. It stayed pretty much where it was, moving around a little, and every now and then it hit the rock-face with what seemed to be some kind of pickaxe.

Eventually he crouched down again with the boys. 'It's a solitary dwarf,' he said with hushed urgency. 'We could wait until he leaves, or until he finds us, or I could overpower him and try to get him to talk.' He paused, looking into the boys' frightened eyes. 'Actually, I've decided to go for the overpowering option. Stay here and you'll be safe. I'll come back for you in a jiffy. Okay?'

The boys nodded nervously. Toby smiled and winked, then crept out into the sunlight. He shielded his eyes against the harsh glare. The dwarf was still busy, fiddling about at the rock-face, his back to Toby. Toby scampered nimbly over the strewn rocks, ever nearer to his target. He levelled his staff at the dwarf, the tip starting to burn in a fierce blue flame ready for battle – then he tripped over a small boulder. He fell heavily, landing face-down, at the same time losing his grip on the staff, which clattered noisily to the ground.

The dwarf spun around with a startled cry.

Richard and Tom were watching Toby's progress from their rocky hiding place through the viewing crack. They could see that Toby wouldn't be able to get up and get his staff in time before the dwarf got to him, and to their horror, they could see Toby wasn't moving! The dwarf, holding his pickaxe out in front of him, started to circle cautiously around Toby's unmoving sprawled body, seemingly to ensure there was no movement before closing in.

Richard knew he had to act. He waited for the dwarf, still slowly circling Toby, to reach the point in his circular travel where his back was presented to the boys. 'Tom, I'm going,' he hissed.

Before Tom could respond, Richard broke cover and ran

as fast as he could at the dwarf. The dwarf heard his approach and began to spin around to defend himself, but Richard was already there. He leapt and rugby-tackled the dwarf to the ground, landing heavily on top of him, the dwarf's pickaxe spinning out of his hand, fetching up against some nearby rocks with a loud *Clang!* that echoed jarringly around the cave walls.

The dwarf kicked and punched and writhed underneath Richard. Richard tried to keep him pinned down, but couldn't keep a firm hold on the squirming body. He grabbed both of the dwarf's flailing arms, but the dwarf managed to wrench one arm free of Richard's grip, allowing him to twist his body around to face his assailant, the dwarf's hood falling away in the process. Richard froze in a state of complete shock – and so, fortunately, did the dwarf who appeared completely bewildered by this sudden unexpected change of tactic. Richard stared down…at the face of a girl.

'You're not a dwarf! Well at least not a *male* dwarf,' Richard managed to say hoarsely as he struggled for breath.

Richard saw the expression on her face change from one of wide-eyed fear to one of nervous curiosity. 'No, I'm not a dwarf, and I'm not male,' she said, calmly looking up at him.

Richard could feel a blush coming on, then remembered the tunnel. 'Well, whoever you are, tell me on whose orders you dug that tunnel at the back of this cave,' he started briskly, 'although you must have had some help…I would have thought,' he finished less assuredly.

Her forehead creased up with growing irritation. 'What tunnel?' she snapped. 'Look, if I was to dig a tunnel, it would take an awfully long time using my geologist's hammer, wouldn't it?'

Richard averted his gaze sufficiently to see the hammer lying nearby. It did seem rather on the small side, and didn't look capable of doing much more than chipping off little bits of rock. He was losing the conversation. 'Er, if you're not a dwarf, what are you?'

'I would have thought it's pretty obvious that I'm an elf... but what are *you*?'

'Er, I'm also an elf.'

A hint of a smile appeared on her face. 'Very interesting. What kind of elf has rounded ears?'

Richard's hands instinctively went to his head, feeling for the hat that wasn't any longer there. It must have fallen off in the struggle; but before he could think what to say next, she again became very agitated. 'Who's that standing behind you?' she demanded.

Richard's instinct was to turn around to look, but at the same time he didn't want the girl (dwarf, elf, or whatever she was) to take the opportunity to escape or attack him. With an enormous effort of will, he continued to look directly at her. His heart in his mouth, Richard said quietly, 'If there's anyone standing behind me, I hope it's Tom.'

To Richard's great relief, he heard Tom's reassuring voice. 'Yes, Richard, it's me. I've got her covered with my wizard's staff, and I've also got her hammer. You can move away from her now. Fantastic rugby tackle, by the way.'

Richard slowly stood up, turning to see Tom looking like something out of a martial art movie, crouched menacingly and ready to go into action, heavy wooden staff in one hand, hammer in the other.

The elf, rather than being impressed by Tom's Ninja act, was frowning, seeming to be distracted by the staff he was holding. 'Where did you get that staff from?'

'From me.'

Everyone turned to see Toby. He had just got up from the ground, and was dusting himself down. 'Hello Ellie,' he said haltingly, tentatively touching a nasty cut on his forehead.

'Don't worry about those two – they're my friends. But what are you doing here? I told you to stay away – it's too dangerous, too close to black dragon country.'

'You know each other?' gulped Richard.

'I should hope so,' said Ellie, picking herself up from the ground, a smile on her face. 'He's my brother.'

EIGHT

'There's certainly a lot of blood,' said Ellie.

Toby had introduced Ellie to the boys, and now he was sitting on a convenient boulder, wincing as she finished wiping away the dried blood from the wound with a damp handkerchief. The boys stood together, looking on.

'Right,' she said. 'That's you sorted. Keep the handkerchief, just in case the bleeding starts again.'

'Okay, Sis. Thanks,' said Toby. 'Now please tell us what you're doing here.'

'Well…' she said, placing her hands on her hips.

Richard and Tom gazed at her, transfixed, at this point not really caring too much what she was about to say. Her hair was a rich golden-blonde colour, swept back behind her pointed ears, where it reached down to the top of her shoulders. Her face was nearly perfectly proportioned, with full lips and eyes of the deepest blue. Of course, all beauty has its imperfections. The boys were seeing Ellie, lovely as she certainly was, very much in soft focus. They hadn't noticed a spot on her right cheek that she had recently burst, nor had they noticed that her front teeth tended to protrude a little, making her look slightly rabbit-like when she smiled. None of this mattered, or indeed ever would matter – Richard and Tom were deeply under her spell.

She was a little shorter than the boys. She wore a brown

smock, belted around the waist, the hem-line finishing just above her bare knees, and as for footwear – she sported short brown leather boots. Over the smock, she wore a grey hooded cloak, similar to the cloaks Toby and the boys were wearing. The leather belt around her waist had a leather holster hanging from it, in which she had placed her hammer, the combination of cloak and holster making her look a little like a gunslinger in a Mexican cowboy movie.

Richard had decided she was the most beautiful girl he had ever laid eyes on. Then he became aware she was explaining why she was here. 'It's the school holiday, and I needed some rock specimens for my geology project, so I came up here today to get them. Mum and Dad are used to me disappearing for days on end – they know I can look after myself.'

Toby sighed. 'You're certainly very capable, Ellie, but you probably didn't tell Mum and Dad you were heading in this particular direction, did you?'

'Of course not,' she replied without hesitation. 'They would have tried to stop me.'

'Typical,' he muttered. 'Well, you found out how dangerous it can be around here. I couldn't see you properly against the blinding sunlight, and reckoned you were a dwarf working for Drusilla.' Toby looked away from Ellie towards the boys. 'I'm sorry I let you down, boys. Silly of me to have stumbled like that. I was lucky it was my sister, and not a dwarf. A dwarf in Drusilla's service would have plunged an axe into me without asking any questions.'

'There's someone else who played a very important role in all this,' announced Tom, turning towards Richard. 'My friend here. He thought Toby was about to be killed, so he ran out and tackled Ellie without anything to defend himself with.'

Richard smiled at Tom. 'Thanks, Tom, but you were brave too. You were my back-up.'

'My friends,' said Toby, gesturing to the boys. 'You both

showed great courage today, and I thank you for it. I'm proud of you.'

The boys smiled, not sure what to say next. Silence took over, but not for long. Something had been troubling Richard about the recent action in the cave. 'Ellie, when Toby fell over, why didn't you realise it was him?' asked Richard.

Ellie's blue eyes focussed on her questioner and she smiled. Richard felt himself flushing. Would he always turn into a beetroot when she looked at him? He dearly hoped not.

'Toby's hood was covering his head,' she explained.

'That was unfortunate,' agreed Toby. 'My hood must have flopped over my head as I fell.'

Toby gestured to the group. 'Now we need to move on. It seems that our tunnel builders have long gone. We need to follow their tracks without further delay. I'm sure they lead to Drusilla. Ellie, you must go home now.'

Ellie frowned. 'Not so fast, Toby. First, I'd like to know what's going on here. What is this tunnel you keep going on about, and what has Drusilla got to do with it?'

'Fair enough,' said Toby. 'Let me give you a potted history.'

Toby then proceeded to tell Ellie about the tunnel, the book, how the boys were humans from the other version of the world, what Drusilla was up to, and so on. Soon Ellie had the whole picture.

Toby pulled out his fob-watch. 'It's midday, Ellie,' he said. 'You need to leave now if you're to get home before nightfall.'

'No,' she replied firmly. 'I'm going with you three. You need all the help you can get. Besides, I'm not going to give up an opportunity to get to know humans. I thought they only existed in fairy tales!'

Toby considered this, then stood up and said, 'Well, I suppose that's it then. There's no point in fighting it. You're as stubborn as I am. Ellie, welcome to our little band!'

Toby proceeded to lead the group to the cave mouth. The

sun brought welcome warmth, as they crouched down in a circle to examine the dusty ground of the deserted track that ran past the cave.

'You can see the ground is pretty churned up here,' muttered Toby, pointing at a muddle of footprints. 'I would say, judging by the size of the prints, that they were made by dwarves, in fact quite a few dwarves – I reckon in the region of ten. Thinking about it, it would need at least that number of dwarves to cut the tunnel as quickly as they must have done. Now, notice where the footprints are leading.'

Toby stood up, everyone else following his lead. 'They came out of the cave and turned left, heading down the track in a north-westerly direction.'

Ellie and the boys peered in the direction he had indicated. They could see the track meandering into the distance like a thin grey ribbon, following the edge of the mountain range. Where the mountain range ended, the track continued on through green hills sprinkled occasionally with houses and copses of trees, until it was finally lost to sight. Beyond the hills, on the distant horizon, they could just make out another mountain range.

'Those mountains over there are where Drusilla's stronghold is,' said Toby grimly, 'and at the rate dwarves move when payment in gold is involved, they're probably within spitting distance of her fortress by now.'

For a moment, nobody said anything as they stared at the distant mountains, lost in their own thoughts. In the warm summer sunshine, birds were singing, butterflies were fluttering, bees were buzzing – everything was as it should be, yet in those far-off mountains, an evil power was gaining strength and expanding.

Richard was the first to break the silence. 'You know,' he said, 'whenever I visit somewhere new, the first thing I want to see is a map. I don't suppose you've got one here, have you Toby?'

'I certainly have. No self-respecting traveller should leave home without one!'

Toby took a well-used map out of a pocket and unfolded it so that all could see.

'This is a map of the country I live in – Dracofarne, which means Land of Dragons,' explained Toby. 'My ancestors could have named it Elvenfarne (Land of Elves), but I think Dracofarne was chosen on the basis that of all the folk that live around here, dragons are the more eye-catching. Now – '

'Blimey!' interrupted Tom, stabbing the map with a finger. 'There's Grindleshorn! It must be the same Grindleshorn Richard and I know, because it's in the right place. It looks like Dracofarne encompasses what I know as Wales, and also what Mum calls 'border country', to the east of Wales. So what's the history of Grindleshorn, Toby?'

'Well, as you've probably guessed, Grindleshorn was around before the world divided, and the two worlds subsequently kept the name on. Grindleshorn means 'Meeting Place' in the ancient elvish tongue, and it is simply a place, or should I say, *the* place, where the elvish elders meet to discuss matters of great importance. In fact, to be specific, Grindleshorn is actually the outcrop of rock in Richard's garden. The spiritual life-force of the elves is held in that ancient rock.'

'Which explains the great feeling I get whenever I'm near it!' gasped Richard.

'Yes,' smiled Toby. 'As a result, even the human world's version of Grindleshorn and the surrounding area has managed to retain a strong elvish life-force. It's that life-force that has awakened the elvish ancestry in you and Tom, and brought you into this world – with a little help from me.'

'Well, I'm not sure I should climb The Rock any more, now I know its significance,' said Richard, frowning.

'I wouldn't worry about that,' grinned Toby. 'The elders

would simply be pleased to know you get so much pleasure from it.'

Then, pointing at a mountain marked on the map on the edge of a mountain range, Toby said proudly, 'Here is Mount Mystic, rather appropriately named, given that generations of wizards have lived here. My house is to the south on the far side, and we are standing at the bottom of the mountain on the north side. So you can see that those industrious dwarves tunnelled straight through the mountain from the bottom where we are now, to my house halfway up on the far side.'

Then Toby moved his finger along the map. 'Now, Ellie has journeyed about twenty miles from the west to get here. You can see that west of this mountain range is an area known as The Hills of Plenty, which is an area brimming with villages and farms, and that village – just there – is called Sweet Meadow, where Ellie and my parents live.'

He paused while he moved his finger further up the map. 'The track we're standing on heads in a north-westerly direction, crossing my mountain range, The Indomitables, or as it's known in the human world, The Cambrian Mountains, eventually reaching that mountain range fifty miles to the north-west called The Broken Teeth – known in the human world as Snowdonia. Drusilla's fortress is located inside that mountain there – Mount Dracomé, or as you humans call it – Mount Snowdon. Dracomé is ancient elvish for 'Dragon View', and indeed, before Drusilla took the mountain over, it was a favourite vantage point for dragons to stop off at and check out where their next meal was coming from. Now, to complete the picture, moving eastwards, there's Broom Down village, and further east, there's Oakbeam Forest where we saw the unicorns, fell down a hole, and met some fog; and finally, there's Grindleshorn, which, as we know because of its ancient roots, has the same name in both our worlds.'

Toby looked up and put the map away. 'Any questions?' he asked.

'I've got one,' said Tom. 'What's worrying me is how long it's going to take to cover fifty miles on foot. I mean, to walk that sort of distance over rough hilly terrain could take as much as four days. Aren't we going to arrive far too late? Surely Drusilla will have had more than enough time to use the book?'

'I agree,' said Toby, smiling as he observed the fast-developing expressions of horror on his companion's faces, 'which is why we're flying there. Tonight.'

It took a few moments for this to sink in, then everyone started talking at once.

'Great! We'll be flying by dragon!' crowed Ellie, smiling hugely.

'Cool,' said Tom happily.

'Oh no!' groaned Richard. 'I don't want to fly on anything other than an aeroplane! Why hasn't this world invented aeroplanes yet?'

'Let's have something to eat,' said Toby, ignoring Richard's rant. 'It'll soon be dusk, and we've a long night ahead of us.'

He promptly offered travel-biscuits. Ellie and the boys looked at the biscuits despondently, knowing only too well how dreadfully they tasted. Richard fancied that cork soaked in camel sweat would have the same consistency and still taste better.

Toby relented. 'I've an idea,' he said. 'Put your biscuits down on clean rocks, like I'm doing with mine.'

They all looked up at Toby quizzically, but did as he said.

'Now stand back from the biscuits.'

Nobody needed a second bidding, and they quickly moved away.

'You can stop there,' laughed Toby. 'A metre or so would have been sufficient.'

Ellie and the boys rather sheepishly moved a little nearer.

'Another reason,' said Toby looking levelly at his companions, 'for using sorcery sparingly, is that when it is invoked, a sort of 'sorcery signature' is left afterwards, that takes some time to disperse and can be detected by sorcerers if they're close enough. Now, I'm banking on her being in her mountain right now, waiting for her dwarves to return – so she'll be too far away to detect what I'm about to do. And she's the only sorcerer, or should I say, sorceress, I'm worried about. So here goes.'

Everyone instinctively ducked as Toby whirled his staff above his head in a great arc, its tip starting to glow yellow. Suddenly, crackling yellow lightning strikes erupted from it as it swept over the biscuits. Then Toby and the ghastly biscuits disappeared in a great pall of yellow smoke.

'Are you all right, Toby?' choked Richard.

'Yes, I'm fine,' croaked Toby's disembodied voice.

'Hope he's vaporised those damn biscuits,' muttered Tom.

'I heard that, Tom!' shouted Toby from somewhere within the smoke – which then cleared, to reveal a wonderful sight and smell. The biscuits on the rocks had been replaced by what looked to be roasted chicken legs. Lots of them, all perfectly cooked.

'Wow!' said Tom, grinning ear to ear.

'Eat up!' said Toby. 'You all deserve it!'

Nobody needed a second invitation. Soon, all that was left was bones, picked clean.

As soon as everyone had eaten and drunk their fill, Toby walked down the track. 'I'll be back in a few minutes,' he called out.

They watched as he then moved off the track and started to scramble up the mountain-side. He climbed surely and quickly, and before long he reached a ledge, about forty metres up. He paused for breath, then cupped his hands around his mouth to form an impromptu megaphone – and made the most extraordinary deep barking noise. If a lion tried to bark like a dog, it would have produced the same sort of sound. Toby continued barking for about half a minute, the noise echoing and reverberating around the mountains. Then he stopped, and so eventually did the echoes. Finally there was silence.

'What's he doing?' Richard asked Ellie.

Before she could reply, more barks broke the silence, but these weren't at all loud. It didn't seem that Toby had made these noises, thought Richard. Perhaps they were very late echoes?

As Toby started to descend, Ellie smiled and turned to Richard. 'I think I know what he was doing. If I'm right, we'll soon know.' Richard didn't like the sound of this.

Toby had reached the track and was running to the waiting group. 'We're on!' he shouted breathlessly.

There was no time for explanations. Suddenly the group became enveloped in a dark shadow, quickly followed by a buffeting wind that made it hard to stay upright – and then it happened all over again. Finally it stopped. Everyone had instinctively crouched down on the ground with their hands covering their heads. Then Richard and Tom heard nearby laughter.

'Come on, you two,' Ellie giggled. 'You can get up now.'

Cautiously, the boys stood up – to see two huge red dragons standing a little way down the track. Richard could only think of one thing to say. 'Oh no.' Then he decided to elaborate further. 'It occurred to me that Toby might be calling for a dragon,' he said to no-one in particular, as he walked with the group towards the waiting dragons, 'although I didn't expect *two* to turn up – and now, I really would like to wake up from this nightmare.'

The saying goes, that behind every cloud is a silver lining. Richard was about to find how true this can be.

'Don't worry, Richard, I'll ride with you on one of the

dragons,' Ellie said, smiling. 'I've ridden a few dragons in my time!'

'Ellie, I'd like that,' said Richard, returning her smile. Things were definitely looking brighter.

'Yes, that's a good idea, Ellie. I'll ride with Tom on the other dragon,' said Toby.

Tom looked disappointed, but visibly perked up as they drew near to the dragons.

'Boys, you've already met Dave, here,' said Toby, gesturing towards one of the very similar-looking dragons.

Richard wondered how you told dragons apart. These two appeared identical, but now being as close to dragons as he would ever want to be, he started to see the differences. Dave had more pronounced ridges above his eyes, his ears were slightly longer and narrower...and he had a damaged scale on his rear left leg...

'Now let me introduce Dylan, another good friend of mine,' Toby was saying, nodding towards the other dragon.

Dylan smiled as only a dragon can. 'Pleased to meet you, young humans,' he said in a deep gravelly voice, with a distinct Welsh sing-song lilt to it.

Toby continued, 'Dave and Dylan are both committed to ridding the world of Drusilla, and braver more resourceful dragons you won't find anywhere.'

The dragons smiled and started making rumbling noises, rather like the beginning of an earthquake. Suddenly it dawned on Richard that the dragons were laughing, or at least chuckling.

'My dear Toby, less praise please. You're making us squirm with embarrassment! If we weren't coloured red, you'd see us blushing right now,' rumbled Dylan.

'Sorry about that, but a wizard's praise isn't given lightly,' said Toby firmly. 'Now, it's getting dark and it's time for us to start our flight. Mounting positions, please!'

The ground shuddered with a flurry of dust as the dragons dropped down from their standing position to a squatting position, their bellies now flat to the ground, legs hunched up above their sides. Richard felt sure that Drusilla would feel the vibrations in her fortress all those miles away.

Without hesitation, Toby climbed nimbly up Dave's front left leg, and scrambled onto his back, finally sitting with legs astride, just behind his neck. Ellie followed suit on Dylan.

Then Tom scrambled up Dave's leg just as Toby had done, and in no time was sitting in front of Toby, holding onto the red leathery crest in front of him.

Richard peered up at the great beast towering above him, Ellie somehow managing to look beautiful perched on the dragon's back, her legs astride. What worried Richard particularly at this moment, was the fact that although the dragon was lying down, it was still a long way up there.

Ellie smiled down at Richard encouragingly. 'Come on, Richard. I'm getting lonely up here,' she said softly with the most winning smile imaginable.

All Richard was aware of was that smile and those blue eyes. He became vaguely aware that he had started climbing the dragon, but Richard's world had for the moment dissolved into a kind of fluffy soft-focus where only he and Ellie existed, lost in each other's gaze.

The dream ended as suddenly as it had started.

'Oof!' gasped Richard.

Ellie had caught Richard's hand, and hauled him into a straddling position in front of her, his groin landing heavily on what turned out to be an unyielding hard area between dragon crests. For a while, he dared not say anything to Ellie. Instead, he gritted his teeth, concentrating on the long sweep of dragon-neck in front of him, taking care not to look down.

Richard was very aware that Tom was grinning at him, so he threw a 'don't care' kind of look back at him.

It was getting colder as the dark night closed in. Toby looked around, making sure they were all set. Then he raised his staff high in the air, and dramatically cried, 'Let's fly!'

Ellie touched Richard's shoulder and said, 'Hold on tight, Richard. I'll look after you. You've nothing to fear.'

'Thanks,' he said weakly, hoping she was right. And hoping he wasn't about to throw up.

As Dylan moved from lying down to standing up, his body lurched in a series of sickening heaves, reminding Richard of a particularly unpleasant roller coaster ride he had experienced in Skegness when he was eleven.

The dragons were now poised for flight. Richard, valiantly trying to stop his world falling apart, made the most of this stationary moment. Then Dylan's huge wings unfurled with a sound rather like that made by a ship's sail unfurling in a stiff breeze, ending with a 'Thwack!' as the wings opened to their full extent, the folds of leathery skin suddenly becoming tight as a drum.

The wings started beating up and down with ever-increasing force. Richard could feel the air buffeting him with every flap. He held on tighter than ever as he felt his body being lifted then dropped in time with the incessant wing beats. 'Whump, whump, whump!' went the wings.

He carried on looking at Dylan's neck, gradually getting used to the up and down motion, although he wasn't sure that his bottom would get used to it.

Suddenly, he was aware that Ellie was talking into his ear. 'Well done. We're flying,' she said.

'Flying?' thought Richard. How could that be? Don't dragons need to warm up a bit on the ground first before taking to the air? Without thinking, he looked down, and could no longer see the ground, but he could see pin-points of light here and there. As if waking from a dream, he suddenly realised that the lights he could see were coming from houses – far below.

It was at this point that his stomach seemed to leap into his throat. He doubled his grip on his dragon-crest, and kept his gaze fixed on the dim outline of Dylan's neck throughout the rest of the flight, the hammering of his heart contrasting starkly against the slow steady wing-beat of the dragon.

The two dragons and their passengers flew on in silence, in silence that is, except of course for the subdued 'Whump!' noise created by every downward stroke of the dragons' great wings.

Gradually the lights below became fewer, until eventually no lights at all were visible. Looking down, all was now an inky blackness; but ahead, a jumble of dark jagged shapes were looming against the starlit sky. Richard, though still keeping his attention on Dylan's neck, had nonetheless noticed the shapes. The part of his mind that wasn't concentrating on Dylan's neck, was vaguely wondering what the shapes reminded him of. They looked a bit like a giant's lower jaw, filled with broken teeth, in need of an urgent trip to the dentist. Suddenly, his whole mind shifted its attention to the shapes. That was it – broken teeth! He was looking at the Broken Teeth mountains. Then he shuddered. These mountains were Drusilla's. Somewhere not far away, she was plotting her conquest of the world and ultimately her conquest of the version of the world Richard knew of as – home.

Now they were flying into the giant's mouth. The skyline of broken teeth was all around. Richard could just make out the dim outline of Dave ahead, and noticed that he was losing height. Suddenly Richard felt himself being forced forward. He was about to tumble over Dylan's head. 'Aargh!' he yelled.

Ellie's restraining hand was on his shoulder in an instant. 'It's all right, Richard! We're gliding down to land.'

'Okay,' responded Richard, shaking like a leaf and trying to sound a good deal braver than he actually felt.

Down and down they went, the cold rush of air buffeting

Richard's face. He noticed that Dylan's wings were no longer flapping. They were held outstretched, the wind whistling over their leathery surface as the downward swoop into the jagged blackness below continued. Every now and then, Richard noticed Dylan was making flight corrections. Sometimes he would pull his wings in slightly, then extend them again, then flex one wing slightly, causing its tip to drop down as the dragon turned a little before straightening up again. It reminded Richard of that rather bumpy landing he had endured when he and his family had flown to Cyprus on holiday last year – but at least then he had been firmly strapped in! It didn't seem that passenger safety featured very highly on this particular airline's 'things we could do better' list. Richard rapidly put this thought to the back of his mind.

Everything had gone black now. They must be flying between the mountains, Richard reasoned. Then Dylan started flapping his wings violently with accompanying staccato 'Whump!' noises. They rose briefly, then still with wings flapping furiously, rolled to the left, jinked to the right, dipped down – and as Richard hung grimly on, he prayed it would all end before either his heart burst, or he threw up the entire contents of his stomach.

His prayer was soon answered. He could now hear Dylan's increasingly harsh breathing above the noise of the madly flapping wings. It was obvious the dragon was exerting an immense amount of effort. Suddenly there was a hard jarring 'Thud!' that threatened to catapult him from his seating position, followed by an awful scraping sound that went on – it seemed to Richard, for ages – but that in actual fact lasted only a few seconds.

The sickening motion mercifully stopped. All Richard could hear was the rustling sound of Dylan's wings folding up, and the sound of his rasping breathing. 'Bit bloody tight, that was,' Dylan reflected when he had caught sufficient breath.

'Still, we're down and the right way up. There's good for you.' Then he remembered his passengers. 'Are you all right back there?' he asked, turning his head to look. 'Ah, I see you're both in one piece.'

He paused. Richard and Ellie could see in the starlit gloom that Dylan was smiling at them. Then he winked. Richard almost fell off with surprise. There was something rather disconcerting about a huge dragon winking at you.

'I hope you two behaved yourselves during the flight,' Dylan said softly, his smile broader than ever.

Richard flushed bright red, and thanked his lucky stars that no one would notice in the gloom. Before Richard could answer, Ellie stepped in. 'Really, Dylan!' she giggled. 'We've spent the whole flight trying not to fall off! Besides, Richard and I have only just met. I'm here on a strictly professional basis, to help save the world and to keep Richard and his friend Tom out of trouble!'

Richard felt rather deflated on hearing this.

'Professional, is it?' Dylan rumbled in his Welsh sing-song sort of way, still smiling broadly. 'Well, my professional opinion is that you two stay seated while I back up – whoa! That was close.'

Dylan's body shuddered as he appeared to stumble. Richard almost fell off in the process, but Ellie grabbed his arm and pulled him back up into his seating position.

'Thanks, Ellie. I'll return the favour some time,' said Richard shakily.

A rock could be heard clattering down the mountainside, presumably dislodged by Dylan. It clattered and echoed for some time, before becoming swallowed up in the sighing of the wind. Richard was well aware this meant they were very near the edge of a very long drop. He peered beyond Dylan's neck, and could only see blackness – nothing at all was distinguishable; but looking down, he could just make out the rocky ground Dylan was standing on. Then the cold realisation dawned on him. The blackness was a void – Dylan was right on the edge of a precipice and was carefully backing away from it. Cold shivers ran up and down Richard's spine at the very thought of it.

Soon Dylan completed his backward-shuffle. 'Right, you two. Keep your heads down. We're going into a cave,' he said.

Richard could feel the dragon swinging his body around, then felt a rhythmical walking motion. He quickly became aware of a dim light ahead, which appeared to be coming from a large cave situated at the end of a deep gash in the mountainside. It only took a few of Dylan's giant strides to reach the cave mouth.

Dylan was right – there wasn't much headroom. Richard and Ellie ducked as Dylan entered the cave. After a few more dragon-strides, they reached the end of it.

Richard could now see the source of the light. Toby was sitting on a rock on the cave floor, his staff propped up against a nearby wall. The top of the staff glowed with a yellowish light, the same comforting light that had guided Toby and his companions through the dwarves' tunnel. Tom was standing alongside Toby, and was grinning from ear to ear, as he watched the progress of Dylan and his passengers.

In front of Toby was Dave, lying on the cave floor. Dylan swiftly followed Dave's example. This time, Richard remembered to hang on tightly while Dylan completed the uncomfortable lurching transition from standing to lying-down position.

Tom could contain himself no longer. 'What a flight that was! Absolutely brilliant. How about you, Richard?'

'It was certainly exciting,' said Richard quietly, as he and Ellie scrambled down the side of the dragon. He felt enormous relief when his feet finally found the solid floor of the cave.

Dylan was conversing in hushed tones with Dave. 'Hardly

enough room out there to land a dragonfly, let alone a dragon. A bit tricky, to put it mildly. How about you?'

'I think you did a lot better than me, my friend! If Toby hadn't fired off an 'emergency stop' spell at the last minute, I think I'd have gone right over the edge. Then I'd probably have got flying before reaching the bottom of the valley, but I might have lost a passenger or two on the way.'

Dave paused briefly, seeming to be very shaken. 'Anyway,' he continued, 'I suppose the good news is that black dragons would think twice before attempting to land here. So all in all, I think this is a very good hiding place for you and me, while we await the return of our elvish and human friends.'

Dave's quiet rumbling words seemed to hang in the air, as everyone took on board their full import. It would not be long before Toby, Richard, Tom and Ellie started the final stage of their journey to Drusilla's fortress.

The flickering light from Toby's staff played on the faces of the dragons, elves and humans in the cave, faces that were contemplating soberly what lay in store for them in these barren forbidding mountains. As if to underline their solemn thoughts, the mountain wind outside the cave continued a mournful song – which Toby soon interrupted. 'We'll stay the night here,' he said, 'and will set off by foot at first light. It's too dangerous to walk in these mountains in the dark. They're not called the Broken Teeth for nothing – they make the mountains where I live look like a walk in the park. I reckon it's only a couple of hours' scramble to Drusilla's fortress from here. There's plenty of rock-cover around, so we should be able to get to her front door without being seen – '

'Do we simply knock on her door and request a chat?' said Tom cheekily.

'No, of course not,' replied Toby, a thin smile on his face. 'The terrain around here is so difficult that she doesn't expect anyone to arrive on foot. Her visitors are either flying dragons, or folk travelling on flying dragons. The fact that we will arrive on foot is our element of surprise – she'll be looking to the air, not the ground – well at least, that's my theory. We'll slip in undetected…hopefully.'

Toby quickly changed the subject, seeming to realise he wasn't exactly winning his audience over. 'Now we must eat and drink,' he said brightly. 'I'm afraid I can't risk using sorcery this close to Drusilla, and to be honest, I'm hoping with fingers crossed she won't detect the spell I had to use on our flight here. But what all this means is…well, there won't be chicken tonight.' He hesitated, taking in the looks of despair in front of him, his audience seemingly reflecting on a difficult day which was about to be completely sunk by the prospect of travel-biscuits. However, the ensuing silence didn't last long.

'Mum's the er…blimey, what are those things I'm not good with?' A low, deep voice resonated around the cave walls. '*Word*. Yup! Brilliant. *Word*. Love it.'

A shuffling, rasping sound started, getting ever louder. In the dim light, Richard could just make out that something massive was entering the cave. He moved in front of Ellie to protect her. As whatever-it-was came more fully into the light, Richard could see it had many hairy legs. Oh God, a giant spider – probably called Shelob, he thought grimly. Then in one grotesque flowing motion, the legs curled underneath the spider's enormous body, at the same time as a particularly fat leg raised itself upwards. Suddenly Richard realised he was looking at a massive hairy hand, which had momentarily shaped itself into a 'thumbs up' sign. Then it rasped its way out of the cave, the echoing din dying away as the hand disappeared. But suddenly a new sound started. It was a low rumbling that seemed to be shaking the mountain apart. The noise got so loud that everyone started covering their ears. The cacophony reached a crescendo as a wall of

dust burst into the cave, quickly followed by an actual wall –
which came to rest just short of where the dragons were lying
– the dragons seemingly not the least bit concerned that they
had narrowly avoided a severe squashing. The earthquake had
apparently ceased, at least for the moment. Everyone was now
choking as the dust swirled around the cave, and as it started
to settle, Richard became aware that the newly arrived wall
had writing on it, writing that was now unmistakeable in spite
of the gloom. He read these words: 'Giant Pizza for delivery.
Contents may vary, and normally do. Sorry.' As the visibility
continued to improve, it became clear that the wall was one
face of an enormous box that had been pushed into the cave by
the returning monstrous hand, which now waved in a rather
sweet way before noisily withdrawing.

A voice outside the cave could be distinctly heard muttering
to itself. 'Blimey. How did I get up here? Mum always said,
in times of trouble, put your best foot forward. Well, I don't
know which foot is best, so I'll put both forward. Yup. That's
it.'

Richard could imagine only too well what was about to
happen. A sickening thud shook the cave, followed by the
crunching sound of cascading rocks. Then all was still, save
for a distant voice on the breeze: 'You know, that wasn't the
way I got up there.'

Still recovering from the experience, Richard smiled
weakly at Toby and said, 'I'm guessing that Giant Pizza
means…'

'Yes, you've got it. Pizza for Giants, although it is also
undeniably a giant pizza. I didn't want to risk more discontent
with my travel-biscuits, so I got Flo to deliver a pizza – '

'Flo?'

'Short for Florian. Giants can never remember the full
versions of their names.'

'Just a thought, Toby. Perhaps next time you order fast

food for delivery, you could find someone a little smaller and less dramatic than a dragon or giant to deliver it?'

'Hmm. I don't think that anyone else actually delivers anymore. Dragons and giants have long sewn up the delivery market – it's all about 'economies of scale', which is another way of saying that dragons and giants can shift so much stuff in one go that no-one else can compete with them. It seems to be the way the whole world is going – small local personal businesses being replaced by big corporate operations. Anyway, tuck into this mega-pizza. It's not for our dragon friends – they ate before the flight. They'll slow their metabolisms down while they wait for us, so that they won't need to eat for several days. Mind you, they'll stay alert, ready to go into action, won't you?'

'That's right,' rumbled Dylan, 'but I'll murder a steak when I get home!'

Toby nodded. 'After we've eaten, we need to get some sleep. I've got sleeping bags that will keep everyone warm, well everyone except Dave and Dylan – dragons are designed for sleeping in cold caves!'

Dave and Dylan glared at Toby with expressions of utter disdain.

After much effort opening the enormous lid of the pizza box, Toby, Richard Tom and Ellie literally dived in.

'I'm going for this bit with what looks like pepperoni covered in cheesy stuff,' said Richard, tugging at the edge of the enormous pizza, the 'cheesy stuff' covering the discs of pepperoni stretching into increasingly thin yellow strings as he pulled. 'Oh, no way!' he gasped, dropping the pizza as though it had just given him an enormous electric shock.

Everyone turned to look.

'Hmm,' said Tom. 'That's not actually pepperoni, is it? Seems your food only has eyes for you.'

'Very funny,' retorted Richard. 'Hope you choke on yours.'

This was food that looked at you disapprovingly as you ate it, the circular shapes now having revealed themselves as staring eyes.

'Sorry, forgot to tell you,' grinned Toby, his words almost indiscernible through a mouthful of food. 'Giant Pizza is best eaten with eyes closed. Not the eyes in the pizza, that is. Your eyes.'

'Great,' said Richard, giving Toby a withering look. 'Now everyone's a comedian.' But finally, Richard plucked up courage and followed Toby's advice, finding that at one moment he was tasting something like normal mozzarella pizza, then roast chicken, then fish pie. Clearly Giant Pizza contents really did vary, as indicated on the box – it was just that the variation was from one mouthful to the next. But none of this seemed to matter, because, judging by the wide smiles on everyone's faces it was obvious that Giant Pizza was infinitely better than Toby's horrendous travel-biscuits. Soon, they had eaten their fill, leaving an enormous amount left over for everyone to stash away in pockets and bags for future use.

Now it was time to go to sleep. Richard and Tom looked at the cold, hard rock floor of the cave. It looked like they were in for an uncomfortable, sleepless night. Then Toby produced from one of his pockets a number of what looked like folded beige handkerchiefs, which he handed out to Ellie and the boys. Next, he took his own 'handkerchief' and shook it. Its folds fell out, creating a large quilted sleeping bag. It seemed impossible that such a small folded package could produce such a thing. Of course, sorcery had to be involved.

Keen to follow Toby's demonstration, Richard and Tom shook out their sleeping bags, marvelling at the transformation from small scrap of material to large sleeping bag, but not relishing the uncomfortable night they were going to have, on the cold hard floor. They lay their sleeping bags down next to Toby and Ellie, who were already inside theirs. The boys duly

121

got inside their bags, and were amazed yet again. The sleeping bags were not only keeping them nicely warm, but somehow made them feel as though they were lying on a comfortable mattress, rather than on the rough hardness of the cave floor. And the material under their heads felt like luxurious pillows.

Toby looked at his companions and said, 'Sleep well, everyone. Dave and Dylan – please take up your sentry positions.'

The dragons stood up, and turned awkwardly around so that eventually they ended up facing the cave mouth, somehow avoiding knocking into each other in the confined space as they performed the manoeuvre. Then they both lay down heavily on the cave floor.

Finally, Toby said softly, 'Light out. Goodnight.'

The light at the end of Toby's staff extinguished, allowing the darkness of the cave to rush in. They all slept soundly that night. The knowledge that the dragons were guarding the cave mouth, combined with the cosiness and warmth afforded by Toby's sleeping bags, but most of all the fact that everyone was completely worn out – helped.

NINE

Richard was dreaming about walking along sunlit mountains with Ellie, when he was rudely awakened by Tom. Blearily, he became conscious of the fact that the cave interior was now dimly lit by growing daylight from outside.

'Sorry to wake you,' said Tom cheerily. 'You looked so peaceful – but some of us have an important mission to complete! The others are up and about.'

When all had breakfasted on remnants of Giant Pizza, Toby marshalled everyone at the back of the cave. The two dragons, lying down side-by-side, looked on with interest. 'I suggest you put the sleeping bags I've given you into your pockets,' he said. 'As you've seen, they fold up into almost nothing, and you never know when you might need their warmth and comfort – I really should copyright the design, don't you think? Anyway, now to the plan, or at least the nearest I have to a plan. Myself, Richard, Tom and Ellie will walk the remaining five miles to Drusilla's fortress. The object is to get inside without being noticed, which is why we won't be flying there. Dave and Dylan will stay hidden in this cave, awaiting our return. When we're in the fortress, we'll find the book and invoke the padlock spell, and that will stop her using its powers. I'll do my best to sort Drusilla out, and then we'll walk back to this cave, whereupon Dave and Dylan will fly us back home, hopefully safe in the knowledge that Drusilla has been neutralised or destroyed. Any questions?'

'How long do you think it will take to get back here?' asked Richard.

'If all goes well, we should arrive at Mount Dracomé – that's the mountain she's built her fortress inside – in the evening. We'll find a way into the fortress tonight under cover of darkness, do what we have to do, then journey back here the day after, probably arriving some time in the afternoon. Any more questions anyone?'

'I've got something else, and it's been worrying me for a while,' said Richard in a hushed voice, looking left and right for anyone listening who shouldn't be. 'None of us have weapons to protect ourselves with if we're attacked. Ellie's got her little rock hammer, but that's not going to get her very far if she's cornered by a black dragon.'

'Good point,' replied Toby. 'But we have a serious form of defence, which is this.' Toby held his staff high for all to see. 'You know, unless you're very proficient with a weapon, I believe you're safer without it. If your attacker sees you're unarmed, there's a chance you won't get hurt. Of course, you might be captured, but then I should be around to stop that happening.'

'But what happens if things go wrong and Drusilla captures *all* of us?' asked Tom. 'What's the fallback plan?'

'Er, I'll let you know that in good time.'

'So no fallback,' said Tom under his breath.

Toby hurriedly carried on. 'Richard and Tom, please put your hats on – we need to keep your human ears out of sight of the eyes of Drusilla and her followers. Okay, band of four! Let's move out.'

They walked past the dragons, pausing at the cave mouth.

'Farewell my good dragons,' said Toby, dramatically wielding his staff. 'We will be back!'

'See you,' said Dave simply.

'Good luck,' said Dylan, aiming a mischievous smile and a wink at Richard and Ellie.

Richard could feel his cheeks starting to get a little warm, and was glad to be following Toby out of the cave. Ellie gave Dylan a quick smile, seemingly unaffected by his teasing, and joined the group outside in the early morning sun.

Toby led the group away from the cave mouth, past the rocky ledge that the dragons had landed on the night before. The problem that Dylan was dealing with during his 'final approach' last night was now blindingly apparent. The ledge was just about wide enough to take a dragon with its wings outstretched, but one false move and a wing could easily smash into the steep mountain wall at the back of the ledge. The length of the ledge also left a lot to be desired – it was no more than three dragon-lengths long, and over-running it would result in a glancing collision with the mountainside, followed by a sheer drop onto the rocks far below. Richard shuddered as he peered down, thinking how he had been teetering here on the back of a dragon, literally on the edge of disaster. He was thankful it had been too dark last night for him to see any of it.

Fortunately, Tom could usually be relied on to see the brighter side of any situation. 'Impressive mountains, aren't they Richard?' he said, his hand sweeping in their general direction.

Richard looked up and took in the soaring sunlit beauty of the jagged rock peaks all around them.

'Snowdonia is definitely a much more fitting name for these mountains than The Broken Teeth,' Tom continued. 'You know, I recognise exactly where we are. I climbed all around here with the Scouts last year – in our version of the world, that is. There is a difference though. Somehow this version of Snowdonia seems, well, more wild.'

Then all was quiet, except for the sound of feet crunching

125

on the slate-strewn path and the calling of eagles. Having walked along the ledge, they climbed the mountainside, finally reaching a broad ridge that stretched for a considerable distance. For some time they walked along the ridge. For the most part, the ground at this altitude was barren rock, but occasionally there was a patch of coarse grass or a wiry bush that had somehow, against all odds, found sufficient soil in cracks in the rock to grow in. Eventually, they reached a point where the ridge started to climb steeply to a summit.

Suddenly, Toby ducked down behind a small rock outcrop, and urgently motioned to the group to do the same. With everyone now huddled out of sight, he hissed, 'I saw something move on that slope. I'm going to take a look.'

He peered cautiously over the line of rocks. 'Oh, it's only goats,' he sighed with relief. 'You can all get up now.'

Now standing, they could see a small group of goats with brown shaggy coats and long curved horns. The goats were preoccupied with the task of teasing out the sparse vegetation from the mountainside. Then without warning, they all stampeded down the slope.

'What's spooked them…?' Toby started to say.

At that moment, a huge black shape appeared over the summit, moving at great speed.

'Get down!' snapped Toby.

As one, the group ducked down behind their rocky protection again, Richard sneaking a view over the top. The black shape was a black dragon. It flew fast and low over the ground, overtaking a straggling goat – then with a single swipe of a claw, the dragon knocked the poor animal to the ground. The great black beast flew on, turning gracefully while losing speed, finally landing next to the prone goat. The dragon's cruel yellow eyes flashed in the sunlight, taking in the surroundings, as the beast ambled up to its victim. It paused, looking around and listening, then placed one clawed foot on the carcass and brought its head down to tear the flesh. The head came back up with a large hunk of blood-stained meat in its massive jaws. With one convulsive backward throw, it swallowed the meat whole.

'What are you doing?' hissed Toby, as he pulled Richard down from his viewing position. 'It's not a blind dragon!'

'Sorry,' whispered Richard, 'I just couldn't take my eyes off it.'

Crouching behind their rocky outcrop, Toby, Richard, Tom and Ellie hardly dared breathe. After what seemed like hours, the awful sounds the dragon was making as it ate its meal – stopped. All that could be heard was the sighing of the wind. Surely they would hear the sound of the beast taking off? What was it doing?

'I advise you not to move,' said a harsh, gravelly, cruel voice.

TEN

The group of four looked up to see the huge terrible head of the dragon directly above, hanging over the rock outcrop. It must have crept up on them.

'You hid well from me, but that didn't prevent me from smelling you,' said the dragon with an unpleasant grin, its massive nostrils flaring as it sampled the air. 'In fact, I smell not just elf, but something else.'

The dragon moved its head a little closer to Richard and Tom who were crouching together, shaking with terror. Richard was all too aware of rows of huge curved teeth, still stained by the recent kill.

It sniffed long and deep, and muttered, 'That's a scent I've not come across before. I'll wager you're the group of folk I've been asked to look out for. Tell me if I've got things wrong, but the two of you who smell different – I reckon you're the young male humans. And to think I used to believe that humans were the stuff of fairy tales! Now – the other two are clearly elves. You, holding the stick – you must be the wizard, Toby Nonsuch. As for the lady elf, I wonder who *you* are?'

The dragon smiled smugly in anticipation.

Richard had never seen Toby look so fierce as he stood up and brandished his staff at the dragon. 'There must be something wrong with your sense of smell, my friend,' growled Toby. 'We are all elves, and I am no wizard. We're simply a group of elves taking in the air in these beautiful mountains.'

'That piece of wood you're holding looks like a wizard's staff to me,' said the dragon, still smiling.

'It's simply the stick I take with me when I'm walking in the countryside,' retorted Toby.

The dragon's smile grew larger and even more unpleasant. 'I'll let Drusilla decide whether or not you're the people she's interested in seeing,' it said. 'If you're not the people, then... well, that really would be the best outcome for all of you. For the life of a unicorn, nobody in their right mind walks for pleasure around here, at least not these days. Now, all do what I say, and no-one will get hurt. I want you to come over here, and form a group in front of me. Then we'll walk to Mount Dracomé. It's not far.'

The dragon had spoken with the air of someone who was bending over backwards to be reasonable. Richard, Tom and Ellie looked nervously at Toby for direction.

'I'll come over to you on my own to start with, to make sure that you don't mean to harm us,' challenged Toby, staring directly into the dragon's fearsome eyes. 'Then and only then, I will ask my friends to join me.'

Briefly, the dragon's forehead furrowed in thought. 'All right,' it agreed. 'Don't forget that if anyone runs off, I can fly, and I will be the fastest. I'm very good at eliminating problems, which is why I'm a captain in Drusilla's elite Personal Guard.'

Toby looked at the terrified expressions of the others still crouching behind the rock. 'Stay where you are until I call you. It'll all work out,' he said, with what he was clearly hoping was a confident smile.

As agreed, Toby climbed over the outcrop to where the dragon was standing. He stood defiantly in front of the great black beast. 'I have to say that I lied about my walking stick,

Captain!' he announced, at the same time pointing his staff at the dragon's head. An intense blue flame sprung from the tip and leapt towards the dragon, hitting it between the eyes with a mighty 'Crack!'.

The dragon lurched and howled with pain, as the residue of the flame continued to crackle around its head. 'You've just made a foolish mistake, elf,' slurred the dragon, slowly recovering its senses.

'You're a great lumbering stupid creature. You'll never catch me!' shouted Toby, hitting the dragon with yet another burst of flame.

The dragon, swaying with pain, reared up on its haunches to its full monstrous height, its eyes blazing like a demon's. 'I'll kill you, elf!' it roared. So saying, the dragon lurched towards Toby. Toby turned and ran towards the edge of the mountain ridge. The dragon crashed its way behind him, getting ever closer. Toby reached the edge, and ran along it, the dragon in hot pursuit, now half galloping and half flying. Suddenly, Toby stumbled, falling headlong, landing face-down, right on the edge of the precipice. Quickly, he turned over, so that he now faced the dragon that had just landed with an earth-shaking 'Thud!' next to him. It roared triumphantly and raised a massive claw over Toby's prostrate body, poised for the kill. But Toby suddenly pulled himself up, and pointed his staff at the ground on which the dragon was standing. There was a 'Crack!' and a blue flame erupted from the staff, covering the ground around the dragon with a blue rippling effect, rather like ocean waves, but waves that crackled.

The dragon seemed completely nonplussed, almost in a trance. It gazed down at the weird blue light show at its feet, its claw still held high in readiness for the downward stroke. The ground started to vibrate, and an ominous deep rumbling sound quickly grew in intensity, accompanied by fissures snaking out in all directions.

As Toby continued the onslaught, drawing every last ounce of sorcery energy into the flame spouting from his staff, the edge of the mountain ridge started to break up, shattered rocks falling into the abyss. A trickle of rocks quickly became a landslide. The ground under the dragon literally started to fall away, taking it inexorably towards the edge. Suddenly, it seemed to wake up to the danger. Desperately, it clawed at the moving ground and started to flap its wings in an effort to pull or fly itself to safety, but it was too late. It howled and screamed as it plunged into the void, its awful cry echoing around the mountains. Toby quickly stopped the flame and ran from the precipice to safety, narrowly avoiding the fast-moving cracks in the rock that now threatened to engulf him.

The dragon tumbled as it fell, flapping its wings frantically, but before it could counter the tumbling motion and get airborne, it crashed onto the sharp rocks at the bottom of the valley – and the terrible screaming mercifully stopped.

Toby, shaking uncontrollably from the horror and exertion of the experience, slowly walked back to the battered edge of the mountainside.

'Are you all right, Toby?'

It was Ellie's voice. Toby turned to see her and the boys standing behind him. He turned his gaze back to the valley below. 'I'm fine,' he said quietly. 'Unfortunately there's one member of Drusilla's Personal Guard who is definitely not.'

Richard gazed down at the body of the great beast, utterly broken on the valley floor. He was thinking about what Toby had just done – he knew they couldn't have allowed the dragon to deliver them to Drusilla – so there was no alternative but to kill it. Logically, Toby had done what needed to be done. Yet Richard felt sadness, and he could see that Toby felt it too. A creature had been killed that was simply doing its job. Then he had another thought – actually, it was a creature that could have killed them all at the drop of a hat, and wouldn't have lost any sleep over it.

Eventually, Toby turned away from the scene of carnage to face his companions. 'I had to do it. If Drusilla finds out we're heading for Mount Dracomé, she'll make sure we never get anywhere near The Book, and our mission to stop her is as good as over.'

'We all know you did what had to be done,' said Ellie, squeezing his arm. 'To be honest, all we care about is that you're unharmed, and that you saved us from the fate of dying horribly in the jaws of a dragon! Mind you, you almost messed up, didn't you? You fell over again!'

'I did not fall over!' he protested, a hurt look on his face. 'It was all part of the plan!'

'Of course, brother,' she teased.

Toby ignored her and carried on regardless. 'Look, I zapped him thinking I could kill him outright,' he resumed, his voice rising, 'but it seems that Drusilla has done something with these black dragons to make them resistant to sorcery. So I ended up only giving him a headache and making him very angry. I then realised I had to lead him away from you folk – and then what? I could see the edge of the ridge in the distance, and it dawned on me that if I could get him to follow me there, I might be able to get him to take a long tumble. So I led him along the edge, then deliberately dived to the ground, hoping that he'd be sufficiently surprised by this to hesitate just long enough for me to energise my staff and disrupt the ground he was standing on – and thank goodness, it worked!'

Toby had been so keen to explain all this, that he had forgotten to breathe. As he inhaled, he noticed that everyone was smiling at him. The strained look on his face slowly gave way to an embarrassed grin. 'I'm sorry,' he said ruefully. 'I think I'm a little wound up.'

'You were brilliant, Toby,' affirmed Tom. 'An ace wizard!'

'Absolutely!' agreed Richard.

'Thanks,' said Toby. 'Well, we must move on. As long as

we stand here, a passer-by might think we had something to do with this dragon's demise. Otherwise, it looks like an unfortunate accident – he simply got caught in a small landslide and plunged to his death. Now follow me, and keep your eyes peeled for dragons, or any other folk for that matter. We're very close to Drusilla's fortress, so anyone you meet is likely to be working for her.'

Toby led the group up the slope, towards the summit over which the dragon had so recently flown. As they stomped their way ever higher, Richard half expected another dragon to appear; only this time, they would be in full view. Eventually, they reached the summit – without incident – and stopped to admire the view. Directly in front of them, soaring above the lesser mountains surrounding it, was the majestic Mount Dracomé, or as far as Richard and Tom were concerned, Snowdon. A valley peppered with rocks and gullies lay between their vantage point and the mountain.

'We need to cross that valley,' said Toby grimly, 'and find our way to the foot of Mount Dracomé before nightfall, ready to sneak into the fortress under cover of darkness. We'll need to stick together and avoid prying eyes.'

As if to demonstrate Toby's last point, two black shapes flew out of Mount Dracomé and headed eastwards. Instinctively, everyone crouched down, not wishing to be spotted by what they all knew must be black dragons. Fortunately, the dragons didn't deviate from their course, and they soon disappeared into the distance.

Toby continued, 'We need to make sure that those dragons don't spot us when they return to Mount Dracomé for the night. I suppose they're some kind of patrol, looking for troublemakers like us, ensuring that the terrorised local population stays terrorised.'

Cautiously, they headed down the slope to the valley below. In places, the descent was very steep, causing little trickles of shale to be dislodged now and then as the group picked their winding way downwards. Each time one of these minor rock falls occurred, the resulting clatter seemed to echo off every mountain in the vicinity. Surely unwelcome ears would hear it, and come along to investigate? But no visitors appeared. All that could be heard apart from the scrabbling sound of elvish and human feet negotiating the mountain, was the sighing wind and the occasional distant cries of eagles and the bleating of mountain goats.

Eventually they reached the valley. A mad jumble of strewn rocks and clumps of vegetation now stood between them and the foot of Mount Dracomé. They walked on doggedly, ever vigilant for black shapes in the sky. Soon it was late afternoon, and the sun finally disappeared behind the mountains, infusing the air with a cool foreboding. As they neared Mount Dracomé, its vastness seemed to loom ever more menacingly in the failing light.

Was it Richard's imagination, or had the landscape become more bereft of life as they neared Drusilla's fortress? They hadn't seen so much as a fly for the last couple of hours. It seemed that the mountains were holding their collective breath, anticipating the moment of a showdown with Drusilla. And that moment was not far off, because at long last they had reached the upward slope leading to the great lofty peak.

Toby led them to a nearby overhanging rock. Soon, they were all hiding beneath it, hungrily eating what remained of their Giant Pizza. Toby beckoned Richard, Tom and Ellie to lean towards him. He spoke so quietly they could only just hear. 'We are literally at Drusilla's front door,' he whispered. 'It's located a few hundred metres up the slope to the east. It's a great stone door in the mountainside, cut so skilfully by dwarves, that you have to look very closely to spot its outline in the bare rock. Of course, we won't need to find the door, because we shan't be going anywhere near it. We need to find another, less obvious, way in, and if I'm right, we shall soon know where that way in is. For the next few minutes I want everyone to keep silent, and not to move.'

Richard, Tom and Ellie looked at each other with bewilderment, then shrugged their shoulders in resignation. Time moved on sluggishly. Soon it was dusk. Then they heard it. A loud deep barking sound, shattering the silence. Definitely the sound of a dragon, and, it seemed, one not very far away.

Toby hissed, 'I'll be back in a minute. Keep quiet and don't move.' Then he picked up his staff, and wraith-like, disappeared silently into the night.

Minutes seemed like hours. Huddled in their rock shelter, they were all willing Toby to return. What was he doing? Had he been captured? Or worse? Richard was sure that only a deaf dragon could possibly fail to hear his pounding heart. Then a 'bark' broke the stillness of the night, this time not quite as loud as the one they first heard. And then another – and another. Soon the air seemed full of 'barks'; then the cacophony stopped, and silence resumed.

No-one hardly dared breathe. Suddenly, from the corner of his eye, Richard spotted some movement. His hammering heart seemed to leap out of his chest in abject panic, then he realised the approaching shadow belonged to Toby. Richard let out a sigh of relief. He stole a quick glance at Tom and Ellie, and smiled inwardly – their faces, illuminated by the twilight, betrayed the fact that they too had been experiencing the full range of emotions that terror has to offer.

Toby was smiling triumphantly. He crept silently into the rock shelter, crouched down next to Ellie and the boys and whispered earnestly, 'It's as I thought! She has dragons out on patrol during the day, and at dusk they return for what they, no doubt, think is a well-earned rest. The good news is that I can see where some are returning to – a point on the eastern flank of the mountain, about a third of the way up. That point is almost certainly a cave, probably housing a single platoon – that's six dragons. Of course, there will be other dragon caves dotted around the mountain, providing accommodation for however many dragons she has in total. As you've probably guessed, those caves can't all be natural. Drusilla probably used dwarves to carve them out – '

'That's all very interesting,' hissed Ellie, 'but how does that help us get inside the mountain?'

'The dragon's cave is how we get in – tonight,' he replied. 'We can't wait for tomorrow when the dragons should be out on patrol, because we need to get to the Book before then. It may already be too late for all I know.'

'What!' she gasped. 'Toby, if we walk into that cave right now, we'll be killed. This seems to me a bit of a drawback.'

Toby considered this. 'Look, if we find a way of getting past the dragons without them noticing, then I think we'll be able to walk straight into her fortress. You see, dragons favour open caves for accommodation. They simply don't like being shut in. Drusilla was happy to give them caves, knowing that no-one in their right mind would try to infiltrate her fortress via a cave stuffed with watchful dragons – and if they did, they wouldn't get far.

'I'm sure that each cave connects with her fortress. Why wouldn't it? After all, her dragons are her most important servants. I reckon there will be elves and dwarves moving to and fro between the corridors of the fortress and the caves all the time, delivering Drusilla's orders for the dragons, and returning to Drusilla with reports on the dragons' progress. I bet that any door between cave and fortress is often left open with all that communication going on – and why not? Drusilla will reckon that no-one is going to get past the dragons. All we need to do is find the door in the cave above us and slip into the fortress.'

Richard had been listening to this discourse between Toby and Ellie with increasing disbelief. 'I'd like to get one or two things straight, Toby,' said Richard. 'How do you propose we *slip* past the dragons, and what happens if the door is closed and locked?'

'Don't worry,' said Toby. 'Remember I'm a wizard. I'm sure I'll get us to that door without being noticed, and if it's locked I'll unlock it – yes, that's right – then we'll be inside.'

'Toby,' said Tom, adding his voice to the debate, 'what if you're completely wrong and there isn't a way into the fortress from the cave?'

'There has to be a way in,' said Toby firmly. 'I'm sure that's how Drusilla keeps in close touch with the dragons. Definitely. Absolutely!'

Richard wondered at this point if he was the only one with confidence at an all-time low. Then to make matters worse, Toby disappeared again. After a few minutes he returned and hissed, 'There's no more activity, so I think there's a good chance that all the dragons are back in the cave – which actually doesn't sound too good put like that, does it? But at least we shouldn't be spotted on our way up there. Besides, the fact that the cave is packed full of dragons could be to our advantage...I wonder...?'

Richard, Tom and Ellie were wide-eyed. Richard couldn't see how Toby could possibly think that a cave full of dragons might be to their advantage, but there was no time for debate. Toby whispered, 'Let's go. Follow me, keep silent, and look out for anything that moves.'

They left the relative safety of their rock shelter, and walked in single file behind Toby, up the starlit rock-strewn slope of the mountain. As Richard climbed, he thought briefly about happy times with his family, in the same world, yet a world apart – and here he was, tramping up Snowdon in the darkness, straight into the jaws of goodness knows how many nasty dragons.

Mind you, it wasn't completely dark; the stars were shedding just sufficient light to see where you were going, which meant of course that you could be easily seen. Richard looked around nervously. Keep your mind on the job, he thought.

It seemed they had been climbing forever, then suddenly Toby halted. All was quiet, save for occasional snatches of distant conversation wafted to them by the playful night mountain wind. The conversation was that of deep, harsh gravelly voices. Black dragon voices. From a point above them and a little to the left, a glow could be seen – it was light spilling out of the dragons' cave.

The conversation on the wind was hard to discern, but occasional snatches could be clearly heard: 'Captain Dracon?... looks like he fell off the escarpment at Raven End...he wasn't bad for an officer...the eagles are feasting there.'

Approaching the cave from one side, Toby led the group right up to the edge of the cave mouth, avoiding the pool of light emanating from it. They finished up standing together, with their backs pressed against the mountainside, in an effort to make their profiles as small as possible. Toby was right, thought Richard, as he took in the precise square outline of the cave's mouth. It certainly wasn't natural.

Now they could hear all too plainly the dragon-talk within. 'So now, number two platoon needs a replacement captain,' a voice growled. 'I'm going to go for that position.'

'You, Caspen!' another voice rumbled. 'I never thought of you as officer material! Besides, if you leave this stinking platoon, where are they going to find a dragon prepared to take your poxy place, eh?'

There was a momentary silence, which was quickly broken by much grating laughter of dragons, but it seemed Caspen wasn't prepared to leave it at that. 'Thanks a lot, Rantor,' he snarled. 'I think I've got what it takes to lead a platoon, so I'm going to give it a shot.'

The conversation fizzled out at this point, an impasse seeming to have been reached. But shortly afterwards, Rantor resumed the discussion. 'Caspen,' he goaded, 'I don't suppose you had anything to do with Dracon's death? Since you seem to want his position, maybe you had something to do with his demise?'

The silence that followed was electric. You could have toasted bread with it.

Richard, Tom and Ellie stared at each other with open mouths. They knew that what Rantor had just said, came not from Rantor, but from Toby. Toby had his hands cupped around his mouth and was mimicking the dragon's voice, 'throwing' it into the cave.

Rantor spluttered, 'I didn't say that! Who's mucking about? Look, didn't you notice that my mouth wasn't moving then? For the life of a unicorn, someone's been putting words in my mouth!'

'You're sick, mate!' roared Caspen. 'Not content with accusing me of killing Dracon, you add insult to injury by doing some kind of pathetic ventriloquist act you probably learnt in a circus! Take back your lies, or it'll be the last circus act you ever appear in!'

'Look, I didn't say those words! Now don't you dare call me a liar, Caspen,' spat Rantor, his voice dripping with menace.

Caspen snarled, 'I do call you a liar. Take back what you said or else.'

'Let's settle this outside,' growled Rantor, or at least someone that sounded like him. 'Come on everybody – outside! Let's get well away from the cave – we don't want *her* to find out about the fight, do we?'

'Can you believe it?' roared Caspen, 'Rantor doesn't know when to stop, does he? There he goes again, doing his stupid circus act!'

Rantor wailed, 'For God's sake I didn't say that! You've got to believe me!'

But Rantor's protest fell on deaf ears. 'Everyone outside! Everyone outside!' chanted the rest of the dragons.

Suddenly there was a great crashing and thundering of heavy feet, and a tide of great black beasts burst explosively out of the cave mouth, Rantor at the front, still protesting, swept relentlessly onward.

If any of the dragons had glanced to their left on their way out, they might have noticed four shapes in the shadows trying to look like part of the mountainside. Fortunately for them, the dragons were totally intent on the prospect of a fight. The group of dragons halted their mad scramble a little way down the slope from the cave mouth, then haphazardly took to the air, the ragged airborne group heading swiftly away from the mountain, presumably for somewhere out of sight and earshot where they could stage their fight in secrecy.

Toby turned to his companions, whom he could see, even by the poor light, were absolutely terrified. 'I counted six dragons,' whispered Toby. 'That's a complete platoon. With any luck, the cave is now empty. Stay quiet and follow me – we're going in.'

ELeven

Toby moved quickly to the edge of the cave mouth, peered into it, then looked back at Ellie and the boys and beckoned for them to follow him.

In spite of Richard's fear, he was taken aback by the sheer scale of the space they had entered. The cave was rectangular, and deep, so deep it seemed it must end up close to the centre of the mountain. The walls, floor and ceiling were all smooth and flat, presumably the work of dwarves. Lines of burning torches were fixed to the walls, lighting the space with a bright flickering yellow glow. Richard felt rather like an ant in a cathedral.

Thankfully, the cave seemed devoid of anyone other than themselves. The space was, to say the least, uncluttered, save for large wooden vats placed at regular intervals against the walls. As Richard ran with the others behind Toby, keeping close to the side of the cave, he saw that some vats held either what was – presumably – water, and others the remains of what looked like some kind of lumpy meat stew. Richard learned to hold his nose whenever they ran past a vat containing stew. It smelt awful, even worse than the worst school dinners he could remember – so it really was bad. He couldn't imagine that Toby's red dragon friends would eat anything like that.

As they neared the end of the cave, Richard could see that

there was what looked like a metal door set into the back wall. So Toby was right – this would hopefully be the door leading to Drusilla's inner sanctum. The only fly in the ointment though, was that it was locked. 'That's unfortunate,' muttered Toby. 'I'll start by trying to open it with a door jemmy spell – '

But he never got to find out whether the door jemmy spell would do the trick, because there was a clanking sound and the door opened without his help. A young male elf dressed in typical male-elf fashion (brown belted smock and sandals), walked in holding a long black wrought-iron implement with an upside-down cup at its end, which Richard realised must be a torch-snuffer. He was obviously about to put out the lights, presumably meaning it was time for all good dragons to go to sleep.

The elf was confused. 'Where are the dragons, and who are you people?' he asked politely. Then he saw Ellie. 'Wow!' he gasped, eyes resembling serving plates, jaw sagging to an astonishing extent, tongue hanging out limply like a thick slice of salami. Unfortunately for the hapless elf, he never got further than 'Wow!' because Toby had thrust his staff out towards him, a white beam of light fizzing from its end that went on to surround the transfixed elf in a shimmering glow.

Toby intoned, 'You will forget all about us and continue with your duties. You are not worried that the dragons are not here. You know they will be back soon. You will wait until they return, then you will put the cave torches out. You will say nothing about the dragons' absence, because you do not want to get them into trouble, and besides, you are frightened of what they might do to you if you upset them. Off you go.'

The white beam disappeared as quickly as it had appeared, and the stunned elf walked past them as though they no longer existed.

'We're in!' hissed Toby triumphantly. 'Follow me and keep close.'

They all fully intended to keep very close. Toby ushered them through, shutting the door quietly behind them. They found themselves in a narrow straight carved-out stone corridor lit by torches, the ceiling a little more than elf-height. Toby led them swiftly on until they came to a much larger corridor. He peered cautiously up and down. It was empty save for the torches that lined its walls. He noticed that the whole corridor was curved. He turned back to face his wide-eyed companions. 'I think I've worked it out,' he whispered. 'I reckon the passage we're about to enter runs all the way around the mountain in a great big circle. I imagine there are passages like the one we're in at the moment leading outwards at regular intervals to the other dragon caves. I'm guessing the circular corridor is the outside of a kind of spoked wheel, and I bet some of the 'spokes' take the form of corridors leading into the centre of the mountain where I feel sure we'll find Drusilla.'

He poked his head out once more to check the circular corridor remained empty, then headed into it, waving for everyone to follow. Again, in spite of his terror, Richard couldn't help admiring the workmanship of those who had fashioned this impressive geometrically perfect passageway. It had been cut directly out of the mountain rock, its smooth shiny surfaces looking as though they had been polished. They moved quickly along, expecting to meet someone at any moment. Incredibly the corridor was deserted – perhaps everyone was turning in for bed? Soon they came to a passage leading off to the left, presumably to the centre of the mountain.

Having convinced himself the passage was empty, Toby led them quickly into it. Soon, they passed a narrow set of stairs on the left, leading upwards, but Toby carried on to the end of the passage. It adjoined yet another corridor, which had doors set into it at regular intervals along its length. Suddenly they heard approaching footsteps and voices. Toby pulled his head back into the corridor he and his companions were currently in, and gestured for them not to move.

'I'm off duty now, mate,' said a voice. 'I'm knackered, so I'm going to have an early night. See you in the morning.'

'Yeah, I think I'll be doing the same soon. Goodnight,' replied another voice.

They heard the sound of a door being opened and closed, then the sound of footsteps resumed, becoming ever louder. Everyone flattened themselves against the corridor wall, trying to be as inconspicuous as possible, not daring to breathe. The owner of the footsteps, an elf, walked past their corridor without a glance, the sound of his footfalls dying away into the distance.

Toby whispered, 'This seems to be a dormitory area for Drusilla's staff. I have a hunch that the stairs we passed back there might lead to Drusilla's inner sanctum. Let's see.' Without waiting for a response, he retraced his steps, Ellie and the boys following him like bloodhounds. They reached the stone stairs and climbed them. The top of the stairs led to a level straight corridor, terminating in a closed metal door at its end.

Toby hesitated at the door, his hand hovering indecisively over the handle. Ellie and the boys craned forward, listening for any sounds coming from whatever might lurk inside. All was quiet. Toby decided to try and open the door. He slowly moved the handle downwards until it reached the end of its travel, and to his surprise – it opened. He had expected it to be locked; after all, there was no-one standing guard. The door moved slowly (and fortunately, silently) under its own weight, but Toby quickly restrained the motion, holding the door barely ajar. A sliver of light streamed through the narrow open gap. The only sound that could be heard from within was an occasional muted crackling.

Toby waited for a while, listening. Still all that could be heard was the crackling sound. Finally, holding his staff protectively in front of him, he slowly pushed the door open further, all the time peering through the ever-widening gap. Soon, the gap was wide enough for Toby to see directly inside. Then he opened the door completely, stepped in, and beckoned for everyone to follow. They found themselves in a large circular chamber. Toby shut the door behind them noiselessly as they gazed at their new surroundings.

They appeared to be standing on a circular balcony. The balcony followed the perimeter of the curved wall. The wall, balcony and ceiling all seemed to be carved out of the grey rock of the mountain, but the surfaces were as smooth as glass, so smooth that they glistened with ever-changing colours in the strange flickering light. It seemed that Drusilla had reserved the very best dwarf handiwork for this room. The balcony was well-lit by oil lamps, placed at regular intervals around the circular perimeter of the chamber. It was edged with a safety-wall, which, from their current position, prevented any view of the area below. They would have to move right up to the wall in order to see over it, and Toby wasted no time in doing this. He led the group to the wall, gesturing for everyone to crouch down as they neared it. When they reached it, Toby straightened up just sufficiently to see over. An incredible sight met his eyes. He quickly bid the others to take a look.

Now they were all taking in the enormity of this strangely beautiful circular room, set in its improbable location deep in the heart of the mountain. The reason that the walls were flashing with myriads of colours was now clear to all. There was a dazzling multi-coloured light show taking place directly below them. At the heart of the display, was a wooden lectern with a large venerable book placed on it. The book was open, and occasional jagged flashes of red crackling light flickered from it, rather like miniature red lightning strikes. There were two huge horizontal circular ribbons of white light, hovering at lectern height side-by-side, overlapping at one point only – directly above the book. Standing on top of the ribbons, filling the entire perimeter of both circles, and depicted in full-colour light, was a large assortment of three-dimensional elf-like figures, human-like figures and animal figures, all in frozen poses. The elvish and human figures looked as though they were drawn from some noble ancient mythology, dressed in flowing garments or cloaks, and in some cases, hardly dressed at all. The animals included a lion, tiger, dragon, winged horse, scorpion, crab, and a wolf – to name but a few. The figures all faced outwards from the centre of their circle.

The two circular rings were rotating very slowly at dissimilar speeds. Every now and then, a new pair of characters would meet directly above the book, causing a burst of crackling red lightning-flashes. The figures looked real, but they shimmered in much the same way that holograms shimmered in the science fiction films Richard was so keen on. He was mesmerised by the eerily beautiful merry-go-round below. Eventually he wrenched his gaze away to see how they might get down there. There was a single wooden staircase with banisters, positioned nearby to their left, which led down to the ground floor where he could now see a large wooden writing desk covered in paperwork comprising of scribbled writing and assorted strange-looking diagrams, a scattering of various comfortable-looking padded chairs, and several large wooden bookcases, brimming with books.

Suddenly his eye was caught by movement on the merry-go-round. Yet again, two characters were approaching each other, this time an elf and a human. The red lightning flashes started as expected, but now grew in intensity beyond anything he had seen before. The crackling echoed around the room. Suddenly a three-dimensional fog of colours appeared above the rings, rapidly dissolving into intense full-colour

146

clarity, depicting a scene that Richard was very familiar with. Then the lightning flashes and the crackling returned to their original subdued level.

'It's…it's my house,' stuttered Richard, 'and everything, including the Wild Wood. It's where this whole mad adventure started.'

'And it seems so fitting that this should be where the next chapter of your adventure starts. I shall now freeze the wheels so that this connection in time and space between our worlds is not lost.'

The voice they had just heard had come from behind them. It was a calm conversational feminine voice, a voice talking for all the world as though its owner had known the group huddled on the balcony for ages and was pleased to meet up with them again. As one, the group turned in its direction. A beautiful slender woman stood there, smiling, her astonishing green eyes taking in everything. She looked to be about the same age as Toby. She wore a free-flowing thin grey dress, reminiscent of a Roman toga, with a simple cord around the waist, and she had abundant long rippling auburn hair that fell in a carefree way below her shoulders. She wore simple open leather sandals, elf-style. Surely this lady standing before them couldn't be Drusilla? She seemed so elegant. She certainly didn't seem to be the sort of person you would expect to be in the advanced stages of planning one-world domination, let alone two-world domination. The only thing that slightly jarred with her graceful image was the wooden staff she was holding. It was similar to Toby's, but less gnarled, making it seem more feminine. She had just nonchalantly waved it at the glowing wheels below, and they had instantly stopped moving, the image of Richard's home remaining in suspension above the now-frozen wheels.

'I hope I didn't frighten you,' she said. 'I've been working here most of the day, but even sorceresses have to pop out to 'powder their noses' every now and then. I don't generally lock doors in my area – in fact I operate an 'open door' policy with my employees – it helps to keep everyone happy, motivated, and most important of all, trustworthy. I haven't had to worry about unannounced visitors until now, since my dragons have always taken care of them, but somehow you all managed to slip through. Only you, Toby, could pull off a stunt like that – some time you really must tell me how you managed it – but for now, please take the stairs down to the floor below where we can sit down and have a chat. I imagine we all have issues we'd like to air – oh, I've just remembered – I need to do something.' She momentarily closed her eyes, and at the same time her staff briefly glowed with a pink light. 'Good,' she murmured. 'Now my dragons have their orders and know when and where to go. So where were we? Ah, yes.'

She pointed to the nearby stairs, still smiling, still being the perfect hostess. Richard, Tom and Ellie looked anxiously at Toby for guidance. Toby smiled at his companions and said quietly, 'Let's go down the stairs as Drusilla requests. We certainly have one or two issues we'd like to discuss with her, haven't we?'

Drusilla shepherded them all to the area below, where she arranged four chairs in a semicircle in front of her writing desk, and invited her four visitors to sit down, before sitting down herself at the desk. She carefully placed her staff on the desktop, within easy reach. Richard had already worked out that sorcerers (and it would seem, sorceresses) do not like being separated from their staffs, which was certainly why at this moment Toby was holding on to his staff like a limpet.

'Toby, I'd be a lot happier if you'd put your staff down on the floor,' she said, smiling far too brightly. Toby reluctantly obeyed.

Richard's whole body was shaking with fear. Here they were in one part of this improbable room, sitting in comfortable chairs, in the audience of the most feared person in the world, about to have a chat, while a few metres away the ultimate fate of two worlds was in the process of being dictated by a bizarre double carousel ride. Out of the corner of his eye he could see his home hovering in space. Everything he loved most, his family and his home, were now all too graphically part of a monstrous space-time game.

Drusilla gazed at the boys, from one to the other, and back again. It felt to Richard that those amazing green eyes were drilling right into his soul, exposing his most intimate thoughts and memories. It was like one of those awful dreams when you're taking a school examination and realise halfway through you haven't any clothes on. Just when he thought she was about to tear his mind completely apart, she seemed to lose interest, abruptly abandoning her scrutiny. 'Please take off your hats, my young elves, if it is elves that you are,' she said, smiling just as she had the whole time.

The boys turned in panic towards Toby. 'It's all right,' he said quietly. 'Do as she says.'

Richard and Tom slowly removed their hats, exposing their human ears. Drusilla sighed, leant back in her chair, cupped her chin and gazed up at the stone ceiling. 'So, the prophecy is fulfilled,' she murmured. 'Two human boys have arrived to padlock The Book in order to stop me from reuniting the elvish and human worlds. Of course, the prophecy doesn't indicate whether or not the boys succeed. And I'm sure that the writers of the prophecy didn't intend to stop *me* from using the book. Surely the Ancients would have been overjoyed to know that I, a true visionary, would be taking on the task of reuniting the worlds, my aim to create an undivided world all the stronger for its blend of elvish and human qualities? The difficult part of course is convincing the aggressive technology-focused human world that they need to submit to my rule in order to reap the benefits. I'm afraid I will have to show a little aggression myself – to get their attention.'

She seemed to be talking to herself, momentarily oblivious of the presence of her visitors. Suddenly her mood changed and she leant forward, beaming her gaze like a spotlight at Toby. The smile she'd been wearing had now vanished. 'You've hurt me, Toby Nonsuch,' she said quietly, her brow furrowed. 'You know, you still have a special place in my heart, so it's particularly painful for me to find you're working against me. When I heard you had two new trainees who always wore hats, I began to wonder if it was possible that they were the humans described in the prophecy. Then I thought that with your misplaced sense of right, you might be taking the humans to the book to stop someone like me accessing the human world. Suddenly it made sense that you had to be the guardian of the book! The Order of Sorcery has always had a soft spot for you. But if you had the book, where were you keeping it? An obvious place was your house – so obvious, I almost decided you wouldn't possibly keep the book there. Thank goodness I didn't take any chances and sent my elite tunnelling dwarves to investigate just in case. My dear Toby, you've always had a misplaced faith in the safety of your house. I'm afraid your ever-watchful dragon friends were blissfully unaware of my tunnelling operation. Now, I'm pleased to say, the book is at long last with its rightful owner.'

She allowed herself a smug smile as she momentarily looked across at the precious book and the images hovering above it, before returning her gaze to the group in front of her, quickly homing in on Ellie. Drusilla's eyes narrowed with interest, her lips curling into a thin smile. 'You've got spirit, young lady,' she said thoughtfully. 'Feisty and very pretty – a potent combination. I see a resemblance to Toby – I wonder – are you the kid sister Toby told me about all those years ago?'

Before Ellie could answer, Toby intervened. 'Drusilla, my young friends are not going to answer your questions,' he said earnestly. 'I'm their guardian, and I'd rather you talked to me.'

'For old times' sake, Toby, I'll respect your wishes,' she replied, her smile fading. 'Like you, my training in sorcery has honed the gift of insight, and there's much that I know without need of confirmation. I simply *know* that this girl is your sister – Ellie is her name, as I recall.'

Toby looked stonily at Drusilla and didn't say a word.

Having just gone through the uncomfortable experience of Drusilla dissecting his soul, Richard was very confident that she really did know that Ellie was Toby's sister. He had been keeping quiet the whole time, mainly out of instinctive self-preservation, and now he had reached the point where he simply couldn't hold back any longer. 'Drusilla – can I call you that?' asked Richard nervously.

'That is my name,' she replied, smiling with sudden warmth that contrasted starkly with the polite reserve that up until now had preceded it. 'I considered 'Supreme Empress' among other titles, but decided I prefer the less formal 'Drusilla'.'

Richard was starting to realise that Drusilla was a complex character. It was difficult to know where you were with her. She clearly had a strong ruthless side, with a potential for evil, but there was a part that was gentler, even humorous. On one hand she was powerful and in control, yet she had the 'common touch' – could even be your friend, as long as the ruthless part was allowed to do what it wanted to do.

'You obviously know Toby quite well, at least it seemed you did some time ago,' said Richard with growing confidence. 'Were you friends then?'

She paused before responding, her mind presumably reaching back through the years, her eyes taking on a far-away look as the memories returned. 'We were more than friends. We were very much in love,' she said quietly, with what seemed to be heartfelt sadness.

Richard felt betrayed. He turned angrily to Toby. 'Toby, why didn't you tell us that Drusilla used to be your girlfriend?'

'At the time, it just seemed to be information you didn't need,' shrugged Toby. 'Drusilla, or Betty as she was then, was my girlfriend many years ago when we were both learning sorcery. We were mentored by the same Grand Master – '

'And they broke up soon after completing the training,' interrupted Ellie. 'Toby was miserable for months afterwards. Whenever he visited us at home, it was about as much fun as being continually rained on by a dark, brooding cloud – '

'Thank you, Ellie,' said Toby hastily. 'We broke up because as the training progressed, it became increasingly evident that we had very different approaches regarding the use of sorcery. Drusilla has always felt that Elves have failed to progress as a nation because they tend to lack the ambition that many humans have, and wanted to use her sorcery to lead Elves into a more aggressive way of doing things. At the same time I think she would like to teach humans a lesson for not believing in non-human folk, this non-belief having caused the ancient division between our worlds. I believe that Drusilla and I both wish to see all the races of people reunite, but where we differ is that I want it to happen in a natural way, not to be forced into it by fear and violence.'

Silence ensued while Drusilla gazed at Toby for several seconds without speaking. Then she said, 'I suppose that's a reasonable summary. But I think you lose sight of the fact that sometimes you have to be a little cruel to be kind. I think that if someone doesn't provide proper leadership for a better world, the world won't get better. My destiny is to be that leader, and I will demonstrate strong leadership. People respect and follow strong leaders, when they realise that in the end everyone benefits, except for a few misguided souls who get in the way during the process – but that's an unfortunate fact of life. A few individuals suffer, whereas the vast majority of people benefit beyond their wildest dreams!'

Toby's face had become red with anger. 'We're still as far

apart as ever, aren't we?' he growled. 'I don't believe that the use of aggression is the way to make any world better. Why can't you simply show people a better way, and let them decide whether they want to take it, instead of trying to ram it down their throats? And can't you see that people don't follow you out of respect? They follow, because they know they'll be less dead and better off if they do! You keep them loyal to you through a mixture of fear and bribery.'

Richard was fully expecting Drusilla to explode and was steeling himself for it, but she was to prove she was anything but predictable. She smiled, and without even a trace of annoyance said, 'Toby, you and I have grown to have different perspectives on life. I think we should agree to disagree, and, so to speak, move on. Now, is there anything that anyone wants to ask me before I deal with the subject of where we all go from here?'

'How did you find out about the human boys?' asked Toby. 'I was careful to keep them away from other folk as far as possible. Whenever it was necessary to involve anyone, I chose those I trusted – and I'm pretty sure you didn't receive any reports of sightings from your dragons.'

'Well, you're right about my dragons,' she agreed. 'No reports from them, although I wonder if I might have had a report from Captain Dracon, if he had survived to provide it. He seems to have been standing on the ridge at Raven End, lost his footing in a landslide, then hit the ground below before he could get airborne. I suspect you might have had something to do with it, but I'm happy to let that particular 'sleeping dragon', as it were, lie. Captain Dracon was certainly dependable, but I have to say I would always back you Toby to win in any contest.'

It seemed to Richard that she really didn't want a confession from Toby. It was as though she was certain Toby was involved – and that was the end of the matter as far as she was concerned.

Suddenly Drusilla smiled. 'I've just realised that I've been a very poor hostess,' she said briskly. 'I haven't offered any refreshments. I've also just realised that the solution to the lack of refreshments will provide the answer to your question regarding how I knew you were accompanied by the humans. Please wait a moment.'

She touched the wooden staff lying on her desk, and a pink glow briefly surrounded it. Immediately, a bell tinkled faintly, presumably from somewhere in the mountain. After what seemed a very long time, but actually was no more than half a minute, a muted clattering sound was heard, followed by the balcony door opening wide. The clattering resumed, now echoing loudly in the room, then as quickly stopping. Everyone turned to look up at the balcony – and collectively gasped.

TWELVE

'Can I help yer, Madam? Oh my gawd – it's Toby Nonsuch!'

'Ben?' blurted Toby. The landlord of the Green Goblin inn gazed down on them.

'Ben has been working for me for some time,' said Drusilla, smiling smugly. 'When Ben visits, he kindly carries out barman duties for me, among his other duties. He recently told me that you were passing through his pub with two lads who always wore hats, and who generally seemed like fish out of water. It really is amazing how much useful information you can pick up from a busy pub. Ben gallops here every now and then, to let me know what he has learnt. On these occasions he leaves his son Bill in charge at the pub. I probably ought to recruit Bill some time – that would give me overall coverage twenty-four hours a day, seven days a week. Let's face it, if I'm to lead the world, I need to know what's going on in the world. Folk like Ben act as my eyes and ears. You see, Toby, my secret army is growing out there, and with it, my ability to control events.'

Toby gazed icily at the centaur who appeared to be shuffling about nervously, making scraping sounds on the hard floor. 'How long have we known each other Ben?' he shouted. 'Many years. I wonder over how many of those years you've been betraying your friends?'

'I-I'm sorry, Toby,' stammered Ben. 'I really am. I don't expect yer to forgive me, but when yer offered a lifestyle you've only ever dreamed of, it's hard to resist. Not only that, but I really do believe that in the end, the Lady will create a better world for all of us.'

Before Toby could reply, Drusilla became the perfect hostess again. 'Now, can Ben get you all something to eat and drink?' she inquired breezily. 'We can rustle up most things.'

Her invitation was met with a wall of silence. Everyone appeared to have lost their appetite. Toby looked long and hard at Drusilla, and finally said, 'We'd like to leave now, Drusilla.'

She laughed, then quickly regained her composure. 'You know as well as I do that I cannot let any of you go, at least not until my plans have progressed a little further,' she said flatly. 'I insist that you stay as my guests for a while. I'll ask Ben to return when you change your minds regarding refreshment. I'm sure you're all thirsty and hungry. Thank you, Ben, you can go for the moment.'

Ben nodded with obvious relief, then quickly clattered out of the room, closing the door behind him.

Drusilla scanned the grim faces in front of her. 'I think that in time you'll all realise that it's better for everyone if you join my cause. Come with me and let me explain how that book over there is going to help fulfil that cause,' she said, rising from her chair, staff in hand, pointing towards the eerie light show. 'And Toby, don't even think about picking up your staff.'

Toby stopped inching towards his staff, and made a show of giving it a wide berth as they all followed Drusilla. She led the group directly to the book. On the way, they had to walk through life-size images of people and animals. Each time Richard walked through an image, he could feel its energy interacting with his body, just like in those static electricity experiments at school.

Drusilla stopped at the lectern, looking as though she was

about to preach a sermon. Then she motioned for everyone to form a semicircle in front, facing her. How surreal is this, thought Richard. Everyone was illuminated by patchworks of bright colours emanating from the mystical light-show. In a sense, they had now all become part of it.

Drusilla was smiling, looking down at the ancient leather-bound book. It was lying open roughly halfway through its great thickness. Its beautiful handwritten pages were obviously the result of a labour of love, which presumably, thought Richard, must be an essential part of the book's sorcery. The book seemed to be alive – shimmering waves of white light rippled outwards from its pages, with occasional red crackling lightning flashes reaching out rather alarmingly, before fizzling out into the surrounding air. The whole effect was mesmerising. Richard couldn't tear his gaze away from the beauty of the strange living light.

Suddenly he became aware that Drusilla was speaking. 'You are all witnesses to the beginning of the first interaction between this world and the human world, since the time they became separated many thousands of years ago,' she intoned grandly, rather as though she was sending a ship off on its maiden voyage, or was opening a great new building to the public. 'It's fitting that an elvish philosopher and human inventor should be positioned closest to The Book,' she continued, glancing at the shimmering images directly to her left and right. 'When my work is done, the mystic world and creative world will be reunited, and mysticism will forever combine with creativity in one marvellous whole!'

'Blimey. She really is mad,' Richard muttered under his breath.

'As a barrel of ferrets,' hissed Tom.

Drusilla held out her hands to the two dazzling figures facing each other across the book. One figure was that of an elderly elf, who looked rather like a great Greek philosopher, his balding grey hair and full beard contrasting with the whiteness of his robe-like garment, the folds of which flowed all the way down to his bare sandaled feet. He looked like Plato with pointy ears, thought Richard.

The other figure was that of a youngish man. He wore a simple crude belted garment made of brown furry animal skin, perhaps taken from a deer. His long tangled black hair fell untidily onto his shoulders. He too had a full beard, but like his hair, it looked like it had never been near a pair of scissors. He wore simple shoes on his bare feet. They were probably the first shoes ever worn, consisting of a section of animal skin formed into a bag around the foot, and tied off with leather cord around the leg just above the ankle.

In spite of the tension in the room, Tom's curiosity overcame him. 'I can see that this guy is the philosopher,' he said, pointing at the elf figure. 'But if the guy in the animal skin outfit is an inventor, what did he invent?'

Drusilla seemed impressed with Tom's impetuosity. Her demeanour visibly thawed, and she allowed herself a smile. 'The guy in the animal skin, as you put it, is from an early time in human history,' she explained. 'I believe your people refer to humans from this period as Cro-Magnon. This man was called Barradorf, and he invented the wheel. Other members of his tribe wondered why they didn't think of it first, and quickly stopped moving heavy objects over rolling logs, instead building carts with wheels – which made haulage jobs a lot easier. In fact they were so irritated they didn't think of it first, that they never gave Barradorf the credit he was due, which is why his name wasn't passed on down the generations of humankind. He died an early death under a runaway cart.'

'So how do you know he's who you say he is?' asked Tom.

'Well, at that time the elvish and human worlds were one world. Barradorf's elf-friends in a nearby village were very impressed by his wheel – which they gratefully started to use –

and recognised that it was a turning point (forgive the pun) for the human race. They saw that humankind was at the dawn of a quest for creativity and invention, and that is why elves have continued to remember Barradorf. When I recombine the worlds, I'll make sure that Barradorf finds his rightful place in human history as a father of invention.'

'That's all very interesting, Drusilla,' said Toby, 'but what exactly are your plans, and how do we fit into them?'

Drusilla responded with a chilling detachedness – as though she was discussing a chemical treatment for the removal of greenfly from a rose bush. 'Well, Toby, before I recombine the worlds, I need to get them both under my control. This world is shaping up nicely, but now I need to get the human world to fall in line – and I'm starting the process by sending my dragons through the portal at Grindleshorn, where they will kill a few humans in order to get the world's attention. It's a small price to pay for what will prove to be a major step towards my vision of a unified world – with me fulfilling my destiny as leader.'

'What?' spluttered Toby in disbelief. 'Why don't you and I see if there is a way of reuniting the two worlds without violence? Why put Richard's innocent family in danger and countless others, when you and I could put our heads together, like in the old days, and work out a solution that's good for everyone? Come on, Drusilla. Let's leave the book alone for a moment and talk.'

She considered this, but not for long. Suddenly the look of hard resolve returned, more fiercely than before. 'I'm sorry, Toby,' she said coldly. 'I have no need for discussion. Now is the time. It all makes sense. The human boys come through a portal to stop me fulfilling my destiny. I obtain The Book and invoke its power, and find that the two images on the wheels of light that meet each other represent the key strengths of elvish and human cultures! It can't be coincidence! Not only that, but the time lines are such that the same portal has been selected. So now the portal that was used against me shall become my salvation – and the world's!' Drusilla's features softened a little as her gaze settled on Richard. 'Richard, I really hope your family isn't harmed. I like you – but what must be must be. My dragons have been briefed only to go for easy targets, in order to reduce the chance of dragon injury. They'll pick off a few people and then return safely home. My aim is to inflict only the minimum pain necessary to get the undivided attention of humankind.'

Richard felt sick at the pit of his stomach. 'Can you warn my family before the attack starts?' he asked quietly.

'I'm afraid not. They would warn others. Mind you, I doubt anyone would believe the suggestion that they were about to be attacked by dragons – but no. I cannot leave anything to chance. I really am sorry.'

Then without warning Drusilla held her arms out wide, her staff in her right hand. She suddenly grew hugely in stature, her head almost reaching the ceiling. Her eyes had become yellow, like the eyes of a dragon, thought Richard. 'Now is the time!' she proclaimed. 'Make time and space as one! The ancient souls again unite! Magrimasté! Magrimasté!'

The lightning flashes around the book grew more intense than ever, reaching out towards the wide-eyed audience. Toby, Ellie and the boys quickly took a step backwards. The crackling sound now filled the room – it was deafening. Then the figures either side of the book – which were now crackling and heaving with electric energy – moved. In perfect synchronisation, the venerable elf and young human thrust out their hands towards one another, the movement ending in a discernible *Thunk!* as their hands met in a robust hand-clasp above the book. And that is how they remained, frozen in greeting, gazing into each other's eyes. Then the lightning flashes and the harsh crackling of raw sorcery started to diminish.

Drusilla swiftly returned to her normal size and closed her eyes – it seemed that the exertion had taken a lot out of her. When she opened them, they were her own green eyes again.

In spite of his fear, Richard whispered to Toby, 'What does Magrimasté mean?'

'It's ancient elvish for 'May the force be with me',' he whispered back. Richard frowned in disbelief. He wondered if it could possibly be that there was some weird connection between the roots of the elvish language and certain science fiction sagas from his own world, but also was aware that right now he probably should be concentrating a little more on the immediate issue of staying alive.

Drusilla suddenly opened her eyes wide, beaming a triumphant smile. 'It is done!' she cried. 'Time and space between the worlds is as one! The portal will stay open for two full days, whereupon the synchronism between the worlds will have faded to the point that it closes. Two full days is sufficient for me to marshal my dragons, get them through the portal, then to safely return. I've already given them their orders, and in a matter of hours they'll be ready to leave.' Nothing could have prepared anyone for what Drusilla said next. 'I'm gasping for a cup of tea,' she said breezily. 'I imagine you all are, too.'

Drusilla had changed character again, just like that. Now she was everyone's best friend. Her staff, which she was still holding, pulsed with a pink glow. Almost immediately a distant clattering of approaching hoof beats on stone could be heard. The balcony door opened and in came Ben. He clopped his way to the balcony wall and peered over it. 'Ben, I think we could all do with tea and cakes,' said Drusilla, as though it was the end of a perfect day.

But Ben didn't have time to respond. Ellie had reached boiling point. 'You're a monster!' she screamed, waggling an outstretched finger at Drusilla. 'Here you are, calmly ordering tea while you unleash your dragons on Richard's family or any other innocent people that get in their way! Have you no compassion? Have you no feelings?'

'So I was right!' Drusilla snapped back, her face contorting with rage. 'There *is* a fire burning inside you! But how dare you speak to me in that way! I shall teach you how to behave!'

'Ellie, watch out!' shouted Toby. Drusilla had thrust out her staff at Ellie, energy already starting to dance visibly over its surface. But Ellie's reflexes were fast. She groped for anything to use as a weapon. In a flash, she threw her geologist's hammer at Drusilla. Drusilla ducked, and the hammer flew over her head hitting the wall, clattering harmlessly onto the stone floor. As she ducked, she lost her balance and started to fall backwards, instinctively grabbing the lectern in front of her in an effort to save herself. Drusilla and the lectern rocked backwards and forwards as if they were engaged in some kind of manic dance. Then gravity took over. The book took its leave of the lectern and hit the ground, literally sucking the lightshow into its pages as the covers slammed shut, leaving only the flickering wall lamps to illumine the room – closely followed by Drusilla who ended up in an undignified heap on the floor with the lectern on top of her.

Still dazed, she managed to push the lectern off. Somehow she had kept hold of her staff, and now was waving it around wildly, its tip starting to glow green as she tried to get up from the floor. Suddenly, a football-sized sphere of green crackling fire issued forth from the flailing staff, hitting the ceiling with a dull 'Whump!', causing shards of rock to shower down. Again and again, spheres were loosed off as she struggled to get up and mount an attack. Everyone was running about in an effort to dodge the barrage. The walls and ceiling were becoming increasingly embellished with football-sized pockmarks. Fireballs were also reaching the balcony, causing Ben to canter to and fro in order to avoid being hit, rather as though he was part of some grotesque arcade game.

Taking advantage of the chaos, Toby thrust out his arm, and immediately his staff leapt from where Drusilla had forced him to leave it, straight into his waiting hand with a 'Thwack!'. Then he pointed the staff at Drusilla who was increasingly 'getting her aim in' on Ellie – who in turn was proving a hard target to hit, dodging the fiery missiles with the prowess of an athlete.

'Drusilla!' bellowed Toby. 'Stop! I've got you covered!'

Now standing, Drusilla turned around in surprise, the barrage of fireballs instantly ceasing. She was staring at the end of Toby's staff, but she didn't act like someone who was at a disadvantage. 'My dear Toby,' she snapped, her face red and pinched into an ugly sneer, 'My sorcery is infinitely more powerful than yours. Don't try to take me on.' So saying, her head transformed into that of a black dragon, its terrible mouth opening wide and unleashing a blood-curdling roar.

But Toby stood his ground. 'That may be true about the sorcery,' he shouted above the awful din, 'but it's not sorcery that I intend to use against you.'

'What then?' snarled the dragon-head.

Without further ado, Toby hit her sharply on the side of her (dragon's) head with the end of his staff. She slumped to the ground, her head transforming back into her own as she fell, her staff clattering lifelessly onto the floor.

Toby smiled. 'Good old-fashioned elbow-grease, my dear dragon.'

He looked around. 'Is everyone all right?'

There were murmurings in the affirmative as Ellie and the boys cautiously approached the prone body on the floor.

'Excellent job, brother. She's dead!' announced Ellie brightly, then, 'Damn! She's breathing,' after having taken a closer look.

'Don't bother about her,' said Toby briskly. 'We've more urgent matters to attend to.' So saying, he stood the lectern upright, picked up the book and placed it on the lectern, then thumbed through its pages until he reached the one he wanted. He opened the book fully at this place. 'Richard and Tom,' he called. 'Gather around.'

'Are you going to close the portal?' asked Richard.

Toby looked at him sadly and said, 'My dear friend, I wish I could. The wheels are in motion for your particular portal, and cannot be stopped. Nature will take its course, and in two days' time the portal will close. All we can do now is padlock The Book so that Drusilla or anyone else can't use it again. Then we need to move very quickly. Now, both of you put your open hands on the book – here, and…here.'

The boys placed their hands on the ancient text where Toby directed. Then he placed his own hand on the page. He intoned, 'The open minds of these young humans shall blend with the understanding of the elves. With our hearts, we implore the Book to protect itself from manipulation. We invoke the padlock spell, to protect the mystic and creative worlds from each other until they are ready to rejoin as one. Magrishan!'

The boys suddenly pulled their hands away from the book as if it had bitten them. The ancient text had vanished. 'Blimey!' said Tom. 'What's happened?'

'The Book is now padlocked, Tom,' said Toby, smiling with relief. 'What better way to prevent someone from using a book than to remove the words?'

'I suppose that makes sense,' replied Tom thoughtfully.

'Okay Toby, what does 'Magrishan' mean?' asked Richard, with a slight air of resignation.

'It's ancient elvish for 'Divert all auxiliary power to the shields'.'

Richard looked up sharply at Toby, who was now wearing a broad smile. 'Okay, I'm joking,' laughed Toby. 'I know a lot of things about you and your world, and I have to say I wish we had some of your science fiction dramas here. Of course, we don't even have television or cinemas. Actually, 'Magrishan' is ancient elvish for 'Make it so'.' Before Richard could follow this up, everyone's attention was taken by sounds of movement coming from the balcony.

Ben had taken advantage of the preoccupation with The Book, and was inching his way towards the door, as quietly as a hoofed creature can on a stone floor. He was just preparing to gallop the last few metres, when a voice dispelled any further thought on the subject of galloping. 'Hold fast, Ben!' called Toby from below. 'You'd better help us out of here, or you'll be meeting your ancestors sooner than you expected!'

'Whatever yer say, Toby,' said Ben, who clearly had no intention of taking on a wizard, let alone one that definitely meant business. At that moment, muffled voices could be heard, getting closer. Soon there was a knock on the balcony door. 'Are you all right, my Lady?' asked a nervous quavering voice.

'Answer the door, Ben!' hissed Toby. 'Get rid of them! If you try anything, the dragons will be having roast centaur tonight!'

'I won't let yer down, Toby,' he hissed back.

Just to make sure, Toby ran up to the balcony and stood behind the door, staff at the ready. Ellie and the boys joined Toby moments afterwards. Then Ben clopped to the door and opened it. A group of elves stood in the doorway, nervously brandishing swords they plainly didn't feel entirely at home with. It underlined the fact that the only real soldiers in Drusilla's household were the dragons, thought Richard. Intruders weren't expected to get past *them*.

'Rest easy,' said Ben with authority. 'Everything is under control. The Lady has had a bit of a problem with some sorcery, and wishes to be left alone while she works it out. She is not to be disturbed by anyone until the morning. Right now, the Lady has instructed me to escort a group of elves out of the mountain. They have an important mission to undertake. So, everyone back to their posts please. I'll bring the group along shortly.'

This seemed to satisfy the would-be soldiers. Their leader said, 'Very good.' Then they left, seemingly much relieved, whereupon Ben shut the door.

'Well done, Ben,' said Toby. 'At least you've done something right today.' Then he turned to the boys. 'Go and fetch your hats, and cover your ears up. And Richard – please bring the book to me.'

'Okay, but what are we doing about Drusilla?' asked Richard.

'Well, Drusilla isn't our most pressing problem right now. The dragons already have their orders and in a few hours they'll fly to the portal – somehow we have to stop them. I'm certainly not about to kill Drusilla, although it is tempting! I think the greatest punishment for her is to lose power. Besides, because she's bribed so many people, a civil war could easily erupt if she came to harm. No, she's lost The Book, and now…she's going to lose her beloved staff. Yes, that's it – bring me her staff as well, please.'

'Will it let me pick it up?' asked Richard, frowning.

'You'll be fine. It's the relationship between sorcerer and staff which makes a staff more than a long thin lifeless piece of wood,' said Toby reassuringly, 'and while she's unconscious, that's all her staff is – lifeless wood.'

Richard now felt a little more comfortable about collecting the requested items. He brought them to Toby with great care, as though to drop either item would result in the destruction of this world, and perhaps even his own. The scary thing was that he had an inkling he might actually be right about the consequence of dropping the items.

Toby took Drusilla's staff, placed one end on the floor, and held the other end. Then he broke it in two using his foot. It snapped with a resounding 'Crack!', without any fizzing or flashing. It was no more than old wood. Then he dropped the broken pieces onto the floor and pushed them to the side. Finally, he took The Book and placed it inside a cloth bag that he had produced from a pocket, hanging the bag with its precious cargo over his shoulder.

'Right,' said Toby, smiling grimly. 'That's her power-base gone for the moment. We've shown compassion by giving her a second chance – maybe one day she'll understand that it really is possible to make the world a better place without harming people in the process. Now, Ben is going to get us out of here. Let's go, Ben.'

Ben, looking suitably forlorn and chastened, opened the door and beckoned for the group to follow. Toby was first, staff at the ready in case of any trouble from the centaur, then Ellie, Richard and finally Tom. Ben led them briskly via a maze of corridors and flights of stairs, his hooves creating a constant cacophony of staccato sound. Occasionally they met elves going about their business, but it seemed it was just the start of another long night as far as they were concerned, unaware of the spot of bother their employer was in. In fact they hardly glanced at Ben or his charges.

Eventually, the group reached a closed metal door at the end of a narrow corridor. Ben banged the door with a hoof several times. A muffled voice on the far side said, 'This is a restricted area! State your name and business!'

'It's Ben Nevis, 'er Ladyship's Personal Assistant! I have some folk in tow who need to leave the mountain immediately.'

'Right, Mr Nevis. My wild boar has no nose. How does he smell?'

'Awful,' growled Ben.

There was a clanking sound, and the heavy door started to slowly open.

'That's what passes for security around here?' whispered Toby.

'Yes,' said Ben. 'The Lady thought jokes would be more fun than boring passwords, and more memorable. Don't for a moment think that we'd be asked the same joke if we tried to get through this door a second time!' Toby rolled his eyes in disbelief.

In spite of their predicament, Richard simply couldn't keep Ben's surname out of his mind. 'Toby,' said Richard. 'I'm amazed that Ben's surname is 'Nevis'. In my world, Ben Nevis is a mountain!'

'That's right,' replied Toby. 'One of Ben's ancestors, his namesake, set up his home on a mountain to which he gave his own name, 'Ben Nevis'. Later, the world divided, and both the elvish and human cultures passed the name on. I suppose Mr Nevis wasn't imaginative enough to think of a name for the mountain other than his own.'

'Oi, I heard that. Old Ben was as imaginative as – well, as he needed to be,' finished Ben lamely.

The door was now wide open, and a young elf with a sword in a scabbard at his waist, waved them through with a welcoming smile. Unfortunately, what then greeted their eyes, ears and noses, definitely wasn't welcoming.

'Parrrrpp!'

'Who dropped one?' growled a voice.

'Probably you, mate!' snarled another voice.

'Less talking if you don't mind!' barked yet another voice. 'It's not far off midnight. I want everyone to turn in now. We're due to fly out tomorrow morning at seven o' clock sharp, so look lively about it!'

They had walked into one of the dragon caves, only the difference between this cave and the cave they had arrived by, was that this one was filled with dragons, in fact a platoon of dragons – six dragons to be precise. The flickering yellow torchlight contrasted starkly against the great black scaly forms stomping around. Two of the beasts were lying on the ground, trying to get to sleep, whereas the rest were bumping into each other and generally cursing.

Ben led them down the side of the cave, near to where one of the dragons was resting. Its huge head was lying on the ground only a metre away from the walkway they were using. As they approached, its huge yellow reptilian eyes suddenly opened wide. Everyone halted, self-preservation uppermost in their thoughts. Basically, the dragon was much like Dave or Dylan (the red dragons), the obvious difference being that this one was jet black, although this close, everyone could see its undersides were lighter in colour (more of a dark grey). But why was this dragon so scary? Well, thought Richard, one reason was that it worked for Drusilla, and was therefore particularly dangerous. Another reason was that although it had the same features that red dragons possessed, such as a jagged crest along its body length, harsh brows sweeping over piercing eyes, huge flaring nostrils at the end of a massive mouth packed with steak-knife teeth, and really, really, bad breath – this dragon, like all Drusilla's dragons, somehow looked especially cruel.

'Mr Nevis!' rumbled the dragon. 'You are a busy fellow, always coming and going! I won't ask what you're doing leaving the mountain at midnight with these folk,' it said, nodding its head in the direction of Ben's little group, 'but if it turns out anything is amiss, rest assured I will deal with it.'

'I'm sure you will,' replied Ben shakily. 'Nothing is amiss.'

One by one, they all filed past the great beast, its harsh eyes moving from one person to the next, its mouth gaping slightly to show a great red tongue flailing about within its fearsome jaws, seemingly as though it was tasting the air, or perhaps even tasting their fear, thought Richard. Richard was the last in line, and as he walked past looking straight ahead, the dragon's enormous head suddenly lifted from its resting position on the ground and lurched towards Richard, almost causing him to cry out. Its nostrils ended up a matter of inches away from Richard's head, its fetid breath almost causing him to retch. Richard simply froze – it seemed the wisest thing to do. The dragon's repeated sharp intakes of air through its nostrils were deafening, sounding like some kind of monstrous vacuum cleaner.

'There is something about you,' it said quietly. 'You have a spirit I have not felt before – and you smell very strange for an elf. I have a feeling we may meet again, in which case be prepared.' The dragon smiled a chilling smile, withdrew its head back to its resting position, then closed its eyes, the audience apparently at an end.

The others had moved on some way ahead, presumably not having noticed that Richard had been detained. He walked quickly to catch up, fearing the dragon might decide to have another chat with him if he stayed in the vicinity too long. Finally he caught up with the group at the cave mouth, just as they stepped out into what for all the world looked like a monstrous rectangular black painting, framed by the cave's flickering light. Ben kept the group walking until they were some considerable distance down the slope, well away from the cave, before stopping and waiting for everyone to cluster around.

Richard savoured the fresh night air. It was such a welcome contrast to the stench of the cave. The stars twinkled above as if to say that the visions of hell they had experienced in the mountain were simply bad dreams.

'Yer free to go where you will,' Ben was saying. 'Just keep clear of the dragons. They're trained to check out anything that moves.'

'Well, Ben, in spite of your unforgivable deception, thank you at least for getting us here,' said Toby. 'As far as I'm concerned, you're free to go, providing you stay away from me and my friends. I imagine you won't want to return to Drusilla – she's bound to see through any excuses you might come up with.'

'Don't worry, Toby. I'm out of here,' said Ben, his head hanging in shame. 'Thanks for showing me more mercy than I deserve.'

'Yes Ben, you don't deserve it – but before you go, tell me this. What had you done to upset that dragon back there?'

'Ah. Well, I'd bought several barrels of cider at a rock-bottom price from a nearby apple orchard, yer see, and thought I'd try and get that dragon to air-lift them to my pub. So I spun him a yarn that weapons were concealed in the barrels for a Top Secret mission that Drusilla was personally leading, and the weapons needed to be dropped off in Broom Down for mercenaries who were waiting there. Well, on the way, one of the barrels fell and smashed, releasing a torrent of cider without a weapon in sight, and to cut a long story short, I've had to keep that dragon supplied with free fresh lamb ever since.'

Toby shook his head with disdain. 'Go, Ben,' he said.

Ben took one last look at everyone, then turned and galloped down the mountain, soon lost to the night.

Richard seized his moment. 'Toby, Ben isn't the only one who seems to have upset that dragon.'

Toby gasped, more loudly than he intended. 'What do you mean?'

Everyone huddled around Richard as he described his unwanted meeting.

'You did well not to say anything in return,' said Toby. 'Dragons are very good at finding their way into creature's souls if they want to, and had you spoken, your voice would have given away the last piece of the jigsaw. It was an escape for us all.'

'But it said it might meet up with me again. It was just a threat, right? Toby?'

But apparently Toby now had other issues on his mind. 'Er, hopefully only a threat,' he muttered, almost to himself. 'Hmm, I need to tell old Gandledore – he's a fellow wizard in Broom Down – that a portal has been opened and that a dragon threat is imminent. He'll also need to know precisely where the portal is, and he'll want an estimate of the time of arrival of the dragons. Then he can get the word out. Right, I think I've got all that straight in my head – now to send the message.'

He closed his eyes, and his staff glowed orange. A moment later, his eyes opened and he smiled. The staff stopped glowing. 'Excellent,' he said brightly. 'He's received the message, and wishes us a safe journey back.'

'That was a staff-to-staff call?' ventured Tom.

'Yes, that's it. I guess in your world you'd call it wizard e-mail.'

'Cool. So what's your friend going to do?'

'He's going to mobilise some help for us. But help or no help, I fear that without us there, things will not turn out well. So, no more questions please, Tom – or from anyone else for that matter – and let me hail some transport.'

Whereupon Toby cupped his hands and directed several dragon-barks into the darkness. In less than ten minutes, a huge wind and dust storm came up from nowhere, and Richard, for the first time, was very relieved to see the shapes of Dave and Dylan in the gloom, waiting for passengers. Soon all were on board, and the dragons flew them back to the cave where everyone had slept the previous night.

Dave and Dylan had spent an uneventful day in the cave, and were keen to hear all about the adventure in the mountain. As soon as all had been told, Toby urged everyone to get to sleep. They would have to make an early start in the morning to get to the portal before the black dragons did.

172

Thirteen

It was early in the morning. The sun had yet to scale the peaks of the surrounding mountains, but the cloudless sky promised a warm summer's day. Toby, Ellie, Richard and Tom were now outside the cave preparing to board Dave and Dylan.

Suddenly a shadow swept over the mountain ledge, closely followed by another. 'Stay where you are!' growled a harsh voice from the sky. 'I'm Sergeant Carnor, and this is Trooper Balron. You shall come with us. Reinforcements will be here in a moment!'

Carnor barked several times, presumably to summon other dragons.

'Dammit!' cursed Toby. 'We've been spotted by a patrol! I can just about deal with one dragon, but two is going to be tough. Well here goes, before more of 'em turn up – '

But Dylan had another idea. 'Everyone onto Dave!' Dylan hissed, so that the circling black dragons wouldn't hear. 'He's a strong flier, and with frequent stops he'll be able to get you to the portal! It's your only chance! Go!'

Then before anyone had a chance to say anything, Dylan took off, sweeping upwards to meet the circling dragons. In no time he was circling with them. 'I hear what you say,' growled Dylan breathlessly, 'but we don't wish to go with you.

I suggest you leave us alone, and we'll leave without causing any trouble. What do you say?'

'I say you do what I tell you, or you'll regret it,' snarled Carnor.

'In that case you give me no option, boyo!' roared Dylan, as his tail whipped out without warning, slamming into the side of Carnor, dislodging a dragon-scale, and exposing a patch of red raw flesh. Carnor screamed, and his flight dipped as he felt the first stabs of pain. Balron responded by trying to take a bite out of Dylan's neck, but Dylan saw it coming and jinked out of the way, causing Balron to overshoot and narrowly miss flying into a mountain.

Now the black dragons were snarling, 'Kill him! Kill the red dragon scum!' And they flew with renewed vigour after Dylan who was desperately leading them away from his companions as fast as he could, only to see two more black dragons coming directly at him. He was caught in a trap with two dragons behind and two in front. He was hopelessly outnumbered.

Just before the dragons in front reached striking distance, Dylan dived vertically down into the valley below. The four black dragons responded by swooping down after him. As he neared the ground, he pulled out of the dive, and flew along the valley at very low level in an attempt to make it as difficult as possible for the black dragons to get to him, so low in fact, that he couldn't avoid scraping the rough ground with his claws and tail on a painfully frequent basis. He was tiring fast. One of the dragons had overhauled him and was slashing at his back with its claws. He tried to gain height, but the dragons above were preventing him from doing so. Dylan, increasingly tired and wounded, now had no option but to land. He hit the valley floor at speed, using his great claws to stop himself. Rocks and dirt went flying everywhere. The black dragons overshot, and turned around while losing height. Dylan managed to limp to a nearby rock face, and backed up against it. The black dragons were by now on the ground, moving in from four directions to finish it. But even as they closed in for the kill, Dylan allowed himself a little smile. Out of the corner of his eye, he could see a red dragon flying away up the valley, low but steady.

FOURTEEN

'We can't leave Dylan on his own, Toby!' yelled Richard above the howling of the wind and the explosive 'Whump!' accompanying each of Dave's laboured wing-beats.

Richard was so preoccupied with the recent series of horrific events, he hadn't had time to register that once again he was perched precariously on the back of a dragon with the ground many gut-churning metres below. He was clinging to the dragon-crest in front of him behind Ellie, craning his head backwards to keep an eye on the fast-developing plight of Dylan. He was shouting at Toby past Tom who was feeling increasingly like piggy-in-the-middle.

'There's nothing we can do, Richard!' Toby shouted back. 'Dylan's one hell of a fighter! He's giving us the time we need to get to the portal before Drusilla's dragons do. I reckon I can whip those dragons – I really do – I've seen him get out of loads of tight spots before.'

But Toby's words rang hollow. Four dragons against one.

'Couldn't you have used your staff on them?'

'I was about to, but Dylan took over! I think he did the right thing – he's created a diversion allowing us to escape, and stopped a massive sorcery fight that Drusilla would have homed in on in no time!'

Richard nodded. He knew Toby was right. Dylan had

knowingly risked his life for theirs, and of course there was that little matter of preventing two parallel worlds from destroying each other.

He turned his head to face forward. Ellie's blonde hair twisted and turned in the air-stream, occasionally tickling his face, prompting happier thoughts. Richard couldn't take his eyes off her. The problem is, thought Richard, that his shyness always gets the better of him when anything to do with girls is concerned. But now, somehow, he knew he must overcome the shyness and let Ellie know his feelings for her. I'll do it – tomorrow, he promised himself. Assuming there *is* a tomorrow, came the sober afterthought.

The journey seemed never-ending. Every few miles, Dave landed in order to get his strength back. He always made sure that he landed on a high point, so that he could get airborne with as little effort as possible by jumping off into a glide to maximise his speed before having to beat his wings to maintain flight. Richard hated these glides – they always started off so steeply. He found the best solution was to close his eyes and hang on like grim death until horizontal flight set in. Ellie and Tom on the other hand, seemed to be getting an adrenalin rush out of it.

After a particularly steep swoop, Tom cried out, 'Wow! Beats anything at Alton Towers, eh, Richard?' Richard nodded woodenly. He really couldn't comment. He'd never actually been to Alton Towers. In fact, he hadn't even graduated beyond the relatively tame rides he'd sampled at travelling fairs.

In time, they left the mountains behind to fly over sunlit woods and pastures with sheep and cows grazing, and over little cottages, some with fairy-tale wisps of smoke spiralling into the clear morning air. It all seems so perfect from up here, thought Richard.

Soon they were skirting Toby's mountains, the Indomitables, then onwards over yet more woods, fields and cottages until they came to a village that Richard thought he recognised.

'Broom Down!' shouted Toby, rather as you might expect a bus driver to call before reaching a bus stop. But this particular bus wasn't going to stop. Poor Dave, so very weary now, flew low over the roof tops, scaring the living daylights out of folk making their way to the Green Goblin for a lunch-time pint, the down-draught from his wings causing the inn's sign to swing wildly, then fall off – narrowly missing a very startled thirsty green goblin.

Before long, they were flying over a great swathe of trees which Richard realised was Oakbeam Forest, the forest that ended as his beloved Wild Wood. Dave flew on eastwards over the forest, finally reaching the far edge. He then started to circle, as though searching for something.

'Dave!' yelled Toby, 'I can see the lake! It's to your left!'

Dave spotted the distant strip of water by the forest edge, and steered straight for the twinkling silvery expanse. As they neared it, Richard could see the lake was actually a bloated section of a river that wound its timeless way along the edge of the forest.

Dave swooped down, landing between the forest and the lake. 'Everyone off,' he gasped, fighting for breath. 'I'm going to drink that lake dry, then rest my wings for a while.'

'And well deserved, my friend!' said Toby as he found his way to the ground. 'You have to be the strongest dragon in the world!'

'I'm certainly the thirstiest,' he replied as he waited for everyone to climb down. Then he wearily shuffled to the inviting water, lowered his head and drank the best (and probably the longest) drink he had ever had. Unfortunately, the respite was short-lived.

'Look out!' warned Tom. 'There's someone over there!' He was pointing towards the forest, from which somebody armed with a sword had just emerged.

'It's all right,' said Toby reassuringly. 'He's a friend.'

The friend ran up to Toby, and they briefly embraced, slapping each other on the back in the hearty way that friends who haven't seen each other for ages sometimes do. The friend was an impossibly handsome young elf, probably in his late twenties. His golden hair fell in a cascade of waves down to his wide shoulders, almost tending towards curls, but not quite. A head of hair like his on a less muscular frame would have looked distinctly effeminate, but on him, it simply looked – cool. His short sleeves showed off arms sporting rippling muscles, which were probably needed to lift the huge gleaming sword out of the scabbard hung at his waist.

Toby introduced the newcomer. 'Ellie, Richard and Tom, this is Marrick from ELF – er, the Elvish Liberation Force, that is,' said Toby rather self-consciously. 'I suppose someone must have stayed up all night concocting that name!'

Marrick smiled in the direction of Ellie and the boys, eyes opening wide as he took in the vision that was Ellie. Richard noticed that it seemed to take a very big effort for Marrick to wrench his gaze from her and return it to Toby.

Toby continued, 'ELF is a resistance movement set up some years ago to oppose Drusilla's creeping empire, and I've enlisted their help to ward off the dragons. I'm hoping that they'll be able to prevent them from entering the portal.'

'How will they do that?' asked Tom.

'Remember when we visited Shamus' house in Broom Down? Well, Shamus has developed a weapon that we believe will prove very effective against the dragons. Marrick and his people have several of them in the forest, ready for use.'

'What sort of weapon?'

'Tom, you'll know soon enough,' said Toby, smiling. 'No more questions. The dragons will be here soon.'

Toby turned to Marrick. 'Marrick, are you completely prepared?' he asked.

'Everything is ready,' replied Marrick confidently, his voice ridiculously deep and vibrant. 'Now tell me, how did you fare at Mount Dracomé?'

'I've broken her staff – ' started Toby.

'Brilliant news!' exclaimed Marrick, beaming, revealing impossibly perfect white teeth.

' – so that effectively makes her powerless until she develops a rapport with a new staff,' continued Toby.

'So she's still around?' asked Marrick, frowning, a perfect eyebrow raised.

Toby took a deep breath, as one who for the umpteenth time is attempting to explain a concept to someone who hasn't been listening. 'As ratified by the People's Council, our mission is to remove her power, but not *her*,' said Toby patiently. 'I agree with the Council that putting her behind bars, or worse still, killing her, would most likely cause a civil war. There are an awful lot of misguided folk in this world who regard her as a holy leader – who, by the way, has helped them 'feather their nests' rather nicely. That's why such folk ignore her sinister side.'

'I suppose that's right,' sighed Marrick.

'Good. Now my friend, don't look too down-hearted! There's plenty to do. Drusilla gave the command to mount an attack through the portal before I was able to stop her, and it won't be long before a company of black dragons is here.'

'How many dragons?'

'I imagine Drusilla wouldn't risk much more than a platoon, as this is something of a trial run for her,' replied Toby. 'That would be six of them.'

Marrick raised his eyebrows as he took this in. After a moment he slowly nodded his head, as if to indicate that six was a manageable number. 'Right. I need to go,' he said somewhat reluctantly, again gazing at Ellie. 'Perhaps I could afford Ellie my personal protection at this difficult time?'

180

Richard then surprised himself, and it seemed, everyone else. 'Ellie can look after herself!' he burst out, 'And I for one hope she stays with me and my friends!'

Ellie shot a warm smile at Richard before turning to Marrick. 'I really appreciate your concern, Marrick, but I will be safe here with my friends.'

'Oh, right,' said Marrick falteringly. 'Er, I'd better be off then.'

True to his word, he turned and ran off back into the forest.

Toby, Tom and Dave who had just arrived back from his drink, smiled at Richard knowingly. Richard thought his face must by now look red as a tomato. Ellie moved close to him and said softly, 'Thank you for that. You don't have to worry. You and I are destined to be together. Trust me.'

Richard was in a spin, but before he could even start thinking of a slick response, she had walked off to ask Dave how he was feeling now he'd had a brief rest. Nonetheless, Richard felt incredibly uplifted. '*Destined*' she had said. '*Together*' she had said. '*Trust me*' she had said.

FIFTEEN

'I'm sorry, Dave, but rest time is over,' said Toby. 'Here's a bag with The Book inside. Take it to your home and guard it well, and I'll visit you and your family in happier times. Now go, my friend, and thank you for everything.'

With a great claw, the dragon deftly took the bag from Toby. 'Good luck to you all,' he rumbled as he took off, gaining height slowly and finally heading westwards.

'Now everyone, quickly have something to eat and drink,' said Toby, 'and then we'll take a walk.'

Richard suspected that the purpose of the walk was something more than getting some exercise and taking in the views. Soon, they were following Toby towards the forest. Just as he reached it, he turned sharply to the right and continued walking with the forest edge immediately on his left. They walked about half a mile to a point where the river turned away from the forest and headed off down the valley, as though it had grown tired of its brief flirtation with the trees. Toby led them a further half mile, still following the forest edge, then stopped and stood with his back to the trees.

'Why are we stopping here?' asked Tom.

Toby pointed at the green rolling hills in front of them. 'If you walk about twenty metres in that direction, you will enter the portal,' he said quietly.

'I can't see a portal,' said Tom, frowning. 'Shouldn't there be an outline or a shimmering or something?'

Toby smiled and said, 'There are no visual signs to indicate the presence of a portal, unless it's opening or closing. Otherwise it's something you have to *feel*. Gravitational and electromagnetic fields become distorted in the vicinity of a portal, and this gives rise to a disturbed, out-of-balance feeling. Many creatures are very good at sensing such fields, such as birds, and yes, dragons. I'm afraid that Drusilla's dragons will be drawn to this portal just as moths are drawn to light.'

'Well, I can't say I feel anything,' said Tom.

'Okay,' said Toby patiently. 'I want everyone to shut their eyes.'

They all closed their eyes, and in no time started swaying about.

'Oh, that's awful! I feel sick!' complained a swaying Ellie.

'Right. Open your eyes everybody,' said Toby.

They opened their eyes, stopped swaying, and felt much better.

'You see, when you close your eyes, you lose your visual reference,' explained Toby. 'There is then nothing left to counteract the unbalancing effects of the distorted fields.'

Richard suddenly became aware of what he fancied were dragon-barks, far away. Toby seemed to have heard them too. 'We mustn't waste any time,' he urged. 'We need to warn Richard's family about what's coming, as well as anyone else we meet. So follow me through the portal. You'll simply suddenly find yourself elsewhere.'

Walking through the portal was easy. But when you suddenly find yourself in another world, it's one heck of a shock. The scene now in front of them was very different from the one they had been experiencing a few moments ago. Gone was the wild beauty of ragged wooded hills and valleys. Instead, the controlling, sanitising influence of mankind was evident. Richard's house nestled in the distance at the end of the wide expanse of sunlit cultivated lawn.

Even with the realisation that black dragons were close on their heels, Richard expected to feel pretty good, returning to his world with the prospect of reuniting with his family – but all he felt was an increased sense of foreboding. Something was very wrong. There was no sound other than their own breathing. No bird song, no voices, no sound of distant traffic. Also, there was no wind – not even a whisper of wind. It was as if the world was holding its breath.

'I can't hear anything,' said Richard, stopping abruptly at the unnaturally loud sound of his voice.

'I know,' said Toby quietly, 'but we don't have time to work it out. Right now we need to get to your house and see if we can find any of your family. Let's go.'

Without a backward glance, Toby sprinted towards the house, his companions quickly following his example. They raced past The Rock towards the yew hedge divided by the steps leading to the upper section of lawn, finally pounding up the steps to burst out onto the upper lawn like a band of marauding pirates.

Richard couldn't believe his luck. The whole family – Mum, Dad and James – were out on the lawn playing croquet, and Tom's mother was with them.

As he ran towards the group, he started shouting breathlessly, 'Everyone, it's me, Richard! Thank God you're all here! Get into the house! No time to explain! Get into the house!'

'Mum!' cried Tom, 'Please get inside the house!'

Toby and Ellie added their voices. 'Get into the house!' they shouted.

They all got to within spitting distance of the croquet game, then as one they halted, horrified by what they could now see.

SIXTEEN

James was readying himself for his next shot; he had lined himself up with the hoop in front, and was preparing to swing his mallet from between his legs sharply onto the waiting ball. Richard and Tom's parents, holding their mallets, stood nearby – waiting for James's shot. But the shot would never come. The croquet players were perfectly, eerily, still. Still as statues.

Richard broke the dumbfounded silence. He gasped, 'Mum, Dad, James, Mrs Bradley! Can you hear me?'

He waved his hands at them, vainly trying to get their attention. They didn't react in any way at all. Their eyes and facial expressions were as unmoving as their bodies. Richard's father's eyes were narrowed, as though the sun was too bright – and it seemed that he had held that pose for some time.

In desperation, Richard ran to his mother.

'Richard!' shouted Toby, 'Don't touch – '

But it was too late. Richard had put out his hands to embrace his mother, lightly touched her, then to his horror – watched her slowly fall over backwards onto the soft lawn. Her pose remained unchanged, even though she was now lying on her back. And most strangely, she continued to hold her mallet in exactly the same way, so that it hovered impossibly above her, held in a loose grip.

185

'Mum!' shouted Tom, as he started to run towards his own mother – before Toby just as quickly held him back. 'Best not to touch anyone again!' he cried. 'I think they're all alive, but frozen in time, as is, I've just realised, everything about this world.'

'But…*we're* not frozen!' blurted Richard.

'That's because, as far as the portal is concerned, at the moment we are of another world,' explained Toby. 'But when the portal closes in the next few hours, we will become part of this world and subject to its timescale.'

'So, as long as I end up in *this* world when the portal closes, my family and Mrs Bradley will start moving, and Tom and I can pick up where we left off?' asked Richard, his spirit rising, having momentarily forgotten about the small matter of imminent dragons.

'That's it,' replied Toby. 'But you see, Drusilla has been very clever. She's set up this portal connection so that our time is running much faster than human world time – that's why everything here appears literally frozen in time. When she talked about easy targets for her dragons, I never thought for a moment she was talking about unmoving targets, targets that have no means of defending themselves – you see where this is going, my friend?'

Richard could indeed see where it was going. Suddenly he realised what had to be done. 'Help me get them into the house!'

'Absolutely!' agreed Toby. 'We need to lift each person carefully, two lifters for one person – '

But at that moment, they heard shouting voices and the sound of thunder. At least, it sounded like thunder, but it was actually the sound of many running feet. The voices were as yet indistinct but getting louder and more discernible. Soon it became clear what was being shouted: 'Look out! They're coming! They're breaking through our defences!'

Richard, Toby, Tom and Ellie turned to see a band of some fifty elves running up the steps onto the upper lawn. Richard was surprised to see that many of them were female.

'Wow! Female elves!' blurted Tom. 'And some are black!'

'Not so different from your own world, then,' smiled Toby.

'No...of course,' said Tom, his cheeks flushing pink.

Leading the elves was none other than Marrick. He didn't look cool and composed now. His sword was out at the ready, its blade tipped with blood, and he had a nasty looking gash on his sword-arm, which was still bleeding. Some of the elves behind him were carrying injuries as well. They all came to a halt in front of the frozen croquet game and its onlookers.

'Toby!' panted Marrick. 'We're trying to stop the dragons entering the portal, but they're attacking with such ferocity that it's only a matter of time before some break through and enter this world, so I've brought some of my people here to deal with any dragons that arrive. We've already killed several of them, but I fear that greater numbers of my own people have fallen.'

'We always knew it wouldn't be easy,' said Toby grimly. 'Marrick, get these people inside the house. They're alive, but in a different time-zone, and I'm afraid they're stiff as boards. Take them through those big doors you can see are open.' Marrick nodded, and sent a number of elves to remove the frozen croquet players from the lawn.

'Now, Richard, Tom and Ellie, I want all of you to also go to the house and stay there where it's safer.'

'No,' said Richard calmly. 'I'm going to stay with you and fight as best as I can.'

Without hesitation, Tom and Ellie moved closer to Richard in a gesture of solidarity.

Toby sighed, slowly shaking his head. 'All right. I can't fight dragons *and* all of you! In which case you will need to have something to defend yourselves with.' So saying, he waved his staff at them. There was a blinding yellow flash, and then they were all wearing scabbards with gleaming swords inside them.

'Wow!' said Tom.

'They're good swords,' said Toby. 'Treat them with care – they can cut through dragon-scales!'

Then Toby turned his attention to Marrick. 'Where are the machines?'

'They're being used – and they work!' grunted Marrick. 'I'm leaving six of them on the other side –'

'– and the other six?' interrupted Toby impatiently.

'They're coming through to help defend this world,' said Marrick with a grim smile.

As if to prove his statement, wooden machines started to appear out of nowhere in front of the Wild Wood. Each machine was being pushed by a team of four elves. The machines made squeaking and rumbling sounds as they were coaxed forward.

'Blimey! They're giant crossbows on wheels!' blurted Richard.

'They're not just giant crossbows,' retorted Toby, clearly offended by Richard's reaction. 'They're our secret weapons, and according to Marrick, it seems the dragons don't like 'em.'

'Right,' said Richard hastily.

By now, one of the machines had been lifted up the steps, and it finished its journey a few metres from where they were standing. Basically it was, as Richard had said, a giant crossbow on wheels, but it had clearly been designed to pack a real punch. The crossbow itself was massive, but had been cleverly mounted so that it could be easily pointed by the user in any desired direction including vertically upwards.

At this moment, an elf was hastily winding a drum, each successive turn causing tortured bow-cord to groan as it stretched towards breaking point, until with a satisfying 'Clonk!' the bow was cocked, ready for action.

Now, thought Richard, we need a crossbow bolt. His gaze fell on hooks mounted on either side of the cart, appearing to be capable of holding a total of eight bolts. He noted that only five bolts remained – he sincerely hoped the missing three had found their targets.

Two elves carefully lifted a bolt and placed it in position ready for launching. Richard stared at the massive metal arrowhead, behind which was a lump of grey gritty material surrounding the shaft of the bolt.

'That's a Tobias Nonsuch Special,' said a familiar voice behind him. 'I rustled up that grey stuff in my sorcerarium. The arrowhead pierces the dragon's armour, enters its body, then my little surprise package explodes inside the dragon. When I was developing it, I carelessly dropped a small amount onto the floor, and the resulting explosion knocked me flat and broke all my glass flasks and test tubes. Not that the broken stuff was a big deal – as you now know, my chemistry lab equipment is just for show.'

'Isn't it a bit unsporting using explosives?' asked Richard, frowning.

'You need all the help you can get when you're being attacked by a dragon, as you'll soon see,' said Toby darkly.

Then Toby turned away and called over to Marrick who was busily ensuring that all the crossbows were ready for action. 'Marrick! If we can make each bolt hit its mark, we should be able to deal reasonably comfortably with a platoon of dragons – '

But Toby never completed the sentence, because the sun had just gone out.

189

seventeen

The sun was masked by a burgeoning black tide of scaly bodies. Everyone looked on in horror as one black dragon after another emerged from the portal, immediately taking to the air on great thrusts of bat-like wings, soon to join its comrades spiralling above the Wild Wood.

Toby swore quietly. '*That* is a lot more than a platoon. There have to be twenty of them – and still they keep coming. Drusilla's sent out just about every last dragon in the mountain.'

Suddenly Toby turned to Marrick who was still gawping at the deadly aerial ballet unfolding before them. 'Marrick! The dragons are under instructions to pick off easy targets and avoid injuries to themselves, but their first objective will be to remove the threat posed by us. If we move the crossbows into a defensive line directly in front of the house, then at least they can't approach from behind us. We'll see them coming and be able to concentrate our fire. What say you?'

'I say, damn good idea! For a wizard, you're surprisingly good at military strategy!'

Marrick glanced around as if looking for someone. 'Crossbow Leader! Make yourself known!' he bellowed.

An elf ran out from the crowd of elves preparing for battle. 'Here, Sir!' panted the elf. 'I overheard your conversation with the wizard, and can report that the bows are being formed into a line in front of the house as we speak.'

'Dawn, as ever, you're ahead of the game!' beamed Marrick. 'Carry on.'

'Yes Sir.'

Tom's mouth was so wide open that birds could have comfortably nested in it. No longer was he aware of the commotion of folk running about, nor was he aware of the giant crossbows being urgently manoeuvred into position. He saw only the beautiful Crossbow Leader, her brown eyes, brown skin and her long black ringleted hair. And her radiant smile.

'Hello, Tom,' she said. 'Yes, it's me. I'm a bit busy at the moment, but after the battle, I'll explain everything. Now, you look after yourself.'

She leant forward, kissed him, then ran off in the direction of the crossbows.

'Tom,' said Richard, 'is she…?'

'I – I can't believe it. Yes, she's my girlfriend, but how is it she's *here*? And surely she can't be an elf?'

Suddenly Richard remembered this was not the time or place to be pondering such questions. 'Come on, Tom, we've a battle to fight,' he said grimly.

Tom nodded at his friend, and pulled out his sword.

'Stay close to me at all times,' shouted Toby to Ellie and the boys. 'Richard, your sword won't be much use to you if it stays in your scabbard!'

Tom and Ellie were already swishing their gleaming weapons about with some enthusiasm, but it hadn't occurred to Richard that it might be a good idea to get a feel for his own weapon before the battle commenced. So he sheepishly drew his sword and did some tentative swishing.

'Good,' said Toby. 'Now listen, everyone. When all the dragons have arrived through the portal, they'll attack.'

It was precisely at this moment that the last dragon arrived.

When it joined the black airborne throng, it came in at number twenty-five. Then one of the circling dragons barked, and six dragons peeled off, flying side-by-side towards the waiting crossbows.

Ellie suddenly grabbed and squeezed Richard's hand. Smiling at him, she whispered, 'It'll be all right. Don't worry about me. I know what I'm doing, more or less...'

Richard returned the smile weakly and squeezed her hand in return. 'That's good...I think,' he said.

'Crossbow-elves!' shouted Dawn, the Crossbow Leader. 'Track your target and only let fly when it's well within range! Make every bolt count! Now hold your fire until I give the command!'

The dragons loomed ever larger as they glided down towards them. Now they could see the cruel yellow eyes, the open mouths full of razor-sharp teeth, the outstretched claws like rows of sickles. It seemed that the dragons were almost within touching distance, yet Dawn still hadn't given the order to fire. Richard could see that the elves manning the crossbow triggers were snatching increasingly concerned glances at her as the dragons drew ever closer. When was she going to give the order? Was she petrified with fear and unable to get the simple word 'Fire!' out of her mouth? Now they could all feel the draught from the great black wings, only a matter of metres away.

They needn't have doubted her.

'Fire!' she screamed.

With a loud swishing sound all six crossbows loosed off their massive bolts, the bow-carts instantly reacting by leaping backwards. Everyone held their breath.

'Thunk-boom! Thunk-boom! Thunk-boom!' Three of the dragons took direct hits in their chests. The screaming howls of pain were blood-curdling. The other three managed to swerve out of the way of the bolts, gaining height in order to circle around and attack again.

192

The explosions inside the three dragons that had been hit caused blood and flesh to splatter all over everyone standing behind the crossbows – but that was the least of their worries, because one of these dragons was coming straight at them. It was tumbling in the air completely out of control, screeching horribly. The elves manning the two crossbows on the left flank deserted their posts very quickly, but it wasn't something they would be court-martialled for. One second later, a ton of falling dragon collided with their crossbows reducing them quickly to strewn pieces of rent wood and twisted metal, having initially been crushed by the dragon and then suffering several explosions as stored bolts erupted.

The hapless dragon was by now sliding along the ground, rapidly losing speed, but unfortunately not stopping before reaching the house. There was a crashing of glass as its head smashed through a closed patio door, whereupon the law of momentum finally gave up and the beast came to rest. It showed no sign of extricating its head from the house, indeed it showed no sign of movement at all. In the unlikely event it had been alive after having suffered the explosions, it should certainly have died as its head passed through the toughened double-glazed patio door unit, thought Richard.

The remaining two dragons that had been hit managed to fly on. One of them veered off to the right, trying to find somewhere safe to land where it could nurse its injury. It managed to fly over the garden wall into the Henderson's garden, whereupon it dipped out of sight. Shortly afterwards, there was the sound of cracking wood followed by a 'Crump!' and a minor earth tremor, which was presumably the point at which the doomed beast finally hit the ground.

The other wounded dragon veered to the left and managed to fly over the garden wall on that side of the grounds, but then its trailing tail smashed into the top of the wall, sending a number of bricks flying as the dragon disappeared into the Laithwaite's garden. Moments later there was a cacophony of smashing glass, quickly followed by a 'Crump!' and the expected accompanying earth tremor. Richard knew that Mr Laithwaite's beloved greenhouse was no more.

The three dragons that had escaped on the first pass had circled around and had been joined by three fresh dragons. The six dragons came in, side-by-side as before, this time only facing four crossbows.

'Fire!' shouted Dawn.

This time, only one of the bolts hit its target. Unfortunately, it wasn't a good strike. The bolt glanced along the side of the beast, exploding and causing serious injury, but not sufficient to kill it. The wounded dragon managed to fly on weakly, turning around and heading back towards the Wild Wood – perhaps for medical treatment, Richard wondered?

The remaining five dragons were now flapping above the beleaguered company of humans and elves, slashing with their claws. Dawn's elves bravely stayed with their crossbows, trying to re-load them with bolts, but before they could mount an attack, the dragons smashed the crossbows to pieces with their raking claws and sweeping tails.

Several of the bolts fell to the ground together, and exploded directly underneath one of the hovering dragons. The explosion was so powerful, it concussed the dragon. It fell out of the sky onto one of the broken crossbow carts, an upward pointing metal shard sinking deeply into its underbelly as it finally came to rest. The great body convulsed three times, then moved no more.

Incredibly, so far no elf or human had been killed, although several elves had sustained some nasty wounds. But this knowledge was of little consolation to anyone. Right now, they were all fighting for their lives.

Somehow Ellie had managed to pick a rather personal

battle with one of the four remaining dragons. The dragon had landed and was steadily pushing her back towards the house, swiping with huge claws and snapping with its massive jaws.

'It'll be the first time I've killed a lady elf,' snarled the dragon, smiling very unpleasantly. 'Still, there's a first time for everything, don't you think?'

'You're not going to kill me! Say your prayers, dragon!' she cried, as she finally made contact. Her sword bit deep across a flailing claw, drawing blood.

The dragon was momentarily stunned as it looked down at its lacerated bleeding limb, but it didn't stay that way for long. 'You'll pay for that, elf!' it roared.

Ellie now had nowhere to go. The dragon had her pinned against the wall of the house. It raised its uninjured claw high above in order to smash her to the ground. Ellie held her sword aloft with both hands, in a last-ditch attempt to protect herself from the imminent dragon's blow.

'No! No! Leave her alone, you stinking black lizard!' shrieked Richard as he ran at the dragon from the side and thrust his sword deep into the beast's underbelly. Holding the sword with both hands, he drew it back and forth cutting ever deeper into the scaly hide, drawing more blood with every thrust.

The dragon roared with pain and swung its head around, searching for – and quickly finding – the new aggressor. 'It's you!' the dragon growled. 'I spoke to you in the cave! I *told* you we would meet again, didn't I, human!'

Richard just had time to think that he no longer needed convincing that dragons really are perceptive, and it was just his luck to meet up again with this one. He was thinking this as he turned to see a mouthful of teeth bearing down on him. Frantically, he tried to pull his sword out of the dragon, but he knew he couldn't remove it in time to defend himself. He could already feel and smell the dragon's hot fetid breath on his face. He let go of the sword and held out his hands in a futile protective gesture, knowing it wouldn't prevent him from ending up inside the dragon's mouth. But, unbelievably, the mouth stayed open in front of him. Why was the dragon waiting? Then Richard noticed a river of blood sliding down the left-hand side of its hideous face. Cautiously, he moved away from the head – to see Ellie spattered with blood, but very much alive and smiling at him. She was in the process of removing her sword from the dragon's head. She had rammed it under the eye up into its brain. As she pulled the sword out, the beast sank slowly to the ground in a growing pool of blood.

Richard and Ellie gazed at each other.

'You saved my life,' croaked Richard.

'Only after you saved *my* life,' she panted, a small lopsided smile playing on her lips.

But the moment didn't last. A nearby flailing dragon's tail suddenly knocked Richard over, Ellie just as quickly helping him back onto his feet. 'Thanks, Ellie. I'm all right,' he gasped.

Then as one, Richard and Ellie turned to take in the scene developing at the other end of the house. The three remaining dragons had landed and surrounded their combatants, and were in the process of pushing them back towards the house wall. But suddenly, the dragons were engulfed by a dazzling blue light. Toby stood before them with his staff outstretched, crackling blue threads of light snaking from its tip.

'You will not prevail!' he cried. 'I call on my whole being to vanquish you! Shengrel marner! Shengrel marner masté!'

'Oh my God, Richard!' said Ellie haltingly. 'He's taking a Sorcerer's Last Stand! He's unleashing his whole wizard's life force against the dragons. It could kill him!'

For now, the dragons were held motionless by Toby's onslaught of raw sorcery, but Richard could see that Toby was quite visibly deflating with the exertion. Then after what seemed like a very long time, Toby suddenly cried out and collapsed, his staff extinguishing and clattering to the ground.

Eighteen

Marrick, who had been standing behind Toby, rushed to tend to the fallen wizard. Meanwhile the rippling blue aura continued to envelop the frozen dragons, but to everyone's horror, after a few seconds it dissipated and the three dragons started to move. Marrick leapt to his feet and held out his sword in readiness for the dragons' attack. Marrick's elves and Tom quickly followed his example.

But the dragons were behaving as if they were recovering from a heavy night at the pub. One of them rubbed its head ruefully with a great scaly clawed foot. Then something strange started to happen. Was it a trick of the light, or were the three dragons changing colour? No, it was really happening. Black was giving way to a dark purple, which in turn was changing into…

'Red! Richard, they've become *red* dragons,' gasped Ellie.

It wasn't just the onlookers who were nonplussed. The three dragons seemed to have momentarily forgotten that they had a job to do, and were looking blearily at each other in total disbelief.

'You've gone red,' said one.

'So have you, mate,' came the prompt reply.

'I feel weird,' said the third dragon.

The dragons' budding voyage of self-discovery was

interrupted by an unsettling sound. It was a sound reminiscent of a boisterous wind rushing through trees in leaf. The sound was getting louder, and then the day started getting darker. Everyone, including the red dragons, looked up to see a swathe of black dragons peeling off from the still-circling throng above the Wild Wood, heading directly for the house.

They glided down onto the upper lawn, one after the other. The sound of flapping leathery wings as they came in to land was deafening, and the draught from all those wings caused a minor hurricane. Marrick's long locks of golden hair were completely blown out of shape, but even *he* didn't seem to give a monkey's about it at this moment. Everyone was much more concerned about the nineteen black dragons that were now assembled on the lawn.

An especially large and fearsome black dragon was at the front of the sea of black bodies, and he now plodded imperiously up to the red dragons. He peered at them for several seconds, then turned his attention to Marrick. 'I am Garlan, Commander-in-Chief of The Lady's Personal Guard,' he growled, 'and who are you?'

'I'm Marrick, leader of ELF,' said Marrick.

'Ah yes, the self-styled resistance movement,' Garlan reflected, with obvious contempt. Abruptly, the dragon's demeanour became brisk. 'What has the wizard done to these soldiers?' he asked, gesturing to the still-confused red dragons.

'I don't know – ' started Marrick.

'I think *I* do,' groaned a nearby voice.

Toby had recovered consciousness, and was picking himself up from the ground. Finally he was standing, albeit rather unsteadily, his staff in his hand. 'I used the ultimate sorcerer's spell for the destruction of evil on these dragons, and you can see the result,' he said weakly. 'I confess I didn't expect the spell to work in the way it has. They should be dead.'

The red dragons were clearly upset by this. They appeared to have become rather touchy-feely recently.

'Turn them back into *black* dragons, Wizard,' barked an increasingly frustrated Garlan.

'Even if I wanted to do that, I couldn't,' said Toby wearily. 'You see, you black dragons are actually red dragons – '

Toby was interrupted by a massed murmuring from the assembled army of dragons, along the lines of 'He says we're what?', and they all started pushing forward so that they could hear more clearly.

'You see,' Toby tried again, 'some time ago, Drusilla went on a trip visiting all the dragon lairs in the area, putting a spell on any unsuspecting male dragon she came across. The spell changed the nature of the victim, making him conform to her will and forget his family, and as an after-thought she included a colour change to distinguish her dragons from others. My anti-evil spell seems to have worked directly against Drusilla's spell, on the basis that her spell on you black dragons – was *evil*. The proof is right before us – the spell on these three dragons has been undone, and they've returned to their former selves.'

The murmuring from the massed dragons swelled again.

'Enough of this nonsense!' bellowed Garlan. 'My mission now is to finish off any remaining resistance you have left, then we'll kill a few humans here and there to get this world's attention and go home. You've killed several of my soldiers and you will pay for that!'

'By the way, it's not nonsense, boyo!' said a voice from the sky.

'And I agree with my friend!' said another.

Dylan and Dave landed neatly between where Richard and Ellie were standing, and where the rest of the company were huddled. Dylan was covered in nasty gashes all over his body.

'Dylan!' cried Richard. 'I didn't think we'd ever see you again!'

'Well, I might look a right state,' said Dylan, winking at Richard, 'but you should see the other guys!'

As Dylan limped past Richard and Ellie, he smiled at them and whispered so that only they could hear. 'Glad to see you two are still together. Right glad I am.'

Dylan and Dave joined the ranks of the beleaguered company, facing Garlan and the massed dragons behind him.

'As I said, it's not nonsense,' growled Dylan. 'My friend Toby Nonsuch is a good and very great wizard, and he is telling you the truth, whether or not you want to hear it. Dave and I know of many families who have mysteriously lost relatives. Let me paint a picture for you. A male dragon leaves his home to get some food, and Drusilla is lying in wait. In no time, the victim has lost any memory of his family and he's being led to his new home in Mount Dracomé. Do any of you black dragons feel a burning in your hearts, a burning that is telling you I speak the truth?'

Dylan gazed at the mass of dragons. All eyes were locked on him. You could have heard a pin drop.

'I feel a burning,' said one of the converted red dragons, 'but more than that, I think I'm starting to remember my family! Now that I'm a red dragon – well, it just feels right. You know, this wizard has turned me back into who I really am, and I for one support him and his cause!' So saying, the dragon sidled up to Toby.

'Soldier, I don't care what colour you are!' barked Garlan. 'You will fall into rank right now!'

'No, Sir,' responded the dragon firmly.

Garlan was by now apoplectic with rage. 'This is mutiny!' he snarled. 'You'll reap the consequence of your actions when my army disposes of you with the rest of these enemies of Drusilla!'

'In that case you'll have to dispose of me as well,' said one of the other converted red dragons.

'And me,' said the remaining convert.

Both dragons then joined their comrade, so that now all three of them defiantly faced Garlan.

The murmuring from the massed dragons returned with greater intensity than before, and some of them started shuffling about uneasily. For the first time, a trace of fear and uncertainty appeared on Garlan's cruel face. Without turning his head, he barked, 'Silence in the ranks! This is all wizards' trickery! We shall destroy this wizard and his friends before he addles more of our brains!'

So saying, Garlan tensed himself, then leapt into the air with a show of raw power, unfurling his great black wings at the same time. A few wing-strokes later, he was hovering above them like an enormous satanic bat. 'Captain Shandor!' he bellowed. 'I give you the honour of engaging the enemy with your platoon! The rest of you, fall back!'

No dragons moved, except for one. Shandor moved away from the mass of dragons and faced Garlan. 'I'm sorry, Sir,' he said, 'but I don't have the stomach for this anymore. Right now I'm questioning everything, and I need to find answers.' He paused while he moved his gaze to the rapt audience of dragons in front of him. 'I don't know about you, lads,' he said with a ghost of a smile, 'but I'm off to visit the Lady. I've got some questions for her I'd like answered.'

Many of the black dragons were now turning their heads, looking to see who might speak next. 'I'm with you, Captain,' said a hesitant voice.

'And me,' joined in another.

Then the floodgates opened, and the air rang with growling voices expressing their support for Captain Shandor. Shandor turned to Toby, nodded, then with a majestic sweep of his wings launched himself into the air. He ignored Garlan, who was still hovering, and flew off towards the Wild Wood. Just before he got to it, he dipped down – and disappeared. He had entered the portal and returned to his own world.

Garlan pleaded from aloft, 'Stay with me, soldiers! This is madness. We've a job to do...'

But no-one was listening. One by one, black dragons took off and followed Shandor into the portal, until eventually only Garlan was left, flapping forlornly. Then he pulled himself together. 'Don't think this is over!' he growled. 'I'll help the Lady finish her business one way or another!'

He paused while he slowly glided down until his head was level with Toby's, then snarled, 'As for *you*, Wizard – I look forward to the next time we meet.'

He gave Toby a particularly unpleasant smile, then with a huge flap of his wings, he shot up into the sky, wheeled around, then headed for the Wild Wood with an impressive burst of speed, before being swallowed up by the portal.

NIᴎETEEᴎ

Richard, Ellie, Toby, Marrick and his elves, Dave, Dylan and the three resurrected red dragons said nothing at all – it seemed that no-one could quite believe that the dragon army had actually gone. Then Richard jumped out of his skin.

'My name's Eustace!' boomed one of the resurrected red dragons, grinning ear-to-ear. 'I remember my name! Eustace Ravenkill!'

'Eustace Ravenkill!' roared Dylan with delight. 'The Ravenkills live nearby me! My goodness, you have certainly grown since I knew you, but yes, now I see it is you! Your Dad's a good mate of mine! You went missing years ago – broke your Mum and Dad's hearts – they thought you'd flown away, or worse. Welcome back, lad! Do you remember when I used to take you sheep rustling? Those were the days, weren't they?'

Eustace didn't reply immediately. Instead, he gazed at Dylan with wide eyes, his jaw hanging down loosely and dribbling slightly. Suddenly Eustace broke into a beaming smile (or at least as close as a dragon can get to one), and blurted, 'You're Uncle Dyl! I can't believe it!'

Fat tears rolled down the dragon's cheeks. He lumbered over to Dylan, and the two gave each other the equivalent of a dragon's 'high five', their clawed feet crashing together with a loud leathery 'Thud!'.

Toby glanced at the other dragon converts. 'Er, how are you two feeling?'

'Well, I can't remember who I am yet, but I think it's almost within my grasp,' said one.

'Yeah, I've got the same problem, but I'm working on it,' said the other.

Toby nodded and smiled.

'Haven't we forgotten to do something?' ventured Ellie.

Everyone turned towards her, wondering what she meant.

'Let me explain,' she said patiently. 'First, we broke Drusilla's staff, destroying her power base. Second, we got the book back, and made it safe so that no-one with less than decent motives will open up portals between the two worlds again. Third, we have just battled with, and seen off, an army of Drusilla's dragons, who if they'd had their way, would have carried out needless killing and put the future of both our worlds in jeopardy. Fourth, it looks like Drusilla's spell is losing its hold on her dragons, and a number of dragon families have some wonderful homecomings in store. So what have we forgotten to do?'

'Clear up the mess?' hazarded Tom, taking in the scene of mayhem around them.

'For God's sake!' exploded Ellie. 'We've forgotten to celebrate!'

So saying, she punched the air. 'We did it! We did it!' she screamed, grabbing Richard, and dancing an impromptu jig with him.

That was it. Everyone's tension was released in an outpouring of joy and relief. Elves hugged each other, jumped about and generally went bananas, shouting and hollering. Dragons barked the loudest dragon-barks ever. Tom performed a frenetic dance, which involved jumping a lot and waving his sword around rather dangerously, which fortunately ended as soon as a battle-scarred but smiling Dawn moved into his arms.

After several minutes dancing with the radiant Ellie, Richard remembered his frozen family. 'Just a moment, Ellie,' he said, separating from her and walking up to Tom and Dawn.

'What is it, Richard?' asked Tom.

'First of all, Tom, please introduce me to your friend.'

'Oh, sorry. This is Dawn. Dawn, this is my best mate Richard.'

'Pleased to meet you, Richard,' smiled Dawn. 'I've heard a lot about you.'

'Dawn!' cried Ellie, pushing the boys aside and proceeding to give Dawn a hug.

'What the heck is going on?' asked Tom.

'Sorry,' said Ellie. 'Dawn is my best friend.'

'How do you know each other?' blurted Tom. 'How – '

'Tom,' interrupted Richard. 'I'm as confused as you are, but right now you and I need to go into the house and see what's happening to my family and your mum.'

'Blimey,' said Tom. 'I'd forgotten about them.'

'Nothing has changed,' said a voice. The boys looked across at Toby who was sitting on the steps leading to the patio doors, his eyes bloodshot and tired. 'I've just checked,' he continued. 'If you go to them, you'll only get upset. They're frozen in time, and only *time* can unfreeze them. So all we can do is wait, I'm afraid. They'll be fine.'

'Oh, if that's what you really think...' said Richard.

'It is,' said Toby.

'You look really knackered, Toby,' said Tom.

'Thanks for that,' said Toby, smiling weakly. 'I'm afraid the spell I pulled off rather knocked the stuffing out of me. I never thought I'd have to resort to the Sorcerer's Last Stand, and I don't know of any sorcerer who performed it without dying as a result. I think I've been rather lucky, all considered.'

The realisation that Toby had invoked the ultimate spell in order to give others a chance of survival, with the knowledge that he was almost certainly going to die – moved Richard to tears. Suddenly he knew what he had to do.

'Listen everybody!' he shouted at the top of his voice. 'Listen to me!' Everyone turned to Richard. 'You've all been absolutely fantastic,' he said, emotion welling in his throat. 'You've saved my family, and our two wonderful worlds. But this wouldn't have happened if it weren't for this brilliant, brave wizard – my dear friend, Toby Nonsuch. He's guided me and my friends unerringly through everything and protected us along the way. So –'

'Thank you, Richard, but it really is –' started Toby.

'Be quiet, brother!' said Ellie firmly.

'So, three cheers for Toby Nonsuch, the greatest wizard of all! Now, for the benefit of everyone other than Tom, I say 'Hip-hip' and you respond 'Hooray' each time, okay? Hip-hip!'

'Hooray!' roared everybody, and each subsequent 'Hooray!' was louder than the last.

When the cheers had subsided, Toby stood up with difficulty, using his staff as a prop to lean against. He smiled at the beaming faces around him, and in a steadily strengthening voice said, 'Thank you all for your unbelievable courage today in the face of death. You stood firm and have made an important step towards ultimately winning freedom for our worlds.' Then he turned to Richard. 'Thank you for your kind words, Richard; and thank you, Richard and Tom, for trusting me at the beginning of this adventure and sticking with it through thick and thin. I've a feeling that now you've had contact with my world, the elvish ancestry in both you boys has been well and truly woken – which probably means it's only a matter of time before we embark on the next adventure.'

'The next one?' asked Richard, frowning. 'This one is quite enough.'

Toby's face became serious again. 'There is much more

to do if we are to eventually see the two aspects of our world brought back together again, and anyway, who said *this* adventure is over? I think not quite yet, my friend.'

'Toby!' gasped Ellie. 'Look over there, where the portal is! What's happening?'

Everyone looked where Ellie was frantically pointing. Every now and then, the trees in the vicinity of the portal dithered, so that straight tree trunks became jagged, then suddenly sprang back to being straight again. It was rather like looking at an old-fashioned television set that was occasionally losing picture lock. Richard realised he had seen this before – on the school bus all that time ago – the shaking Wild Wood.

'Oh dear,' said Toby. 'Surely not!'

Everyone stared at him, hoping for clarification.

He fumbled for his fob watch and peered at its face. 'That explains it,' he said, putting the watch back in his pocket. 'We'll have to move fast.'

'Explains *what*?' demanded an increasingly frustrated Ellie.

'The two worlds' time lines are starting to lose synchronism – that's why the portal is starting to disrupt, or, in other words, close,' explained Toby. 'I didn't realise how time has moved on. I suppose I was rather preoccupied with the battle. If we hurry we can get through the portal before it shuts.'

'How long have we got?' asked Marrick.

Toby pulled out his watch again and glanced at it, before returning it to his pocket. 'Fifteen minutes at the outside,' he said. 'Marrick, take your people now, and get through that portal as quickly as you can. I'll see you on the other side in a few minutes. Wait until the dithering starts, then when it stops, one person can go through, and so on.'

'What happens if someone goes through when it's dithering?' asked Marrick.

'I've never tried that,' replied Toby thoughtfully. 'Best to go through when it's *not* dithering, I think.'

Marrick seemed anxious to follow Toby's advice. 'Well I guess I'll see most of you on the other side in a few minutes...' he said, his voice trailing off as his gaze fell on Ellie, who still looked lovely even when liberally covered in blood.

'Sir?' said Dawn. 'Permission to follow on later? I'd like to spend a few moments with my friends here.'

'Alright,' smiled Marrick. 'You deserve it. See you on the other side.' Then he bellowed, 'Follow me, comrades! Run!'

The elves didn't need a second invitation. They ran like blazes across the lawn with Marrick in the lead, down the steps to the lower level and onward to the Wild Wood. It reminded Richard of the start of the London Marathon.

'Now,' said Toby. 'Dylan, I'd like you to look after Eustace and his two friends. Get yourself and them through that portal now, my friend.'

'Right you are,' replied Dylan, 'but shouldn't we tidy up a bit around here before we go?'

'Dylan, you're in no shape to do any tidying up. It'll be all you can manage to fly home and reunite these dragons with their families. And we owe you a great debt – I've not forgotten how you saved us back in the mountains! Sometime you'll have to tell me how you managed to see off four dragons single-handed.'

'I'd be happy to bore you with that story!' said Dylan with a smile. 'Well, it's been a pleasure knowing my first two humans – and I've a feeling I'll be seeing more of you later.' Then he shot a wink at Richard and Ellie who were again standing together, and with a great flap of his battered wings, he launched into the air, his dragon charges doing likewise, obediently following Dylan to the portal. And one by one, they disappeared into thin air.

Now only Toby, Richard, Tom, Ellie, Dawn and Dave were left.

'Richard, Tom – we haven't time to clear up,' said Toby

as he looked around at the black dragon bodies, the strewn wreckage of crossbow carts and blood. 'But you know, I think it may be a good thing, leaving the evidence behind, so to speak. It might be the start of this world coming to terms with aspects of its past it has conveniently ruled out as myth. Then we'll *really* be on the road to reuniting our worlds. How does that sound?'

'Absolutely brilliant!' said a beaming Richard, stealing a glance in Ellie's direction.

'You bet!' agreed Tom, flailing around with his sword again, Dawn keeping safely out of range.

'Dave,' said Toby, looking up at the great red beast, 'thank you for arriving here with Dylan in the nick of time! Now, could you help me out one more time and fly me, my sister and her friend through that portal? It'll close in a few minutes, so I think we're going to need your speed!'

'My pleasure,' smiled the dragon. 'Maybe on the way home we should pay the Green Goblin a visit? Refreshment wouldn't go amiss, and I thought we might check to see if Ben has wormed his way back there.'

'That's a splendid plan,' said Toby, before turning to look at Richard and Tom. Tom had (thankfully) put his sword away in its scabbard. 'Well, boys – this is where the rest of us must part. Look after yourselves. I will be in touch, one way or another.'

'How exactly are you going to get in touch?' asked Richard.

'I don't know, but I think we've started something important. Life finds a way. It always does, my friend.'

'I'm, *we're*, going to miss you, Toby,' said Richard, with a lump in his throat.

'I'll miss both of you, too. Take care!' said Toby, giving them hearty slaps on the back. Then he went over to the dragon and climbed up. 'Ellie and Dawn,' he called from his sitting position, 'we've got to get a move on. Say your goodbyes.'

Dawn placed her hands on Tom's shoulders. 'Tom, I'm looking forward to more potholing expeditions with you in your half of the world, but for the moment I'm needed in my half to help keep Drusilla under control.'

'But Dawn, you live in Pemberton,' said Tom. 'I've visited your house and seen your parents there...what's going on?'

'Tom,' interrupted Toby. 'This is going to be a lot for you to take in, and I haven't got long to tell you. I sent Dawn and her parents into your world a while ago so that Dawn could keep an eye on you, and through you, also keep an eye on Richard – to keep you both safe, and to report back to me. We rented that house in Pemberton.'

Tom backed away from Dawn. 'So Dawn is a kind of secret agent? She *pretended* to be my friend?'

'She was doing it for the cause, and I'm really sorry we had to deceive you in this way. But your friendship with her is very real, Tom. Over to you, Dawn.'

'Yes,' said Dawn. 'Tom, we elves always know the destiny for our affections – it's a kind of empathy you humans lost sight of a long time ago – and I can tell you that you and I were always destined to meet and be together. Toby just helped speed the process up a little.'

She moved forward to Tom, and this time he didn't back away.

'So if you're an elf,' said Tom, 'why didn't I ever see your pointed ears?'

'You never looked!' she laughed. 'They're well hidden under my hair – which I've been keeping nice and long.'

Tom tentatively pushed up one side of Dawn's voluminous hair up to reveal...

'Pointed ears,' he sighed, with a growing smile.

'Tom, I don't want to, but I have to go. We'll meet again soon, but right now I'm going to leave you something.'

'What's tha – ' spluttered Tom.

211

Dawn's kiss was now doing the talking.

Ellie smiled at the sight of Tom and Dawn before moving towards Richard. She reached out and held his hand, gazing into his eyes. 'You certainly have a novel way of getting my attention – tackling me to the ground in that cave!' she giggled. Then her expression abruptly became serious. 'Don't forget me, Richard Cranfield,' she said softly.

'Never – ' he started. He wanted to kiss her, and vowed to himself at that moment that he would not let his shyness with girls take over. So he moved to kiss her on the cheek, but at the last moment she turned her head so that their lips met. Richard wished the kiss would go on forever, but all too soon, she gently pulled away.

'You and I are meant to be,' she whispered. 'Hold on to that. We will meet again soon.'

'I will, Ellie,' he found himself replying.

Then she turned away and quickly climbed up onto the waiting dragon.

'Dave! Fly like the wind!' exhorted Toby.

Dave unfurled his huge wings, and with great sweeping downbeats he rose into the air. 'Farewell, young humans!' he growled breathlessly as he fought for height.

Toby, Ellie and Dawn waved as Dave wheeled and headed for the portal. Richard and Tom waved back, and kept waving, until the dragon reached the entry point. The portal was dithering very markedly now. Dave hovered, waiting for his chance. Suddenly the tree trunks snapped straight, and he powered in with all his strength. The dragon and his passengers vanished from view. Just before they disappeared, Richard heard Ellie shout something. He could make out his name being called, but nothing more.

Suddenly the portal started dithering so much, that the trees behind it became a hazy blur. Shortly afterwards, the trees snapped back, without any sign of further dithering.

Richard and Tom continued to stare at the point in the distance where their friends had vanished.

'I think the portal has closed,' said Richard.

'It looks like it,' agreed Tom.

For a moment, the two boys tried to mentally grapple with everything that had happened. Then Tom said, 'You're a lucky bloke, Richard.'

'What do you mean?'

Tom turned to his friend, and looked at him as though he was one brick short of a full load. 'Are you serious? Didn't you hear Ellie shout 'Richard, I love you!' just before they went through the portal?'

'Really?'

'Yes, really! Can't understand what the hell she sees in you, though.'

'But it's not really as good as it seems,' said Richard frowning. 'She's gone, and it's not that she's gone somewhere a long way off like New Zealand. No, *my* girlfriend has gone to another dimension!'

Tom placed his hand on his friend's shoulder. 'Richard. Your girlfriend is not the only one that's gone to that dimension.'

'Oh, I'm sorry, Tom. We're in the same boat, aren't we?'

'Yes, but both girls told us we will meet them again soon, and that's good enough for me.'

A further silence ensued, soon broken by Tom. 'Isn't something supposed to happen, now that the portal's closed?' he asked, as they both returned to gazing at the distant Wild Wood.

'I think something *is* happening,' said Richard.

The silence had been broken by what could only be described as a low hiss. It was getting rapidly louder. Now it sounded like the sound you hear when you put a seashell to your ear – a kind of rushing sound. Finally it grew into a

213

deafening 'Zzz-ssst!' and the world around the boys seemed to catch its breath. The view in front of them seemed to wobble briefly, and the normal sounds of life suddenly hit like a tidal wave. The boys almost jumped out of their skin. Everything now seemed very loud. For some time, they'd been part of a world where the only noise was either generated by themselves, or others, such as the dragons or elves. Now, out of the cacophony, they were becoming aware of distant voices, of bird song, and could feel a refreshing breeze on their cheeks. It seemed that time had revved up, and they were at long last truly becoming part of their own world again.

There was a piercing scream from behind them, closely followed by: 'What *is* it? Is it dead?'

No mistaking that voice, thought Richard. It was his mother.

'Jesus! Who put that there?' cried out another voice that Richard knew well. It was James.

'How did I get in here on the floor?'

That's Dad, thought Richard.

'Christ Almighty!'

That's Dad again, thought Richard. Now he's spotted the dragon.

'How very interesting!'

That's Tom's mum. She's probably about to attempt a conversation with the dragon.

Richard and Tom looked at each other. 'I don't think there's ever going to be a good time to make our presence known, so we might as well get on with it,' said Richard quietly.

Tom nodded.

They walked slowly up to the patio doors, and peered in. The ex-croquet players were standing near the dragon's head, staring down at it, their mouths open in disbelief (with the exception of Mrs Bradley who looked more fascinated than shocked). Then they spotted the movement outside and looked up sharply.

Richard waved limply and said, 'Er, hello. It's us. We're back.'

Richard's mother gurgled and promptly fainted, falling like a tree across the dragon's neck.

Richard's father spluttered, 'What the hell's going on here? Is this some kind of joke? Where have you been all this time?'

James babbled, 'Richard! The house is wrecked and there are these incredible dragon creature things all over the place, and…and…hey, it's great to have you back…'

Mrs Bradley said calmly, 'I knew you'd turn up some time, boys. Judging by this dragon, I'd say this world is about to become a much more interesting place! Tell us all about it over a nice cup of tea.' She paused as she noticed the prone Mrs Cranfield. 'Rachel doesn't look very comfortable slumped over the dragon. Shouldn't we lift her up?'

TWENTY

Soon, Richard's mother regained consciousness, and this event was followed by hugs all round for everybody. Even Richard's father and James joined in the hugging. There was, of course, a barrage of questions for Richard and Tom to answer, but when the answers kept referring to another world – well, certain members of the audience were not convinced.

'You both spent time living in another world?' laughed Richard's father.

'Well, you were both away for some time and, I imagine, lost, so you must have been under enormous mental strain trying to find your way home…' suggested Richard's mother.

'Come on guys. How did you *really* manage to create all this mess and these huge dragons?' asked James.

'That's enough!' growled Richard, making everyone jump a mile.

Richard's parents and James gawped at him. There was something in Richard's voice, a certain *authority*, which prevented his mother from saying 'How rude!' and his father from saying 'Go up to your room!'

'Thank you for actually starting to listen,' said Richard quietly. 'Tom and I haven't somehow staged the destruction around us. This dragon and the dragon outside are real,' said Richard, with a gravitas that impressed even Tom. 'Before I

216

talk any more on the subject, I want you to go to the dragons, touch them, and check them over until you're absolutely convinced they're either fake, or real.'

Richard gestured towards the great black beasts. 'Go on,' he encouraged.

Without speaking, they obediently walked over to the creature lying half inside the house and half outside, and started examining it, gingerly poking and probing.

Mrs Bradley was smiling, as indeed she had been from the moment she became unfrozen. She walked over to the two boys. 'I don't need to check out the dragons, if that's all right,' she said. 'I *know* they're real. I detect a deep connection between you two boys, these dragons and our world's ancient ancestry. Am I warm?'

Richard and Tom nodded and smiled.

Richard's father waited for everyone to finish their inspections, before he, the eminent qualified scientist, started his professional inspection. He walked all around the dragon, muttering how this was all the most ridiculous hoax, and that someone was going to have to pay for all the damage to the house and grounds. He touched its scaly flesh, pulled at its great leathery wings, finally ending up at its head. He tugged at its snout, and heaved its heavy jaws slightly apart, revealing rows of massive yellow teeth and rivers of saliva. He peered long and deep into the disturbingly open but sightless reptilian eyes.

Suddenly its head jerked upwards. 'Humans!' it roared, as it attempted to get up, its mighty head ramming into the ceiling, shards of plaster and lumps of masonry raining down on Richard's father and everyone else. Richard's father fell backwards without saying a word, seemingly in complete shock, resembling a wide-eyed doll that had been pushed over. The dragon, the rear part of its body pretty much jammed in the patio doorway, started to writhe its way towards the now sprawled body, snarling and scrabbling with a free leg in an attempt to get a purchase on anything firm – Richard's father's favourite armchair getting in the way of the vast flailing claw, causing it to smash into a wall and break up as if it were made of matchsticks. The huge jaws snapped repeatedly as the dragon strained to move forward those last few inches needed for it to get its teeth into its unmoving target.

'Die, human!' it roared, its hideous mouth now in position for the first bite. Then as Richard's father continued to look on in complete paralysed shock, the awful head of the dragon lunged down, stopping inches from him, toying with him before the kill, before finally sinking down onto the carpet – which was turning red. Richard was crouching on top of the dragon's head, his sword rammed down vertically to its hilt into the creature's brain.

'Tom,' said Richard, calmly pulling his bloodied sword out. 'Please make sure that the other dragon is dead.'

Richard dropped down beside his father who had started to pull himself up into a sitting position. 'I'm all right,' he said, his voice shaking. 'I'm really sorry, Richard. These are obviously very real dragons, and I now realise that you and Tom have indeed visited another world, and I want to hear all about it. And – thank you for saving my life, son.'

'I'm with your father, Richard,' said his mother quickly.

'Me too,' said James, adding, 'Great Robin Hood-type clothes, by the way.'

'At last,' said Mrs Bradley, rubbing her hands in anticipation. 'Now we're going to get to it.'

They all walked outside, found garden chairs and set them out on the patio in preparation to hear Richard relate the whole fantastic adventure. Tom filled in whenever Richard inadvertently left something out. It was such a relief for Richard to be able to describe it all in front of such a receptive audience. At various times they moved over to one

218

of the broken crossbow carts, handled the remains of the great crossbow mechanisms, discussed the effectiveness of the crossbow bolts still stuck in the chests of the dragons (Tom inadvertently dropping a bolt onto the patio, the explosion instantly turning the area into 'crazy paving'), marvelled at the hundreds of dragon footprints covering the lawn, then discussed, felt and handled the boys' elvish clothing and swords. At one point, Richard and Tom demonstrated their amazing magical sleeping blankets – how they transformed from tiny folded slips of material into luxurious sleeping bags.

'Right. So that's how one minute, we were on the lawn playing croquet,' said Richard's father, 'then the next, James and I were pulling ourselves up from the living room floor and your mother and Sonia were extricating themselves from the sofas! You know, Richard, science is all about discovering and explaining new phenomena, but sometimes when faced with something that is completely unexplainable and scary, science tries to rationalise it away. I really am so sorry.'

'It's alright, Dad,' said Richard, smiling. 'It really is.'

'How long were we away, and what did you all do?' asked Tom.

'On Sunday morning we went to check up on you both, and of course found that you and the tent had completely disappeared. So we alerted the police and over the last few days, they searched the house and the grounds, and the surrounding area, of course finding nothing. Sonia has been staying with us while this was going on. We've obviously been going out of our minds, although thankfully Sonia has been an amazing oasis of calm. But all-in-all, life has been pretty ghastly up until now. A week has passed, and today is Sunday. For the first time since your disappearance, we all tried to get some normality by playing a game of croquet, which of course – is how you found us.' He paused, his face full of wonder.

219

'This is just so incredible! It proves the existence of parallel dimensions, of wormholes – '

But his eulogy was cut short by shouting.

'Doreen! Doreen! Come here quickly!' It was Mr Henderson, one of the neighbours. He and his wife, an elderly couple, had been having an afternoon nap, and Mr Henderson had just woken and gone out into the back garden to offer their Labrador dog a bowl of water.

'It seems that something big and black has eaten Larry while we were sleeping,' continued Mr Henderson loudly, but surprisingly calmly, 'and now it's sleeping – or rather, I'm hoping it's died of indigestion or something.'

'Arghhhh!' shrieked Mrs Henderson, who had presumably just sighted the big and black something.

The Cranfields and Bradleys looked at each other, and then as one, they stood up, grabbed their chairs, and ran across to the brick garden wall on the Henderson's side. They hastily placed the chairs at the foot of it and climbed up on to them. Simultaneously, six heads rose above the wall, in time to see Mrs Henderson cowering next to the open back door, and a perplexed Mr Henderson standing on the patio, staring at the prone dragon which had crashed onto their dog kennel, the remains of which lay underneath and around the dragon. It looked like a monstrous black dog that had outgrown its kennel rather suddenly. The nameplate 'Larry', was perched hilariously on the dragon's head.

Just at that moment, Larry appeared from under a nearby bush, where he'd presumably been hiding since the arrival of the dragon. His tail was between his legs and he was whimpering. 'Thank goodness you're not inside this thing, Larry,' said Mr Henderson. 'It's all right, boy. I think it's dead.'

'Gordon, Doreen!' hailed Richard's father.

Mrs Henderson waved limply from the kitchen door. Mr

Henderson looked up, clearly taken aback to see six heads looking down at him.

'It's almost certainly dead,' continued Richard's father, 'but I strongly advise you keep away from the head area for the moment, just in case.'

'How do you know about it?' asked Mr Henderson, his puzzlement deepening. 'It looks like a ruddy *dragon*, as far as I can tell.'

'I know about it,' replied Richard's father, trying to stifle manic laughter, 'because we've got two of them on this side of the wall!

Before Mr Henderson could frame a response, there was a distant wail.

'I think I know what's just happened,' said Richard. 'Mrs Laithwaite has just gone to check on her tomatoes, and has found a badly damaged greenhouse with a black dragon inside it.'

'Sorry – Gordon, Doreen,' said Richard's father. 'I'll explain all of it later. Must dash.'

The six heads disappeared from the wall. If Mr Henderson had been able to see through to the other side, he would have seen a line of six people clutching chairs, charging across the lawn.

TWENTY ONE

A month had passed since the family reunions, and a lot had happened.

Richard's father informed the police that Richard and Tom had arrived home. The desk officer who took the call, promptly accused him of 'taking the Mickey' when he tried to explain where the boys had got to. In the end a compromise was reached, and the desk officer wrote down rather pompously in his log: 'The boys sojourned in a remote area during the period of absence.'

Richard's father went on to mention the matter of dragons. At this point, the officer accused him again of 'taking the Mickey', but then another officer could be heard talking to him excitedly in the background. There was a pause, and the desk officer said, 'Well, Professor, apparently we've taken calls from your neighbours, er, let me see, Mr and Mrs Henderson and Mrs Laithwaite, and like you, they are suggesting they also have a dragon infestation problem. Personally, I suspect you're all barmy, but in view of the number of calls concerning this matter, I will send out a patrol car to investigate.'

The desk officer couldn't resist a parting shot. 'The only dragons I know of are giant monitor lizards,' he said with heavy sarcasm. 'They inhabit the island of Komodo and zoos, and I warn you that these are extremely dangerous exotic animals. If

222

such animals are found in your keeping, you could be leaving yourself open to serious charges. Finally, if all this turns out to be a hoax, I'd like to advise you that you will be charged with wasting police time. Goodbye for now, sir.'

The police duly arrived at The Manor and investigated – and lost no time in calling for back-up. Their initial findings that there were dead animals in Grindleshorn, appearing to be a species of winged reptile modelled on the mythical dragon, spiralled up through the various layers of government authority like a bush fire. The police arrived in force and cordoned the area off. Then wildlife experts arrived, soon followed by large container lorries, commandeered to take the dragon bodies away for analysis and preservation.

Government investigative officials called at various times over the ensuing weeks to interview the Cranfields and Bradleys. The officials quickly came to accept that the dragons must have originated somewhere other than this Earth, and were now actively entertaining the notion of the existence of a parallel world, particularly when they saw Richard's and Tom's elvish sleeping bags demonstrated. The sleeping bags, together with elvish clothing, swords, crossbow bolts and the remains of crossbow carts were taken away for analysis. Richard was at a loss as to how they expected to analyse items such as the sleeping bags, created and operated by sorcery, while using the techniques of scientific analysis. He could imagine the headline: 'Out-of-this-World Sleeping Bags Defy Analysis.'

Eventually the Government's scientific advisors accepted that the only theories that explained the incredible recent events were fantastic ones, and that Richard and Tom's explanation of having visited a parallel Earth through a wormhole, was as plausible as any of the others. They agreed they couldn't rule out the possibility that many of the fabulous creatures hitherto treated as mythological, could have actually existed in ancient times, and somehow in the course of events, their particular reality became consigned to a parallel dimension. Naturally, parallel dimensions and wormholes being one of Professor Cranfield's specialist subjects, put him in a wonderful position to accelerate and publicise his research. Now that the Government had decided that there was no point in trying to prevent the sensational news from reaching the public domain, Richard's father found himself being interviewed by the press, and being invited to contribute to television documentaries on the subject of parallel dimensions and wormholes.

Of course, it wasn't just Professor Cranfield's expert opinion which was sought. Richard and Tom were in enormous demand for their incredible story, and it was proving difficult to balance attending interviews for the press and television, against the demands of school. There were some obvious benefits from all this exposure. They were getting tidy sums of money from the various interviews they were giving, but for Richard and Tom, there was one benefit that was more far-reaching; they had become heroes at their school, and were now treated by their fellow pupils with much greater respect. However, Banghead Brunning was still calling Richard names – but fortunately, Richard rather liked the latest name: 'Dragon Lord'. As for the boys controlling the cricket match – they were letting Richard bat instead of only fielding. He wasn't very good to begin with, but was learning fast!

And for Richard, there was a particularly precious benefit. His father had started to show him immeasurably more respect, treating him pretty much as an equal. Now his father actively encouraged Richard's creative flights of fantasy, and made time to discuss issues with him, and to properly listen to what he had to say. It was the most wonderful thing for Richard – it was like having a new, brilliant, Dad! It was the start of a brighter, happier, more confident, more spontaneous approach to life for Richard, as well as for the whole family.

TWENTY TWO

Richard was watching a fascinating television news report. He, his parents and James with Tom and his mother, were all perched on the edge of armchairs in the living room at The Manor, eyes glued to the screen.

'There you are, boys!' shouted Sonia, clapping her hands with excitement.

Footage was being shown of Richard and Tom when they had been filmed at the secure laboratory that the four black dragons had been taken to. One of the dragons had been wheeled out of a large freezer room, and Richard and Tom were providing interesting details including how you climb up onto, and ride a dragon.

The commentary went on to say: 'The scientific community is still debating the origin of these animals, and is broadly split between two camps. Some tend towards Richard Cranfield's and Tom Bradley's assertion that the dragons are not of this world, or at least, not this particular version of the world, but that they were of this world in ancient times, before the world split into two versions, that is, this world, and what they term the 'Other', or 'Mystic' world. Others tend towards the equally fantastic theory that these creatures were genetically engineered on Earth by some brilliant mind. In a world exclusive, we can now report evidence that supports one of these theories.'

The shot then changed to a mountainside deep inside China

where a fossil dig was in progress. The commentary explained that the palaeontologists were unearthing the fossil bone fragments of what was initially believed to be Quetzalcoatlus, the largest known pterosaur, having a wingspan of some eleven metres. There were a number of bones unearthed at the site that didn't fit the pterosaur's skeleton, and eventually these were attributed to a fearsome four-legged predatory lizard of the same period (the Cretaceous period), known as Protomegalania, a giant forebear of monitor lizards such as the Komodo Dragon.

The shot then cut to graphics showing Quetzalcoatlus and Protomegalania in animated life. This was followed by graphics showing how the bones found at the dig seemed to form part of Quetzalcoatlus' skeleton, and part of Protomegalania's skeleton.

Finally graphics were presented depicting the skeleton of a black dragon. The continuing graphics sequence showed the entire set of bones found at the site moving into place onto the outline of the black dragon's skeleton, fitting perfectly.

The world held its breath as the commentary continued: 'So, what was initially thought to be the skeletal fragments from two animals, is now recognised to be the complete skeleton of the black dragon. This leads to an amazing conclusion. The black dragons are living fossils from the Cretaceous period – or rather we should say, they were living up to the point they died recently! From wherever they came, these dragons have remained pretty much unchanged over a period of sixty-five million years. So, this supports the assertion from the boys from Grindleshorn, that flying dragons were present on Earth in ancient times. Who knows, fossil finds in the future may show that the flying dragon was present in more recent times.'

'Yes! Yes!' whooped Sonia, as the report ended with an animated construction of a black dragon flying along. 'Bit by bit, we'll show 'em that there's a lot more to the world than meets the eye!' Sonia stopped whooping when she noticed that everyone was looking at her quizzically, and slightly disapprovingly.

'What?' she demanded, eyebrows raised. 'I'm just a bit excited, that's all.'

Twenty Three

Richard had finished his homework, and had gone to bed early so that he could carry on reading his novel: 'The Otherworld Agent'. He opened it at the bookmark and turned back a few pages in order to remind himself where Max Manfred had got to. Ah, yes. The Megalonians who were trying to steal the death ray machine from the Megalonians who were living in another dimension, had managed to steal a Universe Field Distortion Scanner. This was standard issue equipment for an Interdimensional Field Agent. It allowed the agent to precisely locate both ends of a wormhole by sensing the field distortions associated with it. The Megalonians promptly used the scanner to locate an appropriate wormhole, which they then entered. When they got to the other side, they found Max Manfred waiting for them, calmly holding the death ray machine at the ready, flanked by the machine's Megalonian owners. Max suggested that rather than one dimension trying to take over another, wouldn't it be better for the two dimensions to combine? They could pool their resources and expertise and become a happier more-fulfilled race of people, without anyone getting hurt.

Max had a radical theory that it was the wormholes themselves that were actually keeping the two dimensions apart. He reckoned that if the wormholes were removed, the two dimensions would naturally become one. Suddenly, he realised that he might be holding the means to do this in his hands. The death ray machine worked by distorting fields at the atomic level – in other words by ripping your atoms apart if you were unlucky enough to be within range. All he had to do was to modify the machine's field distortion modulation in such a way that it could be used to disrupt the field of a wormhole – which should remove the wormhole itself.

Then Richard read: "'Life finds a way,' said Max.'

This caught Richard short. How strange, he thought. He had read these words spoken by Max, but *heard* them as words spoken by Toby Nonsuch. Then he remembered that 'Life finds a way' was something that Toby had said to him just before he departed. What a coincidence!

Reading on, Richard soon learnt that Max managed to modify the death ray machine, successfully using it to remove the wormholes, thereby reinstating the two divided worlds as one. All the Megalonians then proceeded to have a rather nice time together.

Now he had arrived at the last page. He read: 'Max Manfred was proud of another job well done. He sat smugly in his office at the Agency of Interdimensional Management, his feet lounging on his desk. 'Life finds a way, indeed,' thought Max, 'although sometimes it needs a little help.' But Max's thoughts were rudely interrupted by his communicator, which was beeping. He pulled his feet off the desk and took the call. It was some good friends who wanted to see him about an interdimensional problem they had just stumbled upon. He finished the call, muttering to himself, 'Mustn't keep Toby, Ellie and Dawn waiting,' as he stood up to leave the office.

Richard stared at the book in shock. He pinched himself to make sure he wasn't dreaming. He wasn't. A smile steadily grew until he was grinning like the proverbial Cheshire Cat.

He had just become the happiest boy in Grindleshorn. Still grinning, he put the book down on his bedside table and turned the light off in preparation for sleep.

As Richard's breathing slowed, a fly on the wall looked down at him. It was the same fly that had been in Toby's kitchen, observing food that inconveniently disappeared. It was the fly that, to the great disappointment of a certain hungry spider, took to the air in the nick of time, bumbling eventually into Tom's pocket where there were remains of 'Giant Pizza'. Because the fly could only ever remember the *last* thing that had gone through its mind, it had no remembrance of its subsequent pizza feast or indeed of setting up home in Tom's pocket, nor had it registered that it had recently made an interdimensional transition before eventually leaving Tom's pocket as a fatter and happier fly. It had no recollection at all that it had then blundered at various times into just about every room in the house, eventually coming to rest in Richard's bedroom. But what it *did* know, right now, was that there was no food in this particular room – which was why it was very pleased to be able to leave the house now that the window, seemingly of its own accord, had suddenly been wrenched wide open and the curtains pulled apart...

The harsh grating noise made by the opening sash window woke Richard with a start, and with heart thumping he switched on the bedside light, almost knocking it off the table, just in time to see something flap into the room and drop onto the floor. It was a tiny black dragon, the size of a large chicken, but a good deal more menacing. It looked at him malevolently, its jaws slightly apart, revealing rows of needle-like teeth. Then it started changing shape, rising higher and higher.

'Drusilla?' gasped Richard.

She stood at the foot of his bed, gazing down at him with cold unflinching eyes. Richard had always felt she had been on the brink of total madness, but now he could see she had crossed that particular brink.

'My staff is broken, yet I am here,' she hissed. 'Soon I will have a new staff, and my power will be more awesome than you can possibly conceive. I can get to you and your human friend whenever I please, and mark my words, I will be back for you and Tom when the time is right for you both to unlock The Book for me, so that I can at last create a cleansed, combined world! *My* world!'

THE END

The last and only thing that went through the mind of a certain forgetful fly that was buzzing around outside Richard's window as it hit a fast-exiting dragon head-on – was of course, its bottom.

THE BOTTOM END